ROOM 21

ALSO BY JESSICA HUNTLEY

STANDALONES
Horrible Husbands
Room 21

ROOM 21

JESSICA HUNTLEY

JOFFE BOOKS

Joffe Books, London
www.joffebooks.com

First published in Great Britain in 2025

© Jessica Huntley

This book is a work of fiction. Names, characters, businesses, organisations, places and events are either the product of the author's imagination or are used fictitiously. Any resemblance to actual persons, living or dead, events or locales is entirely coincidental.
The spelling used is British English except where fidelity to the author's rendering of accent or dialect supersedes this.
The right of Jessica Huntley to be identified as author of this work has been asserted in accordance with the Copyright, Designs and Patents Act 1988.

No part of this book may be used or reproduced in any manner for the purpose of training artificial intelligence technologies or systems. In accordance with Article 4(3) of the Digital Single Market Directive 2019/790, Joffe Books expressly reserves this work from the text and data mining exception.

Cover art by Nick Castle

ISBN: 978-1-80573-109-2

A NOTE TO THE READER

Please note that this book contains in-depth detail regarding epilepsy and epileptic seizures, incest (inferred) and child abduction, which may be triggering to some readers.

PROLOGUE

The Night of the Party

Family can be both a blessing and a curse. On the one hand, we're bound to them by blood. Literally, by blood. Their cells and DNA, running through our bloodstream, are a part of our own bodies, our own genetic make-up. Hell, we even get antibodies from our mothers before we're born to protect us from illnesses, infections and diseases. Perhaps we inherit our father's strong jawline or high IQ, or maybe our grandmother's high cheekbones or love of sewing. Without family, we would cease to exist. Literally. We are who we are because of them . . . which is great for some people who have loving, adoring families and who are kind, compassionate and there for you no matter what.

On the other hand, what happens if you don't know who your family are? What if you're adopted or fostered or have been abandoned by your family at a young age? How can you ever truly know who you are or why you are the way you are if you've never known your family? Some people may not care about where they come from, but I reckon that deep down, everyone is curious about their DNA.

1

Nothing makes sense. That's how I lived for the first twenty-five years of my life.

Until today.

What if, like me, when you do eventually find your long-lost family, they turn out to be a bunch of vicious, psychotic, bloodthirsty lunatics? Then what? Surely, it would be better to not know about them at all?

Because, let me tell you, there's no book or manual out there, or online forum, which prepares you for finding out your family are serial killers. Or maybe there is, and I just haven't found it yet. In any case, after tonight, I will have to walk around in public knowing that serial killers' blood runs in my veins. Will people look at me differently? I expect they will. It's not like I'll have a sign on my forehead that says, "Has a serial killer family", but I may as well. Every time I get angry or annoyed in the future, I'll wonder if I have it in me to snap and kill someone, to torture them or string them up from the neck and watch them twitch and writhe around until they stop breathing.

The point is that yes, my family are twisted and evil, but I'm no angel from heaven either, especially now. I've changed since arriving here at this hotel. Have I changed because of my upbringing or because my family's DNA has made me this way? It's hard to tell and I expect I'll never know the answer.

All I know is that tonight, I'm about to kill dozens of people. Bad, evil, disgusting people, but still people. Human beings with heartbeats and lives and loved ones. Do they deserve to die? Does anyone truly deserve to die?

I don't know the answer to that question either, but what I do know is that I have a choice to make. I must choose whether to follow in my family's footsteps or choose my own path in life. I only met my blood family for the first time roughly two weeks ago, so what gives them the right to have me choose them?

Also, and perhaps I should have mentioned this before, the fact that they are my family, that their blood runs in my veins, doesn't mean I owe them anything, right? Just because I'm biologically related doesn't make them family because family, true family, are the ones who care about you and love you, who'd lay down their lives for you. They may not be related by blood, but does that make them any less a member of your family?

I don't have any close friends, nor anyone I'd call in an emergency, but these people in front of me now are still strangers. I've survived this long with no family. What makes me think I need them now? I don't. So, surely, the choice is simple?

I'm standing in a banquet hall, wearing the most exquisite gown, holding a glass of champagne and looking at my new family in front of me.

They want me to choose.

Tick tock, Kimberley.

Tick tock.

Choose now.

And . . . go . . .

# PART ONE

CHAPTER ONE

Kimberley
Two Weeks Before the Party

The majority of people in life want to be remembered, to have made a difference in the world, whether it be to have created multiple offspring, solved a complex issue or made the world a better place by saving lives. I'm no different, but I don't want to be remembered as merely a person. I have no dreams of being famous. I don't want to be a celebrity or a social media icon. I want to be remembered for doing something great, something worthwhile, something . . . *unforgettable*, but there's a problem with that dream. I'm a nobody. I have about one hundred quid to my name, and no one knows who I am, not even one of the flatmates I live with. It's a tricky one, I'll admit.

However, most people also want to be remembered by their friends and family when they pass on, whenever that may be, but what happens if you're like me and don't have any friends or family? What happens then? Will I fade away like I never existed, or will I cease to exist at all? What's the point of me even being on this earth if no one knows me enough to remember me when I'm gone? I know that all lives matter and we're on this earth for a reason, but what if you don't know what that is? What if you die before you're supposed to and never make an impact in this world the way you planned?

Life is short, they say, but death is forever.

I've spent a long time dwelling on my own mortality and what it means to be alive and what happens to our bodies when we die. I probably spend more time thinking about it than most people spend thinking about what to eat that day, but then I suppose that's common for someone like me, someone who could drop dead at any second due to a severe and life-threatening health condition.

I have epilepsy.

And yes, there are lots of varying types of epilepsy, some of which are classed as mild and not life-threatening, but mine is classed as severe. I have what they label as generalised seizures, which affect and involve both areas of my brain. Generalised seizures are split into lots of different categories. They can happen at any time and in any order, so that's fun . . .

Tonic seizures cause stiff muscles and can affect consciousness and make me froth at the mouth. Clonic seizures cause repeated and rhythmic jerking muscle movements, and finally, tonic-clonic seizures, the most dramatic type of epileptic seizure, can cause me to suddenly lose consciousness and my body to stiffen, twitch and shake. If those types of seizures last longer than five minutes, then it could be fatal for me.

Several times I've also lost bladder control, vomited when I've come round and bitten through my tongue, which at the time looked more serious than it was due to the amount of blood that poured from my mouth. I'd bitten through half of my tongue and took a chunk out of the inside of my mouth, almost choking on my own saliva and blood. Again, another delightful experience. I'm completely joking, of course. I like to use humour to lighten the severity of my condition, otherwise it just depresses the crap out of me, and people look at me with pity.

It is a life-altering condition I've lived with since I was a child and, if not managed appropriately with medication, could see me into an early grave. I'm only twenty-five, so I don't plan on leaving this world any time soon, especially since I haven't done anything worthwhile yet or done anything that's worth remembering. Since I have no direct family members in my life, I'm not sure if the condition runs in my family. As far as I know, I never suffered head trauma as a kid, other than falling off a swing when I was six after my first severe seizure and I don't have any developmental conditions I'm aware of, but then, since I have zero knowledge of my family history, it's difficult to know what causes my epilepsy.

Perhaps I'm just unlucky.

I've seen the same doctor since I was a kid. Doctor Strong. He's great. He's helped me determine some of my triggers, such as alcohol, skipping doses of medication (which happened purely by accident because I don't make it a regular habit to miss my meds, which I take twice per day, morning and evening), stress and dehydration, not forgetting loud noises and lack of sleep.

Due to my condition, I don't drive, nor do I go anywhere near a swimming pool or other areas of deep water, having learned my lesson as a child when I nearly drowned during a swimming lesson at school and had to be resuscitated. It's a wonder I've even made it this far in life, with the number of times I've nearly died when I've had a seizure in a compromising location.

Anyway, the point is, I live my life as if I'm constantly dangling over the edge of a cliff, waiting for my lifeline to snap. I could be crossing the busy street when a seizure hits or walking down a set of stairs (hence why I use lifts wherever possible) because I've been known to take a tumble once or twice (okay, four times). Black eyes used to be a regular occurrence.

I've been close to death several times and hospitalised more times than I care to remember due to injuries I sustained during a particularly bad episode. At work, two months ago, I had a tonic-clonic seizure while cleaning a guest room.

Luckily, another housekeeper was alerted by my seizure alert dog, Muffin, and called the emergency services, who were able to stabilise and assist me.

Muffin is a black-and-white border collie who is not only my best friend but also my personal lifesaver. I have had her for two years. She's trained to give me an early warning signal that a seizure is imminent, such as pawing, circling or barking. She can even fetch my medication on command, a soft pillow for my head to stop it smacking off the floor as well as provide comfort while I'm in the throes of an attack. She truly is a wonderful companion, and I couldn't imagine life without her now. The thought of being apart from her sends my anxiety skyrocketing because I'd have no warning of an impending seizure without her.

I can't always bring her to work with me though. It depends on what I have on that day. It's the price I pay for working in my dream career. I've wanted to be a housekeeper at a hotel ever since I was a child; cleaning, order and politeness have always been my forte, but it sometimes means when I'm suffering through a seizure, I get a gaggle of spectators, craning their necks to get a good look. However, my boss and everyone who works around me knows my condition and what to do if they find me on the floor or staring absentmindedly into space, which is known as an aura, the first part of a focal seizure (yet another type of seizure I sometimes have), which includes hallucinating and an impaired awareness. I don't always remember where I am or what's going on and it can be very scary. Sometimes, I'll just fiddle with my clothes or stand in one place and stare at the wall until it passes.

My favourite movie as a child was (and still is) *Maid in Manhattan*, but it's not for the reason most people think. Most people expect it to be because of the romance and chemistry between the two main characters and how motivational and uplifting it is for a lowly maid to be noticed by a handsome senator and then rise through the ranks to make it to a managerial position.

Spoiler alert. My bad.

It's my favourite movie because of how the maids of that hotel run the entire show. Yes, they may have to do what is asked of them by demanding hotel residents and it may seem like they are at the bottom of the hierarchy, but that's not the case at all. Without those maids, that bitchy woman, Caroline Lane, wouldn't have had a clue how to function. She depended on Jennifer Lopez to run her errands for her, not because she was lazy, but because she genuinely had no idea how to do it and couldn't be bothered to learn because she thought she was above everyone else.

My first job as a fifteen-year-old was a housekeeper at a shitty hotel with peeling paint on the walls, black mould in the bathrooms and bad smells in the hallways. It was basically like trying to polish a turd, but I worked my butt off in that place and was quickly offered a job working in one of the well-known hotel chains. It wasn't posh, nor was it well paid, but I loved it. I never let my epilepsy hold me back either. I spoke with my doctor who agreed that it was perfectly fine for me to work, as long as my employers were aware, and I had suitable protection. That's why he suggested getting an alert dog a couple of years ago after one too many close calls.

I now work at Harris Hotel in Mayfair, London, one of the best up-and-coming hotels in the capital. I often feel like the British version of *Maid in Manhattan* — *Maid in Mayfair*. However, I should point out that my job title isn't technically a maid, which is now considered a gendered and outdated term. Maid is basically a female domestic servant, which doesn't fit with most of the staff because there are more men who work here as "maids". Therefore, we are known as housekeepers, even though I'm not looking after a house, but a hotel. Who even comes up with these things?

I am a Senior Housekeeper, which means my main responsibilities include maintaining a high standard of cleanliness in rooms, handling any personal issues with residents, and liaising and coordinating tasks with other departments to ensure an excellent standard of care. I also manage other housekeepers, optimise costs, and address any maintenance issues as quickly as possible to make sure everything flows smoothly and efficiently.

I love being at people's beck and call because the residents are totally dependent on me and it's the buzz I get from being needed that keeps me in this job. Some people I meet look down on me for being a housekeeper, while others probably think I'm not smart enough to do anything else with my life, but the truth is, I couldn't care less what anyone thinks of my career choice. They don't know the blood, sweat and tears it's taken to get to where I am today. Nor do they realise that without housekeepers, hotels would cease to exist.

My dream of being a housekeeper started when I was a child, as young as five years old I would clean my surroundings as best I could. Due to having no parents and being a child of the foster system, I rarely had my own room, so was forced to share with other children, most of whom were filthy and refused to keep their side of the room tidy.

As a foster kid, I bounced from one family to the next. Most families found my constant battle with epilepsy difficult to control and deal with. Also, I never fitted in with the other children in their households. Never seemed to be able to stay in one place longer than a year or two. I came from nothing. No stable family life. No siblings. No supportive parents to push me into universities and courses to hone my skills. I am where I am today because of one person and one person only.

Me.

I don't know who my biological parents are. I was told at a young age that I was dropped off with the authorities when I was born. I've thought about searching for them, finding out why they handed me in to live a life alone and scared, but over the years that idea has dwindled away. Sometimes, I see women my age with their mothers, shopping or having coffee together, chatting and laughing like best friends. I wonder why my own mother didn't want to do that with me. I've moved past the point of blaming myself. I'm not to blame for my start in life.

Today is the start of a brand-new week. Mondays are my favourite. While most people drag themselves out of bed, moaning about starting a new week, I bounce out, excited to make a difference in this world, despite living in one of the worst flats imaginable.

The rental flat I share with three other people is situated about a thirty-minute walk from Mayfair. It's literally all I can afford, and I can't be picky since I have a dog too. London prices are astronomical, and I can barely afford to keep myself and Muffin fed, which is why I'm the lightest I've ever been, sitting in at a little over fifty kilos. I've always been slight due to not always eating at regular times. The longest I've gone without eating was almost four days, thanks to my fifth foster family. They used to spend the money they received for me to fund their own lifestyle.

I rip back the dingy curtains above my bed and am greeted by a red brick wall, my view every morning. Muffin gets up and does a big stretch across the bed and yawns, stretching her front paws out and sticking her bum in the air like she's doing a yoga pose. I ruffle her soft head and tickle her velvety ears.

My bedroom is only big enough for a single bed, a two-foot-square space of carpet and a rickety old chest of drawers. I don't own a lot of possessions because when you've been in the foster system, you have to get used to living out of a single bag, especially when you change living arrangements so often. Muffin sleeps on the bed with me. I rarely leave her alone in here. If I can't take her along to work for any reason, then she stays at the reception desk at the hotel while I clean the rooms.

It's time to head to work.

I have the early shift today, so it's five o'clock in the morning, which means none of my flatmates are up yet. I prefer it that way. I'd rather not run into them at all because they are all horrible people who steal my milk and smoke in the flat despite me asking them multiple times not to. They keep the place about as tidy as a pigsty.

Thanks to my epilepsy, breathing in smoke can aggravate my chest and lungs, which in turn can trigger an episode. Therefore, whenever I set foot outside my room, I hold my breath. It would be nice to be able to breathe freely in my own home. It's bad enough having to walk through exhaust fumes every day on my commute. Since I've had the condition my whole life, doing normal things like walking to work without the risk of collapsing to the floor is something I've never experienced. Plus, there's the whole sudden unexpected death in epilepsy to worry about.

I pop on Muffin's lead and peer around my bedroom door, checking the hallway for any sign of life. The coast is clear. The stale smoke makes my eyes water as I step into the small living area. I tiptoe around the cans of lager and leftover fish and chips wrappers, which are emitting a foul odour, sending all my senses into overdrive. Muffin attempts to scoff a cold chip, so I quickly tug her away.

By the time I reach the front door, my body is fighting my brain to release my breath so I can fill my lungs with oxygen, but I can't risk having a coughing fit in the flat, so I wait until I close the front door behind me before releasing my breath in a single, long exhale.

Big mistake.

I should know better.

The combination of holding my breath and the cold air is enough to bring on a coughing fit. I drop my shoulder bag on the ground, all the while tears stream from my eyes and my lungs feel like they're about to escape out my throat.

Breathe. Breathe.

The street lights flicker ominously as my breathing finally levels out. Oh yeah, I also have asthma, which can also mess up my whole day. I have to carry around an inhaler all the time.

I pull my coat tighter around my body and shudder against the cold February air, heading in the direction of Mayfair. I could easily hop on the underground and be at work in half the time, since there's a tube station only two minutes away from my front door, but I need to save every penny I can, so I opt for walking everywhere in London, which suits me fine because I don't need to go any further than a thirty-minute walk in any direction. Plus, the underground scares me and while I can technically take a dog down there, I don't like to because it's too crowded. The few times I have been on the tube, it's felt as if there's no air. The last thing I want is to have an epileptic attack on a crowded underground train. It's my idea of a nightmare.

That and being trapped somewhere I can't get out with no access to medical attention.

I don't have an issue with enclosed spaces, as long as I know I can escape from whatever situation I'm in. Lifts don't scare me as long as the doors open. My flatmates call me weird because of my epilepsy, dodgy breathing and quirky habits, but they don't know the hell I've been through in my life to get to where I am.

Those quirky habits have saved me more times than I can count. Touching each of my fingers against my thumb over and over is enough to soothe my anxiety when in a crowded place or when any number of my foster parents would scream at me for no reason other than because I existed. Biting the left corner of my lip would keep my mind focused on the pinch of pain rather than the hours of solitude or the mind-numbing pangs of hunger when I'd be left to fend for myself for the sixth day in a row. One foster family left me home alone for eight days while they went on an all-expenses holiday to Spain. I was ten and had two seizures during that time, which I managed by myself. So yes, my quirky habits may look odd to most people, but that's okay because deep down I know they are the only reason I'm still breathing.

A large gust of wind catches me off guard and I stumble to the left against a black metal railing. Muffin looks up to check I'm okay. Righting myself, I surge onwards towards my destination.

Every time I turn the corner onto Brooke Street, the huge, red-bricked building that is Harris Hotel never fails to take my breath away. Its numerous windows, Union Jack flags flying high above, and the grand Art Deco design across its walls make it stand out from every other building in the vicinity. I'm proud to work here. I even turned down a job opportunity at Claridge's, which is just round the corner.

I may be a senior member of staff, but I still enter the building via one of the back entrances, especially since I have a dog, so I walk down the small alley, a cut-through so I don't have to walk in a square around the whole building, and open the door.

My first port of call is the laundry, where I pick up my crisp, clean uniform: a smart black-and-white dress, fitted to perfection. I also put on Muffin's ID badge, which attaches to her collar. Every morning a freshly ironed uniform is waiting for me, and I dress in the nearby changing rooms with the other housekeepers. I enjoy the chatter of voices while I get changed, very rarely joining in unless I'm spoken to. Muffin sits quietly by my side.

Mary, the Executive Housekeeper, is already there, changing into her smart skirt suit. She's in charge of everything to do with housekeeping. I may be the Senior Housekeeper, but Mary is my boss. She doesn't clean a single thing, but organises everyone else, does all the boring paperwork and coordinates everything to perfection, ensuring the housekeeping personnel work and communicate like a well-oiled machine.

'Hi, Kim,' she says as soon as she sees me. She glances sideways at Muffin. I get the feeling she doesn't agree with me having a dog while working, since she always complains about finding dog hair in rooms I've been in, despite cleaning them. But I brush Muffin every day and if there's a room where I can't take her in for whatever reason, then I never break the rules.

Mary is much older than me, in her early fifties I think, although I've never asked her for her exact age. I turned twenty-five four months ago, celebrating my birthday alone with a single cupcake I bought from a lavish bakery. One cupcake cost almost eight pounds, but it was worth it. Muffin had a single lick of icing and a small corner of cake.

'Morning, Mary. Anything to report?' I tend not to ask my work colleagues anything personal. I just go straight into work mode when I'm here.

'Room seven has a nasty stain on the carpet. I've closed it off until further notice, but I'd like you to ensure it's clean by the end of the day. Susan is off sick today, so make sure the other staff pick up her jobs. Mrs Londis in the Park Suite would like us not to use lavender while washing her items as she's allergic and she's also allergic to dogs.' At this point she shoots Muffin another sideways glance, then continues. 'And the penthouse has a new arrival today. Jennifer Clifton, an extremely wealthy woman who has a long list of requirements, so I'd like you to take point and ensure she has everything she needs. She's checking in at eleven.' Mary rattles off the list without taking a breath. Her back is ramrod straight and her hair is piled on top of her head in a stylish bun.

I nod. 'Consider it done.' Mary doesn't need to worry about me not remembering anything because I have an uncanny knack for memorising lists in my head even if I only hear or read them once. Another quirk of mine that's extremely handy.

'Oh, and the team meeting is in ten minutes, and I'd like you to lead it because I have to rush off to speak to Alan on the front desk.'

'No problem.'

'Thanks, Kim.'

* * *

The team meeting goes smoothly. Susan being off sick means there's extra work for me and the team to do, but no one complains as I hand out the extra jobs to various housekeepers who are all lined up with military precision with their hands behind their backs in neat little rows.

My main concern for the morning is to ensure the penthouse is pristine and ready for our special guest. Jennifer Clifton has never stayed here before, so I have no idea who she is or what she looks like, but whoever stays in the penthouse is sure to be wealthy and important. Mary provided me with a list of her requirements, but I've already memorised them, so I'm now heading to the penthouse to ensure everything is in order for her arrival. Muffin is hot at my heels.

As the lift doors ping open, the grandeur of the penthouse suite expands before me in both directions across the top floor of the entire hotel. There are already housekeepers milling about, straightening flower arrangements, hoovering perfect lines in the plush grey carpet and dusting the various picture frames adorning the walls.

The penthouse unveils a new level of luxury and covers 11,840 square feet with views across 360 degrees of the London skyline, complete with a 400-metre private roof garden, a nine-metre swimming pool and a state-of-the-art kitchen with an impressive and vast wine collection. It consists of four emperor bedrooms and sleeps up to eight people. The entire penthouse is glass-wrapped and studded with skylights, flooding the entire place with views of the changing skies across Mayfair and London from sunrise to sunset.

There is even a private butler for the penthouse. Today, it's Mr Evans, a greying, handsome man who looks as if he's stepped out of a catalogue. His suit is pressed and expertly tailored.

'Morning, Kim. Morning, Muffin,' he says, tipping his hat to us as we arrive.

'Mr Evans,' I respond. 'You all ready for Mrs Clifton?'

'Of course, although I believe it's *Miss* Clifton.'

'Oh, my mistake. Thank you for correcting me.' Phew, that would have been a disaster. I pride myself on getting everything right for our guests and even an embarrassing slip like that is not up to my professional standard. Everything must be perfect, especially for someone such as Miss Clifton, whose excessive list of demands is beyond anything I've ever seen before from a guest.

I suppose it's time to get started and ensure each one is ticked off the list.

She'll be here in less than four hours.

Come on, Muffin, we've got work to do.

CHAPTER TWO

Jennifer

What I wouldn't give to be young again. I'm not talking about being a teenager. Who the hell wants to go back to having acne and all those crazy hormones? Maybe early twenties. Before my body started aching after a hard day on my feet, when I could dance all night and still have the energy to go to work with little more than a headache.

Now, my body doesn't feel like my own. Then again, it never has been my own, not for a long time. I've never been free to be me and my goal in life is to be exactly that. Me. But who am I exactly? That's the real question I've been toying with for a long time now. Despite my wish to be young again, I know I'm where I need to be.

Right here. Right now.

A twinge in my lower back signifies I may have pushed myself too far yesterday with the stretches in my Pilates session, or perhaps it's merely my age. My body looks in its mid-thirties, toned and tight and defined, every muscle sculpted to perfection from vigorous Pilates, weight training and cardio, but in reality, my body is forty-four. I've had to work hard to transform myself, often working and training long into the night. It cost a fortune too, but luckily money isn't a problem. Not anymore.

Today, I feel my age.

Sometimes, I wonder if I've missed out on the best years of my life, living and working in this hotel, but I know it's for a good reason, a good cause. Everything I do is for a reason.

This morning, I've missed my healthy greens shake and plant collagen mix, and I had to skip my early morning yoga routine because I was told the traffic was bad and if I didn't leave at six, I'd never arrive at my destination in time for my eleven o'clock check-in.

So here I am, sitting in the back of my white limousine, wearing oversized sunglasses despite the dreary and dark morning. I like to hide behind them, especially when my eyes are itchy and puffy, and I want nothing more than to scratch them out. Luckily, the shades accentuate my outfit, a Dior skirt suit with an oversized bow at the back, which does make sitting in a car slightly uncomfortable. The sides of my Jimmy Choos dig into the soft skin of my ankles as I sit cross-legged, but I ignore the sting of pain and focus on the task ahead of me.

I'm travelling to London to stay at Harris Hotel for two nights in their deluxe penthouse suite. I've been told it's the best, so I'm expecting the best. No, I'm expecting complete and utter perfection, in every single way. At least, that's what everyone expects me to want. Being Jennifer Clifton is exhausting and complicated, but it's what people want from me, so I must keep up appearances, and that includes looking and acting the part.

I may be wealthy as the sole owner of Clifton Hotel, but no one outside of a close-knit community knows who I am. The name Jennifer Clifton will fall on deaf ears. My father, Damien Clifton, on the other hand, is quite notorious in certain circles. However, he's taken a long sabbatical for the past year and left me to run things, which is what I prefer. Damien is, shall we say, an acquired taste and although I'm expected to look up to him, love him, respect him, I don't. He's vile, manipulative and controlling and I'm glad he's taking some time out. Besides, I'm more than capable of running Clifton Hotel. The party of the year is only two weeks away and, so far, everything has gone smoothly. I just need one more person to join the guest list.

Clifton Hotel is the most prestigious hotel in the country. And yet it's completely unknown. It is not a chain. It's a single hotel that caters to only a select and specialised clientele. Not celebrities, not the exceptionally wealthy, but guests who are hand-selected based on their needs and demands. It isn't found on any Google search, map or hotel listing. It is, for all intent and purposes, invisible. Clifton Hotel is unique and even though my stomach lurches at the thought of what goes on behind closed doors, I turn a blind eye. Because I have to. I'm Jennifer Clifton.

'We shall be arriving in three minutes, Miss Clifton,' says my driver, Valerie.

I unfold my hands from my lap, disturbing Frankie, my Pomeranian, who growls at me, and press the button on the side to lower the glass partition between the front and the back of the car.

'Thank you, Valerie. Please pull up around the side entrance as we discussed.'

'Yes, ma'am.'

Valerie is my most trusted driver and a dear friend. I have a multitude of staff members, some of whom I like and some I don't, but Valerie has been on my side from the start. However, the past year she's really stepped up and proved to me just how trustworthy and loyal she is. In fact, she's the one who told me that the person I was looking for was at this hotel. She's the reason I'm here today. Valerie found her for me.

Frankie settles back on my lap. He and I have a strained relationship at times. He's never really warmed to me as his owner. I get the feeling he tolerates me to keep getting food, love and attention. Plus, he's a diva and if he wants to continue to be fed and pampered then he has to at least act like he likes me on occasion. I do like dogs, but Frankie isn't a dog. He's an overbred ball of fluff whose sole purpose is to look cute one minute and rip your throat out the next. I don't trust him, even when he's snoring peacefully on my lap like an unexploded bomb.

Valerie stops the car at our designated drop-off location around the back of the hotel. I wait while she gets out and opens my door. Frankie jumps up.

'You know you can't come with me.'

Frankie yaps then plonks his bum on the leather seat next to me.

'Please make sure you take him for a walk,' I tell Valerie. 'I don't want another accident on the leather seats.'

'Yes, ma'am.' She extends her hand for me to grasp, as I manoeuvre myself out of the car, something that is difficult to do with elegance and grace while wearing sky-high heels and a short skirt.

'Thank you, Valerie.'

She gives me a curt nod. We have an understanding about a lot of things. Therefore, we don't need to say a lot to each other to communicate effectively. I wish more people were like Valerie.

A doorman is standing by the back door, ready to receive me, but it's the smartly dressed man in a suit who rushes towards me.

'Miss Clifton, a delight to meet you. I am Mr Evans, your personal butler. I hope your journey was pleasant?'

'Thank you. Yes, it was.'

'Delighted to hear it. Please, follow me and I shall show you to your suite. I am available night and day to attend to your needs. Anything at all.'

I raise my eyebrows behind my dark glasses, but I know Mr Evans can't see me. It's always odd to be treated like royalty, despite no one knowing who I am. To them, I'm just some wealthy woman staying in their hotel who has paid over the odds for a suite and who has provided a list of varied and complicated demands. I know it's all for show. They are paid to be at my beck and call. It's not real respect. In fact, other than Valerie and Courtney, my senior housekeeper, I doubt one member of staff respects me or even likes me. But that's fine. Being Jennifer Clifton means one must make tough decisions, be ruthless, cruel and unlikeable. It's just the name of the game. And in this industry, one must be all those things and more to survive. I should know.

I walk behind my personal butler through the back doors, glancing briefly from left to right, checking out the decoration and attention to detail. This hotel may be posher, more expensive and elite than mine, but my hotel has something that no other hotel has and that's *a big secret*.

My heart rate climbs the further into the building I walk. I focus on keeping my eyes dead ahead, rather than searching the rooms for who I'm looking for. Maybe she won't even be here today. Maybe it's her day off. I cannot make it look as if I'm searching for her. I will know her when I see her. I'm almost sure of it.

We step into the gold-plated lift where gentle music is playing. Mr Evans has his hands neatly folded behind his back as he waits with me while the lift ascends. Perhaps he's nervous, or maybe he's been told not to engage me in conversation. I often find wearing oversized sunglasses makes people wary of talking to me. It makes me look as if I want to hide, which is the truth. Hiding in plain sight is my specialty.

As the lift doors ping open, I hold back a gasp. Gosh, the penthouse is quite spectacular, but it's not the reason I'm here. I am here for one sole purpose, yet the hotel staff don't know anything about it. Nor will they. I don't think I've ever been in a suite as magnificent and glorious as this. The penthouse at my hotel is expensive and grand, but this is another level.

I am pleased to see my request of a high-backed, recliner chair is set up and ready for me by the vast windows which span across the entire floor and look out across the London skyline. I've found London to be an ugly city. I've visited several times in the past year, and it's always been disappointing. There are a few attractive buildings, but mostly it's dingy and dark, especially when you walk through the streets. Not a lot impresses me when it comes to location because my hotel is situated in the most beautiful countryside, surrounded by nothing but fields, woodland and rivers.

I take a seat on the high-backed chair, centring my bottom and crossing my legs at the ankles. A young housekeeper in a crisp black-and-white uniform is waiting nearby. Her eyes dart from side to side and her hands are trembling and I know for a fact she's trying hard not to stare at me. I don't blame her. She's probably wondering who the hell I am.

At my request, I was not given a tour of the suite, but I know there are four bedrooms, a swimming pool, a private roof garden and an entertainment room. I don't care to be shown around when I can easily explore myself later when I'm alone. There is classical music playing quietly in the background and the air smells of citrus. So far, so good.

There is a glass of water with a slice of lemon resting on the glass side table beside me. Small beads of condensation slowly run down the side of the glass, causing a water ring on the coaster. I pick up the glass of water and take a sip. I haven't removed my sunglasses, but I don't intend to, not yet. I find it helps to add a barrier between me and the person I'm speaking to. The less people see me, the better. I wouldn't want them to look too closely for fear of them seeing my many flaws.

I swallow the water and replace the glass on the table. I hold up my hand and the housekeeper immediately springs forward, stopping in front of me.

'Yes, ma'am. How can I be of assistance?'

'This water is too cold. I specifically requested the water be at sixty-two degrees, which this is not.'

The housekeeper picks up the glass. 'I shall get this changed straight away, ma'am.'

'I'm not finished. The temperature of this room is not sufficient. I need it increasing by two degrees. I would also like you to fetch me a packet of cigarettes that are precisely eighty-one millimetres long. I don't care what the brand is. I'd also like a back massage, performed by a young, male masseuse who is exactly six-foot-one and weighs between eighty and ninety-one kilograms. I would like my dog picking up from the front desk in five minutes and he must have a bowl of water delivered to this room no later than ten minutes after arriving. The water must be the same temperature as my own. Please also change these curtains. They are not to my taste, and I'd also like a cup of coffee from Columbia, heated to exactly two-hundred-and-one degrees with a dusting of cinnamon on top decorated in the shape of a rose petal.'

The housekeeper stares at me, a completely blank expression across her face. Her lower jaw drops open, and I can see that she's trying to speak, but I fear she may have forgotten her words, or perhaps they've got stuck at the back of her throat.

'Don't just stand there, girl! Did you hear what I said, or do you need your ears cleaning out?'

'I . . . I'm sorry, ma'am . . . I don't . . .' Her face turns bright red, and I can already see tears brimming. Oh dear, it seems I may have pushed her too far. Perhaps I was too blunt.

I sigh heavily, ensuring she knows exactly how disappointed I am in her. This is the part of being Jennifer Clifton that I hate the most. I'm supposed to be this strict, short-tempered woman who demands perfection. It's exhausting.

'This service will not do. It will not do at all. I suggest you fetch me someone who can not only perform the duties I have asked, but who will also not stand there like a fish, opening and closing their mouths as if they're gobbling up food. Where is Mr Evans, my butler?'

The terrified housekeeper shifts her eyes to the door. 'I'll go get him.'

'No,' I say. 'I don't want him. Who is your Senior Housekeeper?'

'Um . . . that would be Kimberley, ma'am.'

'Then fetch me Kimberley at once.'

The housekeeper's bottom lip trembles and without saying another word, she turns and scuttles out of the room faster than I've ever seen anyone move. I'm left in silence. I know I'm being rude and unnecessarily blunt, but not only do I have to keep up appearances, I'm also looking for a particular person. Someone who can keep up with my demands and who won't bat an eyelid when faced with an impossible instruction.

Kimberley is that person.

It's taken me a long time to find her, but now I get to meet her for the very first time.

She won't recognise me or know who I am. She won't have any idea who Jennifer Clifton is, but I know her, and she belongs at my hotel with me. I just need to get her there.

She's an important part of my plan.

She just doesn't know it yet.

She is the final party guest.

CHAPTER THREE

Emily

I remember being pregnant with you like it was yesterday. Despite feeling like an over-inflated balloon a lot of the time, I loved the feeling of you squirming around in my womb, all safe and cosy and warm. The early days were a mixture of nausea, strange food cravings and heartburn, but as the months wore on, I became accustomed to those things, and they were like background noise to all the wonderful parts of pregnancy that started happening, such as the little flutter kicks low in my belly and the hiccups you'd get randomly. I could have watched those little movements for hours.

However, when I reached eight months pregnant, walking became a struggle to the point where I dreaded my commute into work. At times, I resembled a waddling duck, my skin stretched so tight across my belly I couldn't imagine getting any bigger without my skin splitting. It was hard to believe I still had four weeks left until my due date. I didn't feel prepared, not even close, but you were on your way whether I was ready or not. I couldn't, wouldn't let you down.

Before seeing those two red lines appear on the stick, at nineteen, I always imagined my life would be different.

Eight months earlier, I was at university, studying to be a lawyer with an affectionate and loving boyfriend and parents who supported me. I stayed out as late as I wanted, drank too much, yet still managed to drag myself to class and get good grades. I was young, naive and very, very stupid, thinking I had everything I could ever want in my life.

One night changed everything.

The night I met him, your father.

Now, I was heavily pregnant, single, disowned by my family and living on next to nothing in a council flat in Leeds, working at a checkout counter at Tesco. I wasn't sure how I was supposed to give birth to and care for a baby, since I was still only a child myself. Finding out about you was a huge wake-up call, one I didn't see coming but I thank God every day that it did.

The only perk of working the tills was that I could sit down most of the day, but if I sat too long then my back would start spasming and my hips would seize up, so I'd have to get up and move around. However, I couldn't lift anything too heavy, so I was pretty much useless as a shelf stacker.

I didn't regret keeping you, despite how you were conceived, but I did regret ever thinking I could depend on anyone other than myself. Before finding out about you, I relied on my boyfriend and parents for everything. If I needed help with money, then my dad would bail me out. If I needed my clothes washing, then Mum would do it and if I needed to be picked up drunk from a party, then my boyfriend was there for me and would hold back my hair while I hugged the toilet. I thought I could continue to depend on them, that they'd be happy about my decision to keep you.

I was wrong.

My boyfriend was furious when I told him about you, which may have had something to do with the fact I hadn't had sex with him yet, and my parents were both horrified and disgusted with my life choices. They screamed that I was too young, that I was stupid for getting myself pregnant. They made it very clear either I got rid of you and continued to be supported by them, or I kept you, but would be on my own.

I made my choice.

I sometimes think I decided to keep you just to annoy my parents. I was always headstrong and stubborn but carrying you and knowing I was going to raise you by myself was enough to give me heart palpitations and heartburn. I sometimes cried myself to sleep in those early months when I lived in a shared house with my course mates. I realised I couldn't continue at university. I had very little money left from what my father gave me before I was pregnant, so I quit university and got myself a job.

Anyway, that pretty much gets me to the start of my story because I was about to experience another night that would change my life forever.

Just know that everything I've ever done has always been for you.

Always.

***

It was late at night and freezing cold. Gone ten and walking through the centre of Leeds was not my idea of fun on a Friday night. Eight months ago, I would have joined in with the drunken laughter and worn skirts short enough to be belts, but a lot had changed in that time. Now, I was heading home after a long shift at work, looking forward to standing under a hot shower and washing off the grime of the day. Maybe I could soak my swollen feet in a bowl of cool water too. I suffered a lot with swollen ankles. Water retention, I think my midwife called it.

My small flat was only half a mile walk from work, but my round stomach and aching feet made it feel much farther. I hoisted my shoulder bag up, rearranging it across my bump. I had no idea what I was going to do when you arrived. How was I supposed to look after you and earn enough money to feed us both and keep a roof over our heads? Maternity pay would only go so far and what about paying for childcare while I worked? I could have begged my parents for help, but they had made it very clear that I wasn't welcome back home unless I decided to give you up for adoption when you were born. There was no way that was going to happen. My parents kept repeating in their texts and voicemails how disappointed they were that I got myself pregnant and decided to throw away my career before it had even begun. It's not as if I was only a few months away from graduating. I'd only started university less than a year before, but they didn't see it that way. I had thrown everything away, in their eyes, to become a single mother with no prospects and no future. But it wasn't my fault.

My boyfriend, Daniel, wouldn't return my calls and when I went round to his parents' house to speak to him and apologise a few weeks after I told him the truth, they told me he had transferred to a different university down south. They knew nothing about my pregnancy, so I didn't bother telling them. Daniel had made his decision too. He wasn't your father, and he wouldn't believe me even though I tried to explain that I hadn't cheated on him.

No one was going to help me.

No one wanted us.

I placed a hand on my belly, feeling your little flutters as I walked. We were nearly home. I had to be back at work at seven in the morning, so I'd have to eat fast and get to bed. You drained my energy so fast. I didn't know if you were a boy or girl yet, so I used to call you Baby Bean. I wanted your gender to be a surprise. I didn't care either way. As long as you were healthy.

Footsteps behind me made me turn and glance over my left shoulder. I had moved away from the bright lights of the city centre and was now taking a known shortcut through some narrow back streets to my flat, saving me walking an extra ten minutes or so. It was very unusual for me to meet anyone down the side roads, but as I walked, I kept hearing footsteps, stopping and starting, as if their owner were following me and then ducking out of sight when I turned.

'Hello?' I called out, my voice wobbling.

My hands automatically covered my bump as I turned around to continue my walk home, but I didn't get any further. It happened very fast.

I let out a loud scream just before a large hand clamped over my mouth. I bit down, but the person holding my mouth shut didn't seem to care. I tasted blood; mine or theirs I didn't know. I was shoved up against the brick wall. My eyes widened as a flash of a blade appeared and a stab of pain alerted me to the fact it was pressed against my side, only my soft flesh between its sharp edge and you. My bladder released itself and my legs gave out, but my attacker held me up, pinning me against the cold wall.

'Don't make a sound or I'll slice you open, and your baby will fall out of you right here and now, you got it?'

I squeaked, tears streaming from my eyes.

This was it. That's what I thought.

All I thought about in those terrifying moments was you, safely cocooned inside my belly. Yet I was failing you. I couldn't keep you safe.

My attacker raised a large object above their head and brought it down on my temple.

Everything turned black.

* * *

I found myself in that weird space between asleep and awake where I wasn't sure what was real and what wasn't. I was stuck in that space for ages, it seemed. I couldn't find my way out, constantly fighting to wake up, yet wanting to stay unconscious because I knew that when I awoke, I wouldn't like the reality I'd find myself in.

Once I was awake, it took my brain longer than normal to remember what had happened. The memory of the attack slid together piece by piece like a puzzle and as soon as my brain recognised the picture, my hands flew to my stomach, searching for a little kick or sign that you were alive and well. I couldn't feel any movement, so I kept my hands still, resting on my bump, while I sat up slowly and scanned my new surroundings.

My heart was racing, and I expected my blood pressure was high. I did my best to control my rapid breathing, but as the reality dawned on me, it began to run away with me again. Quicker and quicker. Higher and higher.

I was in a white room, no bigger than ten by ten-foot square, sitting on a single bed wedged in the corner. Stains were everywhere. Brown stains. Yellow stains. Red stains. I won't lie to you, but the horror I felt in that moment was unlike anything I'd ever experienced before. It gripped my insides so tight that I couldn't take a breath. My body had forgotten how to breathe. All I could think about was the room, and what all those stains were. And, more importantly, why was I there?

A small door was directly opposite me, but there was no handle, no keyhole. It appeared to be the only way in or out of this room, but there was a square grate in the wall in the far corner. Again, there didn't seem to be any way of opening it from this side.

A single light bulb flickered ominously above. I was still wearing the same clothes as before: my work uniform of black trousers and a loose-fitting shirt with the Tesco logo on it. The trousers were damp around my crotch and the smell of urine turned my stomach. I clamped a hand over my mouth to force myself not to vomit.

Once I was certain I wasn't going to retch, I reached both hands out in front of me and knelt on the floor on all fours, then grasped the side of the bed frame and pulled myself up to standing. It was the only way I could stand.

The room tilted sideways, and I stumbled against the bed, collapsing back onto it. The bedsprings squeaked and groaned under my weight. I had already put on over a stone during my pregnancy and with still four weeks to go, I was dreading how much more I was going to add on. I wasn't big. In fact, my bump was "fairly neat" as my midwife kept saying, but I felt big, considering I was a size twelve before pregnancy. I wasn't used to carrying the extra weight, and my poor back was suffering. I didn't blame you though, as long as you were big and healthy too.

The room was hideous and had a stale odour. My eyes kept focusing on the stained areas of the walls, floor and ceiling. I decided to investigate. Once I gained my balance, I shuffled over to a stained area of the wall and studied it.

Upon closer inspection, I realised the stains were splatters of . . .

A lump in my throat made me almost choke.

Oh my God . . .

I looked up at the ceiling. Small freckles of blood dotted the entire space, along with spots of black mould. There was blood and mould everywhere.

I glanced down at my swollen feet. My shoes and socks had been removed. The carpet was worn and rough. It was difficult to make out what the original colour had been because it was so discoloured from blood and who knew what else.

My nose wrinkled at the thought.

I hobbled across to the only door in the room and pressed my ear against it. There was no sound at all from the other side. I crouched down, closed one eye and attempted to peer through the tiny crack where the hinges were attached. I ran my hands up and down the door, searching for any sort of hidden button or mechanism.

'Hello?' I called out, pushing my lips close to the crack in the door. 'Is anyone there?'

I was met by silence, but something made me turn and look over my shoulder, a slight breeze. Then, a thud from somewhere below. The grate rattled in the wall.

Swallowing my fear, I walked across to the grate and crouched in front of it. Again, I ran my hands around the edges, trying to hook my fingertips around the metal to pull it away from the wall, but it was tight and solid. The breeze came again, blowing my hair against my face.

'Hello?' I called.

Another thud.

I couldn't see very far through the grate because the wire mesh was so close together and whatever was behind it was dark, or there was something blocking the way.

I shuffled onto my bottom, placed my feet against the grate and used one to kick it, hoping to find a weak point, but it held fast.

I was trapped in this room.

But the question remained.

Why?

CHAPTER FOUR

Kimberley

At eleven o'clock, I reach into the pocket of my uniform and remove my inhaler, taking two puffs as required. My doctor has prescribed it for me ever since he first diagnosed my asthma at age seven. Taking regular puffs from the inhaler helps to prevent a possible attack by opening and clearing the airways. Without regular use of the inhaler, my breathing becomes increasingly laboured, even if I'm not triggered by anything. I suppose I don't have to take it regularly, but I'd rather not have an asthma attack because it's usually followed by an epileptic seizure; the medication for that I take first thing in the morning.

Returning the inhaler to my pocket, I straighten my uniform, pick up the clipboard with my jobs on it and check it over once more. I've made the necessary arrangements and ensured all the general housekeepers are prepared for Miss Clifton's arrival and stay. It's gone eleven now, which means she's in the penthouse and settling in. I checked and double-checked her list of requirements, even adjusting the room temperature by one degree to ensure it was to her liking. I don't see any complications arising, so I head to the laundry to begin my daily routine, but since Mary has left me in charge while she's in a meeting, I also need to complete a walking inspection of the hotel. I have a walkie-talkie attached to my waistband and I don't even make it to my first destination before it goes off. Muffin's ears prick up.

'Senior Housekeeper, please report to housekeeping reception one.'

'On my way.' I sigh, looking down at Muffin. 'Come on, I'll let you out for a quick wee on route.'

Muffin does a cute mlem and follows me. I don't use a lead with Muffin. She's completely trustworthy and fully trained. The only time I use a lead is when I'm walking her outside, but in the hotel she's free.

I turn around and take the short cut back through reception towards the housekeeping reception area. I assume something's gone wrong somewhere, either with the penthouse guest or perhaps another emergency. I'm only ever called to the housekeeping reception when there's an issue or a complaint. It's the worst part of this job, but luckily, due to the high standards expected of us, it's rare there is a serious complaint or issue.

As I turn the corner, a loud sob erupts in front of me, then I see one of the housekeepers sitting on a chair with her head in her hands while another stands over her with a tissue, gently patting her back. Muffin's ears prick up again and she scoots over and sits next to the crying woman, letting her know she's there for her by nudging her leg.

'What's happened?' I ask in a calm voice, even though inside panic is beginning to rise. A crying housekeeper is never a good sign. I recognise her as one of the housekeepers who was assigned to the penthouse. I gave her the job because she's one of the best. Her name is Lucy. She's only twenty, but she has a great work ethic, and her standards are almost as good as mine.

Lucy ignores me to begin with because she's too busy stroking Muffin's head and her velvety ears. I can't blame her.

Muffin is the best at comforting people who are upset. She's not just my seizure alert dog but acts as a therapy dog for the entire staff, apart from Mary who is yet to warm to her puppy dog eyes and wagging tail.

Lucy finally looks up at me, still stroking Muffin with one hand while the other dabs her eyes with a tissue. Her mascara is streaking down her cheeks, her eyes are red, her hair's a mess and she's trembling all over. Good God, what on earth could have happened to cause such a reaction?

'Are you hurt?' I ask.

'N-No,' she says with a sob. The housekeeper standing next to her, Michael, hands her a clean tissue, which Lucy takes, and she blows her nose. I wait until she's finished.

'Michael, thank you, but I can take it from here.'

He nods at me, gives Lucy a sympathetic look and disappears down the hall to continue with his duties. I don't like the fact that with Lucy being here, I'm another housekeeper down, especially since she's from the penthouse.

'I need you to tell me exactly what happened, Lucy, so I can sort it out.'

Lucy sniffs loudly, keeping her eyes on Muffin. 'M-miss Clifton, the guest in the penthouse . . . she . . . wasn't happy and gave me a long list of things to have changed, but they were so complicated that I can't remember them, and she was so rude and mean.' She lets out a small whimper. 'She asked for you.'

'She asked for me specifically?'

'Well, she asked who the Senior Housekeeper was and since I know Mary's busy this morning, I gave her your name. Then she asked me to fetch you.'

I let out a long sigh. 'What about her personal butler, Mr Evans?'

'She didn't want him. She wanted you.'

'Do you remember anything of what she needed changing or what was wrong with the room?'

Lucy shakes her head, but then stops and sniffs. 'Something about a dog, I think, that needs to be picked up from reception.'

'Okay, leave it with me. I'll see to her. I need you to clean yourself up and get back to work, okay? Please go and see to room eight.'

Lucy nods, wiping her runny nose with the tissue. 'T-Thank you. I'm sorry. Please don't fire me.'

'I'm not going to fire you. I'll get this all sorted out. It will be fine, okay?'

'Okay.'

Muffin whines slightly and gives her leg another nudge. Lucy tickles her behind the ears. 'You know, Muffin really is the best dog.'

'That she is,' I reply with a smile.

I then take off towards the lifts, moving as fast as I can without drawing attention to myself with Muffin close at my heels. I need to act quickly and ensure Miss Clifton's demands are met. The last thing I want is this getting back to Mary. Everything had been perfect. I'd checked it myself, so either something drastic has happened and someone has sabotaged her arrival, or Miss Clifton is one of those awkward guests who just like to complain. Unfortunately, those types of guests are not uncommon. I always find, the higher up they stay, the more finicky they are. The penthouse guests are the worst. More money than sense, I always say. Nothing's ever good enough for them.

The lift doors open, and I enter the penthouse. Nothing looks out of place. It's all exactly as I remember leaving it earlier this morning. The only minor difference is the slight smell of perfume — expensive. I wrinkle my nose, hoping it doesn't set off either my asthma or seizures. It's been known to happen. I'm like a walking talking time bomb.

'Miss Clifton?' I call out.

There's no answer, but I do hear a faint noise coming from the dining area, so I turn and head in that direction. As soon as I enter, I spot an extremely attractive woman with blonde hair, perfectly manicured nails and dark, oversized glasses. She's sitting in a chair by the window, staring across the city. I clear my throat to announce my arrival, but I know she knows I'm here.

'Miss Clifton, my name is Kimberley. I'm the Senior Housekeeper here at Harris Hotel. I understand there was a problem with the room. I am very sorry for this inconvenience, and I will get the issues fixed as soon as possible.'

Miss Clifton slowly turns her head to look at me, making it as obvious as possible that I'm an inconvenience by being here. 'I'm extremely disappointed,' she says. Then she catches sight of Muffin sitting at my heels. 'That's not *my* dog.'

'No, ma'am, sorry. This is Muffin. She's my seizure alert dog. I can remove her from the room if you'd prefer.'

'That won't be necessary.'

Is it me or has she softened slightly since catching sight of Muffin? Her shoulders have relaxed, and her tone of voice has dropped an octave.

'I have my own dog,' she says. 'Frankie. They are such wonderful pets, are they not?'

'Yes, ma'am. In fact, Muffin is not only a great pet, but she's saved my life on more than one occasion.'

Miss Clifton's chin lowers a fraction of an inch. I can see her cheeks are flushed behind her huge glasses. She doesn't respond to my comment, so I decide to tackle the matter at hand.

'I am very sorry, Miss Clifton, for the discrepancies. I saw to it myself that all your demands were met. I take it upon myself to rectify them immediately.'

Miss Clifton stares at me for several long seconds from behind her glasses, but then, she reaches up and pulls them down off her face, revealing the most striking set of eyes I've ever seen. She must be wearing special contact lenses because there's no way those bright blue eyes are natural. Or perhaps they are, it's difficult to tell. Her eyes are framed by thick layers of mascara covering exceptionally long lashes, which are most likely fake. I can't do anything except stare at her, as if her eyes are drawing me into her innermost thoughts. Her gaze travels up and down my body, scanning me and I suddenly feel very self-conscious. I know my uniform is impeccable, but with those eyes it wouldn't surprise me if she could see through the material to my underwear.

I gulp, aware my hands are shaking slightly. Why the hell am I nervous of this woman? She's no different to any other self-indulged, rich guests I've encountered before. Maybe it's the way she's staring at me that's making my insides flip.

'Please could you repeat what you told the previous housekeeper, and I will be more than happy to sort it out.'

Miss Clifton finally takes her eyes off me and glances out of the window at the London skyline. 'The last girl clearly didn't remember any of it, so I suggest you get yourself a pad and pen. I won't be repeating myself for a third time.'

I shake my head. 'That won't be necessary. I have an exceptional memory.'

This receives another long stare and an eyebrow raise. 'Very well.' She points at a glass of water resting on the table beside her. 'This water is too cold. I specifically requested the water be at sixty-two degrees, which this is not. The temperature of this room is not sufficient. I need it increasing by two degrees. I would also like you to fetch me a packet of cigarettes that are precisely eighty-one millimetres long. I don't care what the brand is. I'd also like a back massage, performed by a young, male masseuse who is exactly six-foot-one and weighs between eighty and ninety-one kilograms. I need this massage set up for one hours' time. I would like my dog picking up from the front desk and she must have a bowl of water delivered to this room no later than ten minutes after arriving. The water must be the same temperature as my own. Please also change these curtains. They are not to my taste, and I'd also like a cup of coffee from Columbia, heated to exactly two-hundred-and-one degrees with a dusting of cinnamon on top decorated in the shape of a rose petal.' She never breaks eye contact with me during her rapid speech. If I didn't know any better, I'd say it was rehearsed.

I nod curtly. 'I'll get on it straight away, ma'am.'

I turn and am about to walk away when I hear her rise to her feet. 'I'm not finished,' she says.

'My apologies, ma'am.'

'I need three round scones of no more than six centimetres in diameter and the newest book release by Richard Osman in paperback. I would also like you to move that chair over to that corner.' She points out her request.

'I'll get someone up here straight away.'

'No, I'd like you to do it right this moment.'

I stop and hold my breath, momentarily stunned by her request. It's a large chair and I'm not sure if I can even move it by myself. 'I . . . Yes, of course, ma'am.' I glance at Muffin. 'Stay,' I say.

Miss Clifton then sits and watches me while I manhandle the chair across the room. I dare not drag it, for fear of messing up the perfect hoover lines in the carpet, so I have to lift it, shuffle a few feet, place it down, take a breath and repeat the process several times before it's in its new location by the opposite window.

She doesn't thank me, nor does she acknowledge me in any way as I walk past her, slightly out of breath, towards the lift doors. When I reach them, I turn back to Muffin. 'Come,' I say. Muffin obeys.

Miss Clifton keeps her gaze on me until the lift doors ping closed and that's when I let out a long breath. What the actual hell just happened?

The woman makes me nervous, more nervous than I've ever been around another person, but that's not why my heart is racing, and a swell of nausea overwhelms me. I'm taken back to my childhood when my foster parents would order me to do things, their constant gaze criticising my every movement. Perhaps that's why I make such an excellent housekeeper — because I do everything that's asked of me without question and I do it to the best of my ability because if I didn't, I'd be punished as a child. As an adult, I've been moulded by my strict upbringing to never question anything. Just do it.

I'm not one for confrontation either. I hate it. It sends my pulse sky-high and my palms sweating. It felt as if Miss Clifton was testing me, searching for any weaknesses. Clearly, the fact I can memorise a long list of complicated items impressed her, but why all the odd requests?

All these requests are completely unnecessary and contradict her original lists of demands, so there must be a reason why she's making such a fuss. She put on her original list that she hates coffee, so the fact she's requested a cup is ridiculous.

There was a moment when she saw Muffin and seemed to soften, but then she turned into a ruthless . . . well . . . *bitch*, is the only way to accurately describe her. I'm torn because the woman fascinates me yet also terrifies me. She stared at me as if she were trying to read my mind.

I could go round and round in circles trying to decipher exactly why she did what she did, or I could just get on with it and start working my way through her list of demands.

Muffin whines at me.

I look down.

Oh God, not now.

She whines again, then barks. It's her alert signal. I'm about to have a seizure. Perfect timing as always. I put Miss Clifton out of my mind and sit down on the floor with my back up against the wall. Muffin rests her head on my legs just as a seizure grips my body.

CHAPTER FIVE

Jennifer

Not a lot of people surprise me anymore. Even fewer shock me, but Kimberley, the mild-mannered housekeeper who's just left the penthouse, has done both and left me almost speechless. Well, speechless inside my head anyway. I had to speak to her like that otherwise I wouldn't be Jennifer Clifton.

When she told me about the dog and her epilepsy, I almost burst into tears. I hadn't been expecting that. There's a lot I don't know about her yet. It shouldn't derail my plans for her, but it certainly throws a spanner in the works, as it were. I won't be treating her any differently. Most people with disabilities don't want to be treated different from anyone else. They just want to be treated like a human being, as we all do. However, I've not been treated like a human being for the past twenty-five years. Just saying.

Kimberley is clearly a more senior member of staff, but she's more than that. She has an air about her that makes me think she takes a great deal of pride in her work, not because it's just a job, but that it's part of her somehow. Plus, she hadn't needed reminding about my list of new demands, all of which I memorised. They took me hours to learn, which I'd done in the car on the drive here.

She'll make a great addition to my team. Of course, there's more to it than that, but Kimberley needs to believe I've sought her out, picked her out from the crowd. I need her at the hotel, then I'll watch her closely because I need her help.

I'm extremely interested to see how she handles my list of demands and what she comes up with. Her work ethic has already impressed me. Watching her shift that large, heavy chair across the room without a fuss has proved to me that she is willing to work hard, both physically and mentally to keep the guest happy. That's what it's all about.

The guest is always right and must always have exactly what they've asked for. I need a new housekeeper, but it's not exactly why I'm honing my sights on Kimberley. Clifton Hotel only hires the best, most exceptional staff, who have the dedication and pride that elevates them above the rest. I also need them to have discipline, etiquette and discretion. My hotel has some very special and interesting guests, and my housekeepers must be able to work to high standards and not question a single thing that's asked of them. I know that's Kimberley and she'll fit right in.

Twenty minutes later, three housekeepers enter the penthouse, but none of them is Kimberley. One is carrying a cup of coffee on a tray, along with a glass of water and a packet of cigarettes. One immediately approaches the curtains and begins to take them down, replacing them with a different design. And the other adjusts the temperature using the thermostat on the wall next to the door.

'Where is Kimberley?' I ask the one who is changing the curtains.

The housekeeper turns and curtseys. Seriously, curtseys? 'I'm sorry, ma'am. Kimberley is indisposed at the moment, but she'll be here as soon as she can.'

'Is everything all right?'

'Yes, ma'am. She's fine.'

I watch while the housekeepers mill about, fulfilling all the requests I gave Kimberley.

'Your masseuse will arrive in forty minutes' time,' one of the housekeepers says. 'Is there anything else I can get you, ma'am?'

'My dog?'

'Ah, yes, Kimberley will bring him up very soon.'

'Very well.'

The three housekeepers leave the penthouse. I glance at the cup of coffee on the side table, pick it up and admire the artwork sprinkled on the top. I take a sip. 'Perfect,' I say with a sigh.

***

Fifteen minutes pass before the lift doors open and Kimberley walks in carrying Frankie in her arms, who is squirming around, attempting to escape, most likely so he can play with Muffin, who is perfectly well-behaved trotting along at Kimberley's feet.

'My apologies, ma'am. I hope everything has been altered according to your liking.'

'Yes,' I say. 'You may place Frankie on the floor.'

Kimberley nods and places the dog down. Frankie immediately starts yapping and running in circles around Muffin who is sitting patiently with her head up, trying to avoid being licked by a crazed Pomeranian who is frothing at the mouth.

'Your dog is very well-behaved,' I say.

Kimberley smiles, stroking Muffin's head. 'May I let her play with Frankie for a moment? She doesn't get a lot of other dog interaction.'

I nod.

Kimberley gives a command to Muffin, who wags her tail as she and Frankie start bouncing and playing, lightly nipping each other's necks and licking mouths.

'Frankie doesn't usually enjoy playing with other dogs,' I say.

'He seems to like Muffin. He's a cutie,' replies Kimberley.

For a moment, I forget where we are and enjoy watching the two dogs play. Muffin skids a little on the tiled floor, but

Frankie is closer to the ground, his centre of gravity lower, so he can run circles around her.

'I hope you weren't indisposed for long,' I say, glancing at Kimberley.

Her cheeks redden. 'No, ma'am, I wasn't.'

Silence.

'Does it happen very often?' I don't wish to overstep the mark here, but I'm curious about her condition and how it affects her daily life.

'No, ma'am. It usually happens very unexpectedly, sometimes when I'm under stress or am triggered by something. Other times it catches me off guard, which is why I've got Muffin. She's able to give me several minutes' warning.'

'Dogs are incredible creatures, aren't they?'

'Yes, I don't know what I'd do without her.'

'I apologise for causing you stress earlier.'

'Oh, no, ma'am . . . It probably would have happened anyway.'

'In any case . . . I apologise.'

Kimberley smiles and nods. 'Thank you. Is there anything else I can do for you, ma'am? Frankie's water will be delivered in ten minutes.'

'No, thank you, Kimberley. That will be all. However, after my massage, I'd like to speak to you,' I say. 'Please could you return to the penthouse ten minutes after my massage has ended.'

Kimberley raises one eyebrow, but otherwise doesn't appear to look concerned. 'Of course, ma'am. Is there anything else I can do for you?'

'That will be all . . . for now,' I reply.

Kimberley calls Muffin who snaps out of play mode and re-enters work mode by following her to the lift. I turn away from the doors as they close. Bang on ten minutes later, a bowl of water arrives at exactly the right temperature for Frankie.

* * *

The massage is one of the best I've ever had. Not just because it's by a handsome man with strong hands, but because I'm pleased with what I've seen from Kimberley so far and I can relax slightly, but she has no idea what else I have in store for her. How can she? As far as she's concerned, I'm just an average guest who perhaps is slightly more finickity than normal.

She's about to come face to face with the offer of a lifetime. And she has no idea how much her life could change. It all depends on whether she's ready to take a leap into the unknown. If she is, then I'll give her the world. She could be a part of something spectacular, something world changing. I just hope she's ready for it.

* * *

Kimberley and Muffin arrive promptly after my massage. I'm relaxing in a white, fluffy bathrobe with my initials engraved on the front and sipping a cool glass of lemon water. My shoulders and neck feel so supple and relaxed now, smooth like butter. Frankie has fallen asleep at my feet, but as soon as the lift doors ping open and Kimberley and Muffin enter, he leaps to his feet and sprints across the room towards them, straight for poor Muffin who stands her ground.

Kimberley's professional persona slips for a moment as she bends down to stroke Frankie, but then she straightens her jacket and slaps on a smile as she approaches me.

'How was your massage, ma'am?'

'Delightful. I gave the man a very large tip.'

'I'm glad to hear it.'

I look her up and down again, taking note of her expertly tailored uniform. 'Tell me, Kimberley, are you happy working here?'

The question must take her off guard for a moment, but she's very good at covering her reactions. 'Yes, of course. This job is wonderful, and I've been very lucky to have gained such a reputable employer.'

I squeeze my lips together, pick up the glass of water and take a sip. 'Hmm . . . Do you know who I am?'

'I . . . Yes, of course, ma'am. You are Miss Jennifer Clifton.'

I watch her for any sign of doubt. It seems she's telling the truth.

'You don't recognise me?'

'No, I'm sorry, ma'am, but before today I'd never heard of you.'

I smile, amused at her honesty. Most people would attempt to lie and flatter me by saying of course they recognise me, but then I'd question them further and they'd trip over themselves. I don't care that she doesn't recognise me. She's not supposed to. It wasn't the point of the question.

'I like you, Kimberley.'

'Thank you, ma'am.'

'I don't like a lot of people. In fact, I can count on one hand the amount of people I do like. You're clearly a very dedicated, headstrong and intelligent young woman, and I would like to offer you a job.' I replace the glass on the table and watch her reaction.

She frowns ever so slightly. Not exactly the reaction I was expecting.

Frankie gets bored of receiving no attention from Muffin and decides to try his luck with Kimberley instead by pawing at her legs. I focus my eyes on Kimberley while I wait for her to respond. I like to make people nervous, allow them to respond in their own time. Not rush them. Frankie soon realises that Kimberley is also ignoring him and comes and jumps up on my lap, whining.

'A job, ma'am?'

'A job,' I say.

'I . . . Wow, thank you. I'm flattered, but . . .' Kimberley stops, perhaps thinking she might be offending me if she says no straight away. 'What is the job position, ma'am?'

She's interested, which means she's not completely happy here. It's a good sign.

48

'I am the owner of Clifton Hotel, an elite and unique hotel situated in the highlands of Scotland, miles from any town or village. The hotel itself is the most beautiful building you will see anywhere. There's a mystery to it that instantly draws you in. My staff are the best at what they do. You are wasted here. I could offer you much more money than you earn here.'

'I-I'm sorry, ma'am, but is this a housekeeping position?'

'Of sorts,' I reply with a smile. 'While there are duties involved for that of a housekeeper, there are other . . . more unique opportunities available to you.'

'Like what?'

I smile again, showing my perfect, straight teeth, which I had fixed a year ago. 'I'm afraid I can't divulge too many details at this point. You see, my hotel caters to some unique guests and clients. What goes on behind closed doors is not always, shall we say . . . *appropriate* to be spoken about outside of my close-knit community of staff.'

Kimberley's eyes light up with questions. 'I'm afraid, ma'am, that I'm not sure what you mean. Besides, I am very happy here in this position, but I appreciate the job offer.'

'Are you sure about that, Kimberley?'

Kimberley bites her lip.

I continue. 'As I said, this is a great opportunity for you. I am here for the next two days while I conduct some business, so you will have time to change your mind if you wish, but I implore you to think about your life here. I will also add that your medical conditions will be covered, any and all medication you require will be paid for and prescribed by my personal doctor.'

'Oh, I'm sorry, ma'am, but I've been seeing my doctor since I was a child. He knows my condition well. I wouldn't want to change to another.'

'Any doctor can prescribe and treat your condition, Kimberley.' She doesn't reply. Clearly, she has some sort of attachment to this doctor for whatever reason. 'I should also explain that the job is a live-in position at my hotel. All your expenses would be paid for, and you would have one day off per week.'

'A live-in position?'

'Yes, and Muffin would be welcome, of course.'

Kimberley glances down at her dog. 'May I think about it, ma'am?'

'Of course. You have two days. I leave early on Wednesday morning at six. If you'd like to travel with me, then report to reception at that time and we shall go up together. It's a fairly long drive, so you may ask whatever questions you have in the car.'

'Thank you, ma'am.'

'Oh, one more thing . . .'

'Ma'am?'

'If you do decide to take the job, then you'll be required to sign a non-disclosure agreement. What goes on behind the walls of my hotel is something that can never be spoken about outside of it. I take security very seriously. Oh, and please can you take Frankie for a walk? I think he needs to urinate.'

CHAPTER SIX

Emily

My heart rate wouldn't slow down no matter how hard I tried. Even though I wasn't moving, it felt like my heart was trying to leap out of my chest, pounding against my ribs like a convict rattling the bars of a prison cell. I lay on the floor by the grate in the wall, listening out for that noise again, but it didn't come. I yearned for the noise to appear, to provide me with some sort of hope that I wasn't alone. Tears streamed down my cheeks in miniature rivers for a long time until they collected at the lowest point on my chin and dripped onto the cold floor.

You finally kicked, announcing you were alive. You made me smile as I stroked my belly, but the moment I was grabbed in the alley kept replaying in my mind. I tried my best to recall the details, but they all blurred into one at first, so I took a deep breath, attempting to categorise my thoughts. It took a few minutes, but eventually the adrenaline from the attack and the shock of waking up in a locked room wore off and a few snippets of memory came into focus. Slowly.

It was a large man who attacked and threatened us. I didn't see his face, but I did see his lower arm, the one which wrapped around my neck, squeezing the breath from my body. There was a black tattoo on it, but its design eluded me. Possibly tribal, but I couldn't be sure. I also didn't remember the man's age. His voice had been rough, gravelly, so possibly not a young man, but with the balaclava over his face, it was impossible to tell.

The watch I usually wore on my left wrist was gone, so my concept of time was skewed. I could have been here for a day or an hour, although the fact I didn't need to go for a wee yet told me I hadn't been here more than a few hours at most. My bladder had emptied itself during the attack and during my pregnancy, I'd been used to weeing every hour, almost on the hour, due to your constant pressure on my bladder. It wasn't your fault, but you did seem to think my bladder was your first squeezy toy, only there for your entertainment. I supposed there wasn't a lot to do inside, except grow and kick.

The temperature of the room was still on the cool side. Not cold enough for me to shiver and be uncomfortable, but enough for goose bumps to prickle my skin. My jacket had been removed too. I rubbed my arms up and down, attempting to generate some warmth or at least wake my body up because sitting or lying for too long often gave me stiff muscles and joints, another lovely side effect of pregnancy.

The noise came again from behind the grate.

My heart leaped for joy and terror at the same time as I awkwardly knelt and peered through the wire mesh, closing one eye to see if it could adjust to the darkness beyond, but eventually my vision started blurring from keeping only one eye open. I decided to admit defeat and moved away from the grate towards the bed. My long day at work, combined with the physical abuse of the attack, was taking its toll on my tired body and mind. Exhaustion was bubbling behind my eyes, forcing them closed and nausea swelled in my stomach from lack of food and water. I knew you'd be okay, taking whatever nutrients and calories you needed from my body, but it meant I'd have to suffer until I could hydrate and replenish my energy stores.

I'd struggled at the start of pregnancy with severe morning sickness, although I felt that was something of a misnomer because it didn't only occur in the morning. At one point, I was sick all day. I had to keep myself hydrated. That seemed to keep it at bay, or at least reduce the symptoms, and I had to eat every couple of hours to avoid sickness. I hadn't suffered as badly with sickness after the first trimester ended, but heartburn was a constant companion now, especially after eating.

I needed water soon. Bile and acid from the heartburn kept rising up my throat, threatening to make an unwanted appearance. I lay down on the bed, but that made it worse, so I arranged the pillow against the small of my back and sat up against the wall with my legs out in front of me.

There was nothing left to do but rest and wait for someone to come in. I couldn't overexert myself or I'd be at risk of passing out or collapsing from exhaustion. I stretched my left leg out in front of me and gave it a rub. It was sore from the attack. I couldn't remember what had happened exactly. I had a few knocks and bumps, but nothing too serious. The main part of my body that hurt was the back of my head, presumably from where the man had knocked me out.

I still hadn't felt you kick properly since I'd woken up. Just that one small kick earlier. It may not have even been a kick. It could have been just my stomach gurgling. Usually, you'd perform flips and kicks like an expert gymnast throughout the day, but perhaps you were resting too, saving your energy like I was. I just hoped you were sleeping soundly, completely unaware of what had happened to me. The least I could do was ensure you were safe and comfortable while I was locked in here.

I needed answers.

Why was I here? I couldn't work it out. What could anyone possibly want with me? I kept myself to myself mainly. I had no enemies that I was aware of, and I didn't owe anyone any money.

Yet, someone had attacked me, taken me off the street and locked me in a room.

Eventually, my eyelids grew tired and closed. I kept an ear out for any sound, but it was so quiet in the room. Too quiet. I could hear my own heartbeat and breathing.

I didn't know how long I was asleep for, but a scratching sound woke me up. At first, it sounded like a mouse scurrying across a tiled floor, but then the sound got louder, clearer and stronger.

My eyes flung open.

A young, attractive woman stood at the foot of my bed in front of me, dressed in a simple black uniform, like something a housemaid would wear.

Before I could open my mouth and scream, she put a finger on her lips. 'Shhh, don't make a sound,' she whispered.

I shuffled towards the edge of the bed, moving in the awkward way heavily pregnant women did. I felt like a hippopotamus. 'Who are you?' I asked.

'It doesn't matter who I am. What's your name?' she replied.

That was when I noticed the tray she held in her hands. It had a glass of water and a plate with a slice of bread on it. She stepped to the side and held the tray out for me.

I picked up the water glass and began to drink. The first sip made me gag. 'What's in this?'

'Nothing bad. It's just water with added vitamins and minerals to replenish your electrolytes.'

I held the glass up to the dim light, searching for any particles floating around. It looked crystal clear, but it didn't taste right. However, it was either drink the funky-tasting water or risk dehydration and your safety. I continued to drink slowly.

'Why am I here?'

'What's your name?' she asked me again.

'Emily Coster.'

'Nice to meet you, Emily.'

'Where am I?' I tried again.

'I'll leave you to finish your bread and water,' said the woman, turning to leave.

'Wait!' I scrambled to my feet, flinching as a sharp pain in my groin made me almost double over. Lightning crotch, another delightful pregnancy symptom. 'What about the use of a toilet? I'm pregnant. I need a change of clothes too. I . . . soiled myself.'

The woman nodded. 'I'll see you have everything you need in due course.'

'I don't . . .' I sank back down onto the bed as a wave of dizziness enveloped me. Oh God. It must have been the water. They had put something in it. And I'd drunk it. I was so stupid. Of course they put something in it.

'W-What have you done to me? What have you given me? What if it harms the baby?' I screamed.

The woman smiled. It was not a smile that set my mind at ease. Instead, it sent shivers down my spine. 'Don't worry, Emily. Your baby will not be harmed. It is a very precious commodity indeed.'

The last thing I saw before I slipped into darkness and collapsed on the bed was the woman walking out of the door.

CHAPTER SEVEN

Kimberley

As I enter the lift, Muffin and Frankie at my heels, my mind overruns with questions. Did that just happen? It didn't make sense. Why is Miss Clifton here looking to hire me? I've never even heard of Clifton Hotel. Should I have? She said it was in the Scottish Highlands, a place I'm not overly familiar with, having never visited Scotland before.

A part of me wonders if it's all a hoax, but Jennifer Clifton doesn't seem like the type of woman who messes people around for the hell of it. She has set this up from the start with her list of demands and then her even crazier alterations to them, which had been too much for poor Lucy, but the more I spoke to her, the more she seemed to soften. We even watched our dogs play together and I spoke about my condition, something I very rarely do with people, especially strangers.

But she seemed genuinely interested and sorry for causing me stress earlier. And she likes me. I suppose it's better than her hating me and giving me a hard time.

'What do you think, Muffin?' I glance down at my dog, who lifts her head and seems to smile at me by panting a little.

'You're a good girl.' I stroke her head. Frankie yaps, clearly wanting in on the attention. I scoop down and pick him up. He's such a tiny ball of fluff.

Frankie licks my face. Now that I'm alone, I can fuss over him without drawing attention. He squirms and yaps as I tickle his velvety belly. He's the most gorgeous young dog.

The lift doors open, and it all happens in a flash.

Frankie yaps, wiggles free from my grasp and sprints into the bustling hotel reception. He does have a lead on, but not being used to using one, my grasp is weak, something he takes full advantage of, and it's yanked from my hand before I know what's happening.

Dozens of guests shriek in alarm as Frankie barrels into their legs, knocking over luggage and skidding across the shiny tiles. For a little dog, he's causing a lot of damage and mayhem.

'Frankie! Someone stop that dog!' The last thing I want is for him to run into the busy London streets and get hurt or lost. I doubt Jennifer would like me much if that happened.

I sprint across the reception area, all too aware that I'm not acting like a professional. Several staff members gasp and whisper to each other as Muffin and I rush past. Then I see Mary glaring in my direction, her back poker straight, her jaw clenched. She looks as if she's about to self-combust, but I can't think about her right now, or the repercussions of this because Frankie has now reached the front steps of the hotel and is tumbling down them towards the pavement outside, his lead trailing in his wake. Maybe if someone steps on the lead, they'd be able to stop him, but most people are doing their best to get out of his way as if he's a tiny, rolling grenade, ready to explode.

I throw myself down the steps, almost tripping over my legs, looking up and down the road for a flash of fluffy dog butt.

'Where is he, Muffin?'

Muffin glances left and takes off, so I follow. Muffin expertly dodges the city commuters as she chases after Frankie, who seems to be having a whale of a time because every head is turning in his direction as he runs past.

I see him stop and cock his leg on a lamppost, then take off again, his little legs moving so fast they're nothing but a fluffy blur.

I need to stop. Strenuous exercise can trigger my seizures, or I could give myself an asthma attack, but all I can think about is getting Frankie back safe.

Luckily, some careless human being has dumped a half-eaten hotdog by a bin, so Frankie stops to help himself. Muffin arrives next to him merely seconds later, with me bringing up the rear, puffing like a steam train. I grab Frankie's lead and pull him away from his feast.

'Goddamn it, Frankie. You could have been hit by a car!'

Frankie licks his lips and yaps.

I place a hand on my heart and glance at Muffin. 'We good?' I ask her.

She doesn't respond with any of her warning signals, so I assume I'm safe from an attack of any kind. I wrap Frankie's lead around my hand several times to be safe and start making my way back through the London crowds towards the hotel.

I then see a hotel porter running down the pavement towards me. He seems to sigh with relief when he sees me. He leans over and rests both hands on his knees and takes several gulps of air.

'Are you okay?' I ask him. It looks as if he's close to having an asthma attack himself.

'F-Fine, just . . . was worried about you.'

'Oh, well, I'm fine.'

'You got the dog back then?'

'Yes, luckily he was distracted by a half-eaten hotdog and stopped his escape to freedom.'

The porter nods. 'Mary didn't look happy,' he says as we begin walking back together.

'Leave Mary to me.'

'Who does the dog belong to anyway? It looks like it's stuck its foot in an electrical socket. Why's all its fur sticking up?'

'He's a Pomeranian. He's just fluffy,' I explain.

The porter doesn't respond. I assume he's not a dog guy. As we enter the hotel reception, he wishes me luck and returns to his porter duties just as Mary storms across the polished tiles towards me, eyes blazing, nostrils flaring. Oh shit.

'As if one dog following you around wasn't enough, I now see you've upgraded to chasing another one. I hope you have a good explanation as to why I just saw you running across reception chasing after a dog who looks as if he's been backcombed and stuck in a tumble dryer?'

'He's a Pomeranian. He's just fluffy. He belongs to Jennifer Clifton. She asked me to take him for a walk to stretch his legs and have a wee.'

Mary steps closer, keeping her voice low but stern, pronouncing every syllable in every word precisely. 'Your job is not to walk dogs to allow them to urinate. Your job is to ensure each and every room is up to standard and that the guests are happy. Is that clear?'

'Yes, but . . .'

'Give the dog to someone else and get on with your job.'

I nod, knowing better than to open my mouth and argue back. There's a time and a place to argue with Mary, but when her eyes are bulging out of her sockets and the vein in her forehead has its own pulse is not the time.

I hand Frankie to the porter who came after me. He agrees to return him to the penthouse after his walk, although I doubt Frankie will need much more of a walk after the sprint he just completed. I've never seen little legs move so fast before.

Muffin and I continue with our daily tasks. I don't hear any further complaints from the penthouse, although I do hear whispering from a few of the housekeepers regarding Jennifer Clifton, and none of it is flattering. It seems she's causing quite a stir.

***

A few hours later, Jennifer appears in reception. She's changed her outfit and is now wearing a stunning, tight-fitting dress with a black jacket. Her heels are high, and her sunglasses are still on, shielding her bright blue eyes. I'm standing behind the reception desk, checking over a few details with the receptionist when she approaches.

'Good afternoon, ma'am,' I say.

'Kimberley, I need you in the business suite right now.'

'Um . . . Yes, ma'am.'

She nods, spins on her heels and heads towards the hallway leading to the large, private business suite that's used for important meetings, presentations and workshops. Some guests like to hire it out to impress overseas businesspeople, but I get the feeling Miss Clifton isn't using it to impress people. She hasn't included any details about why she's hired the room on her hotel application.

'Wow, rude much?' says Rachel, the receptionist. 'No please or thank you. Not even a good afternoon.'

I sigh. 'It seems the more money people have the worse they think they can treat people.'

'Want me to call up to the housekeeping reception and get someone to cover you?'

'Please. Thanks, Rachel. Hopefully, I won't be long.'

Muffin raises her head as I step out from behind the desk. She'd just settled down for a nap and now huffs loudly as she stands and performs a big stretch. She has lots of places she can sleep around the hotel. A lot of the staff love having her around and ensure they make room for her if she's going to be staying in one place for a long time.

'Sorry, girl,' I say. 'You can stay here if you want?'

Muffin yawns and trots up to me, sticking close to my heels as we make our way to the business suite. I knock before entering.

The suite is set up with a large table that comfortably sits twenty people around it with the capacity to fit more if needed. A huge arrangement of freshly cut flowers adorns the centre of the table and in front of each place setting is a hotel-branded notebook and pen and a glass for water.

Jennifer is standing at the head of the table with Frankie in her arms, speaking to an attractive gentleman who's wearing a tailored, navy-blue suit. Neither of them turns to look at me as I enter. I stand by the door with my hands behind my back while I wait to be summoned.

They are speaking in hushed tones and by the looks of their body language, are quite familiar with each other. However, it's clear that Jennifer is not comfortable with the man's proximity because she's leaning backwards ever so slightly and when he reaches out and brushes a hand against her side, she flinches. The man has a dazzling smile, perfectly straight teeth, but I already know I don't like him.

After another minute of standing quietly, Jennifer breaks away from the conversation. Her whole body seems to relax the further away from the man she gets. The man smirks as he watches her walk away, but then his gaze turns and locks on me like a laser beam.

My insides feel like they've been blasted with liquid nitrogen as his eyes scan my entire body. He tilts his head as he notices Muffin at my feet.

Please don't speak to me. Please don't speak to me.

The man keeps his smirk in place as he makes his way around the table towards me. Then Muffin does something she's never done before. She growls, which tells me everything I need to know about the man walking towards me.

He stops several feet short of me, glancing down at Muffin as if she were a piece of meat. Clearly, her presence is enough to keep him from getting too close, which I am monumentally thankful for.

'Delighted to make your acquaintance,' he says, extending his hand. 'And you are?'

I open my mouth to speak, but Jennifer gets there first.

'None of your business. That's who. She's a housekeeper who I've offered to work for me.'

The man raises his eyebrows. 'I hope you've said yes.'

I stay quiet, pretty sure Jennifer doesn't want me conversing with him.

'She hasn't. Not yet. And if you keep pestering her then she won't ever want to come and work for me, will she?'

The man rolls his eyes so only I can see. 'Strict, that one, isn't she?' He adds a wink.

Muffin continues to growl softly, her eyes fixed on the man, like she's ready to rip his throat out when given the command. I've never seen her show any sort of aggression towards anyone before. Not even Mary who despises her.

'What's with the dog?' he asks me.

'Lincoln, will you stop asking her questions and leave her the hell alone,' snaps Jennifer, slamming an open palm down on the table. It causes a loud bang, enough to make me jump.

Lincoln. That's his name.

As I study his face, there's something about it that catches me off guard. He's attractive, yes, but also very familiar, like I've seen him before in passing. Perhaps he's been a guest of this hotel before.

'I hope I see you again, whoever you are,' he says with a smooth voice. His eyes flick down to Muffin and he sniffs loudly before turning away.

It's only once his back is turned that I sigh, and my shoulders release the tension that's been there since I set eyes on him. One thing's for sure: I don't like Lincoln.

Jennifer waits for Lincoln to walk out of the double doors to the garden adjacent to the business suite before approaching me.

'I'd like you to greet each guest as they arrive into the room. Please take their coats, make them feel welcome and then serve them water or whatever else they need.'

'Um, ma'am, there are waiters who can . . .'

'I do not want a waiter. I want you, is that clear?'

'Yes, ma'am.'

'After everyone has sat down, you may leave. However, I'd like you to come up to the penthouse tonight at eight to discuss.'

I stay silent, expecting her to continue and explain what we'll be discussing, but she doesn't. It's almost like she's cut herself short of finishing her sentence. I dare not ask 'Discuss what?' because I doubt it would be received well.

'Understood, ma'am,' I say instead.

'Is your dog going to be a problem?' I'm assuming she's referring to the growling.

'No, ma'am. She's perfectly friendly, I can assure you.'

Jennifer squeezes her lips together. 'Hmm, pity. Lincoln could use a bite to the balls. Perhaps that would take him down a peg or two.'

* * *

I position myself by the door of the suite while I wait for the guests to arrive. Lincoln has sat down in one of the chairs at the far end of the table and is typing on his phone. His eyes are glued to it, barely blinking or looking up. Jennifer is at the head of the table.

The first guest arrives. An exceptionally posh-looking woman who reminds me of the Princess of Wales. She smiles at me, tells me how adorable Muffin is and that it's lovely to meet me. Her hands are smooth, but her nails are dirty, which throws me off for a moment. She smells divine, like sweet fruit and chocolate.

The second guest arrives. A tall gentleman who barely glances at me when I welcome him to the room. He chucks his jacket at me and demands I fetch him a whisky at once with two ice cubes. He glances at Muffin with derision and walks away towards Lincoln, who greets him with a handshake.

The third and fourth guests arrive. A married couple, who introduce themselves as Mr. and Mrs. Jacks. They smile at me and appear polite, but neither of them has anything going on behind their eyes. They look dead inside, hollow, like they have no souls. In fact, when I look at them, they remind me of dolls, the way they move and interact with each other. Weird.

The fifth guest arrives. An old woman of at least eighty who looks like an evil witch in a fairytale dressed in black with a sharp nose and heavily wrinkled skin, covered in make-up that cakes around her black eyes. She's hunched over too and avoids eye contact with me as I greet her.

The sixth guest arrives. This woman doesn't give me her name. She's around mid-fifties I'm guessing and looks as if she thinks everything, and everyone is beneath her. She looks down her nose at me as she hands me her wrap and demands I fetch her a glass of white wine immediately.

Now that all the guests have arrived, I head to the bar and fulfil the drink orders, returning to the table and handing them out to the various guests and pouring water for those who request it.

Jennifer motions at me from across the room, signalling that I can now leave. What the hell was all that about? Why did she need me to greet all the guests like that? I'm frozen to the spot. A part of me wants to stay and find out why all these people are congregated in the same room. They look like they'd all be at home at the Mad Hatter's tea party, but I know Jennifer doesn't want me to stay. Oh, to be a fly on the wall.

Lincoln's eyes are on me as I close the door. As soon as I'm out of his line of sight, the cold tingles on the back of my neck disappear. I don't think I've ever had such a vivid reaction to meeting another human being before. And the fact Muffin doesn't like him tells me all I need to know about him. Dogs are always right about these things.

***

My shift officially ended at seven, but here I am, at ten to eight, waiting to head up to see Jennifer in the penthouse. I've already been asked by several staff members what I'm still doing here, but to be perfectly honest, I'd rather be here than in my flat. I have nothing to go back home for because it's merely a place to sleep. It's not a home. It's a room, a room I'd rather not be in.

Muffin and I are hanging out at the housekeeping reception area in the back where there are a few sofas and a small kitchen to make cups of tea. I had a staff meal earlier, around six, because if we work over eight hours during the day, we're entitled to a free staff meal, and I've been here since six this morning. Mondays are my longest days. I'm just finishing off a cup of tea when Muffin raises her head and then cocks it to one side. She looks at me and her nose twitches.

I know her signals well enough to recognise an early warning. She gets up just as I place my empty cup on the side. I'm already sitting down, so I rest my head back against the sofa. Muffin jumps up next to me and lies across my lap as a seizure takes hold.

It's not a big one and passes in less than a minute.

When I come to, my eyelids flutter open. I stroke her soft head while my body returns to its normal rhythm, then rise slowly to my feet, fill up a glass with water from the kitchen tap and take a drink. Once my thirst is quenched, I'm ready to head to the penthouse. I often feel a bit weird and dizzy for a while after a seizure, but I've learned to live with it.

I'm a little behind schedule now, thanks to the seizure, but I'm not rushing. I'm off the clock after all. The only reason I'm hanging around is because Jennifer Clifton genuinely interests me, and her offer of a job is still niggling at the back of my mind. I know I've already turned her down, but the fact I can't forget about her offer tells me that clearly, I'm still considering it. Perhaps I need more excitement in my life.

I do hate my flat. To live in a hotel with my own room with no costs is a dream come true. I don't want much out of life, but I do feel like I need to make a change. Maybe this is exactly the change I've been craving. I'm never going to make a difference in the world if I refuse to change my own life.

Muffin and I enter the penthouse at four minutes past eight. The lift doors ping open, and we're met with dim, moody lighting and soft, classical music. Seconds later, Frankie comes barrelling around the corner from the direction of the bedrooms and yaps like a possessed demon-dog while running rings around Muffin.

'You can play,' I say to her.

And she's off.

Muffin is only four years old, still a puppy herself really. She came to me at two, still having a lot to learn, but we've learned and grown together.

I take several steps further into the suite. 'Hello? Miss Clifton?'

'Take a seat, Kimberley. I'll be with you in a moment,' comes the reply from the master bedroom.

I turn and head towards the lavish sofas and perch myself on the edge of one, a little too self-conscious to fully relax into the plush, soft pillows. I'm not a friend to Jennifer; I'm a member of staff.

Jennifer appears two minutes later wearing her hotel robe, her hair wrapped in a towel. The first thing I notice is that she's not wearing a scrap of make-up. In the dim light, it's hard to make out her exact facial features, but it's clear she wears a lot of make-up because there are fine lines and wrinkles crisscrossing her skin. I don't know why she needs to use all that make-up on her face because she's a very striking woman. Without her dark glasses though, I can see her piercing blue eyes. Perhaps they aren't contact lenses after all.

'Good evening, Kimberley. Can I fetch you a drink?'

'Oh, um . . .' It feels weird to be asked if I'd like a drink from her. Surely, it should be the other way around.

Jennifer, seemingly picking up on my nervousness smiles and says, 'Relax, Kimberley. You're off the clock. You're my guest here tonight.'

'Oh, thank you, ma'am. I'll just take an ice water with a slice of lemon if that's okay.'

'You can stop with the ma'am thing too,' she adds with a smile. 'Call me Jennifer.' She walks over to the lavish glass bar in the corner and pours out some ice water from the dispenser and adds a slice of lemon. All bars in the hotel rooms are fully stocked with anything our guests could want, including a selection of mixers, spirits, wines, soft drinks and garnishes.

Jennifer hands me the glass of water and then takes a seat opposite me on her recliner chair. 'Now, I'm sure you're wondering why I asked you to come here, and why I asked you to meet and greet all the guests earlier in the business suite.'

I take a sip to soothe my dry mouth. 'I must admit I am curious, ma'am. Sorry . . . Jennifer.'

'Before I begin, have you paid any thought to my job offer since this morning?'

'I have, yes, but I have a lot of questions.'

'Regarding the non-disclosure agreement?'

'Yes, mainly, but also what exactly your guests visit your hotel for.'

'I'm afraid I can't tell you that until you've accepted and signed.'

'I understand.'

'Now, would you please tell me, in your own words, what exactly you thought of each of my guests who you met earlier?'

At this point, Muffin stops playing with Frankie and comes and lies at my feet. Frankie joins her side, and they lie quietly together, their paws touching, like BFFs.

'Um . . . sure. Well, the first woman who entered the room was very nice and polite. She smiled at me and even complimented Muffin. I thought she was well turned out and attractive. However, I did notice . . .' I stop, avoiding eye contact by looking into my water glass.

'Yes?'

I take a sip. 'Well . . . her nails weren't painted nor were they clean. Everything else about her screamed wealth and prestige, so why didn't she have her nails manicured? They looked out of place.'

Jennifer nods. 'A very good observation, Kimberley. What about the second guest?'

'The tall man who ordered the whisky. He was rude and abrupt, didn't make eye contact with me, thank me or acknowledge me in any way. I'd say he's probably a very high-profile politician or lawyer because he looked a little familiar, like I've seen him before, perhaps on television.'

'What if I told you he's in the running to be the next Mayor of London?'

'I'd be shocked and a little worried about the future of the city.'

Jennifer laughs. 'Okay, carry on. The married couple. What did you think of them?'

'Mr. and Mrs. Jacks were polite and had kind smiles, but . . . and I have no proof of this, but . . . they appeared to be almost faking their personalities. Their smiles felt forced. There was nothing going on behind their eyes.'

Jennifer nodded. 'Another excellent observation. What if I told you that Mr. and Mrs. Jacks are sociopaths who have no ability to interact with the normal population and have no emotional response to anything.'

'It would perfectly explain their cold, dead eyes,' I say. 'Is that true?'

Jennifer shrugs as she uncrosses, then re-crosses her long legs. 'Unverified,' she says. 'The fifth guest?'

'The old woman.'

'Yes.'

'Scary.'

'Hmm, yes, she did have a wicked witch of the west thing going on, didn't she? And the sixth guest?'

'She gave me a look as if I was a piece of poo that she just scraped off her shoe. Also, she asked for white wine, but by the stains on her teeth, I'd say she's more of a red wine drinker.'

Jennifer raises her eyebrows but doesn't expand on my comment. 'What about my seventh guest?'

At this, I take a sip of water because I know exactly who she's referring to. There were only six guests who entered the room, and I greeted them all, but there was a seventh person present, and he was already there when I entered.

'Lincoln,' I say.

'Lincoln.'

I take a deep breath in through my nose. I don't wish to overstep the mark here. There's a strong possibility that Lincoln and Jennifer are lovers, considering the close contact they had, but I have a feeling in my gut that tells me something isn't quite right with them.

'Please,' says Jennifer. 'Tell me the truth. Not a lot of people do.'

'Very well.' I take another deep breath, preparing myself. 'To be completely honest, ma'am, Lincoln set off a reaction in me that I've never experienced before. He scared the living daylights out of me when he looked at me and I know Muffin felt the same because she growled at him. And she never growls. Ever. I'd be more than happy to never set eyes on that man again.'

Jennifer stares at me, not making a sound. Shit, have I said too much?

'Thank you, Kimberley, for your honest opinions. I must say, you have an exceptional ability to read people and notice things that most would miss or overlook.'

'Thank you, ma'am . . . Jennifer. Sorry. Was there a reason why you wanted my honest opinions on your guests?'

'Oh, yes. There's always a reason.'

'Okay . . .'

'I need someone like you to work for me in my hotel, Kimberley. I need someone trustworthy, disciplined and motivated. I want that to be you.'

'I understand, Jennifer. I'd still like to sleep on it. May I give you my final decision tomorrow morning?'

'Very well, I shall await your decision. Please come to the penthouse at ten.'

I rise to my feet. 'I'll say goodnight, then. Thank you for the ice water.' I look down at Muffin who raises her head, preparing to move. 'Let's go, Muffin.' She jumps to her feet and shakes.

'Goodnight, Kimberley.'

'Goodnight, Jennifer.'

CHAPTER EIGHT

Jennifer (Before)

I sat and stared at the recent addition to the collection. She wasn't what I expected at all. Plain, at best. I must admit, I hadn't anticipated her to be almost eight months pregnant. She wasn't huge, like some women get when they're carrying a child almost at full term, but she carried the extra weight well. From the back, it was hard to tell she was even pregnant. My father would be positively delighted that I'd finally found the woman he'd been searching for. I couldn't wait to tell him that I'd found his Emily. My trusty bodyguard had managed to apprehend her without damaging the child inside. The pregnancy may have come as a shock to me, but it would work in my favour eventually.

I was aware Emily was scared and probably had a lot of questions, the most obvious one being why was she locked inside a room. She'd find out in due course, but the main thing I needed to ensure was she remained calm and didn't injure the baby. I'd always heard how a mother's stress could sometimes transfer to the unborn child, and they could develop health problems because of it. It was fascinating to read up on pregnancy. It made me wish I'd had the chance to reproduce myself, but it was not to be. I may not have expected it, but that baby was the most important thing in the world right now. I had no experience when it came to children, but I'd make an exceptional mother. Perhaps this child was my chance to have my own family. Emily was in no position to care for it. From what my bodyguard told me, she worked as a checkout girl at Tesco, had no stable family, nor a man to take care of her. How did she expect to care for and raise a child by herself? How was she supposed to work and pay for food and clothing? Yes, it was a good job I came along and found her, rescued her and the child from a future of poverty and hunger.

Sitting in front of the array of computer monitors, I watched her sleep after drinking the concoction of drugs administered to her via the glass of water that Courtney provided. She must have been very thirsty to continue to drink water that tasted funny, either that or stupid. Her vitals were stable when she arrived, but they were looking a bit dodgy after her fright, so my senior housekeeper thought it was best to give her something to calm her down. I was assured there was no danger to the baby. The more relaxed the mother was, the healthier the baby. And the baby was now all I cared about.

A shuffle from behind alerted me to someone entering the room. I knew it was him without having to turn around. He had an air about him, a presence whenever he walked into a room. I'd been hoping to reveal the news to him in a more elaborate way, but it seemed he was as impatient as I was and wanted to check on our new guest.

He didn't speak as he stood behind my chair, placing a cold hand on my bare shoulder. I resisted the urge to flinch. Not out of disgust or the need to get away, but I didn't feel worthy to be touched by him. Silly really, considering he was my father.

'How's our newest arrival?' he asked.

'Take a look for yourself,' I said, moving aside so he could peer closer to the screens.

He leaned in, studying the woman passed out on the bed, the gentle curve of her swollen belly. 'Is it really her?'

'Yes, Father. It is.'

He straightened his back and took a deep breath. 'She's pregnant.'

'Yes.'

'Mine?'

'Unconfirmed, but once the child is born, it shall be tested. However, the timing of her pregnancy fits with your interaction with her eight months ago.'

My father nodded. I must admit, I was expecting a different reaction. Then again, my father rarely showed any sort of clear emotion in the company of others, even me. I always wanted to be a fly on the wall when he was alone in his room, or when he was with one of his playthings. Did he act differently around them? Was it all an act or did he really not have an ounce of compassion or emotion in his body. It would explain why I am the way I am though.

'Are you not pleased, Father?' I asked.

He looked down at me, then stroked my hair before planting a soft kiss on the top of my head. 'Of course I am, my child. Please make sure Emily is well taken care of. If that is my child, then it must be protected and nurtured until it is born. If it isn't, then dispose of it appropriately.'

'Yes, Father.'

'Tell me when she is ready for visitors. I'd like to speak to her . . . alone.'

I nodded my response and then opened my mouth to ask a question that had been burning inside me, but my words seemed to have gotten lost.

'What is it?' he asked.

'If the child is yours, then I would like to raise it here as my own.'

My father sighed, as if me asking that question exhausted and bored him to death. He placed his hand back on my shoulder, but this time he dug his fingertips into my skin, clenching tight. 'I shall think about it. They would be your half-sibling though.'

'I know that.'

'Very well. I'll let you know my answer soon.'

'Thank you, Father.'

He finally lifted his hand away from my shoulder and my body responded by taking a deep breath without me even thinking about it. I couldn't show pain in front of him. Pain was weakness and I was not weak. All I wanted in life was for my father to respect me and be proud of me, but no matter what I did, it never seemed to be enough.

My brother was his favourite. I knew he was, but since I was the oldest, the first Clifton child, then I was the one who lived here and would take his place when he eventually passed on. It was the way things worked, but I knew my father wished I was a man. He wished my brother had been born first. I didn't show my face too often to the staff and guests. It wasn't my time yet. My father kept saying I had to be patient. I worked behind the scenes, along with a select few staff members. It was a lonely existence, being his daughter, but soon I'd take over and be the face of the hotel.

My father quietly left the room. Only when the door closed behind him, did I raise my hand and rub my shoulder where he had squeezed it. I glanced down. Red finger marks dotted my pale skin.

I leaned forward in my chair, pressing my face close to the monitor. I think it was about time I saw my new arrival up close and personal.

* * *

The smell of urine assaulted my nostrils as I pushed the heavy door open after unlocking it with a large, metal key. From the outside of the room, the door was wooden and carved, like something out of a gothic horror house, but on the inside, it was a piece of sheet metal with no discernible handle or way to open it, designed to keep whoever was in the room from escaping.

This room was designed and built twenty-one years ago by my father to keep his subjects locked up until they were needed. Every year since, a woman has been taken from the streets, usually one who wouldn't be missed, and locked inside, ready to make her grand entrance at the party, which my father hosted at the beginning of March each year. The party was the only time where I showed my face properly to the crowds, although masks were used to hide people's identities, my own included.

My trusted housekeeper, Courtney, followed me into the room and stood silently, awaiting my instructions. My nose screwed up at the smell emanating from the unconscious woman. Why hadn't Emily been provided with clean clothes and been washed? Before I took another step, I turned to Courtney and demanded she fetch fresh clothes and a bowl of soapy, warm water. She turned and scurried out of the room and up the corridor, disappearing round the corner, leaving me to approach Emily alone.

I closed the door behind me as softly as I could. Courtney would be able to gain access when she returned because it was unlocked, but if Emily woke up and decided to make a run for it, she would have no way of getting out. She wouldn't know about the hidden release catch in the door to open it in case of an emergency (i.e. one of the staff or me getting trapped inside).

Emily was fast asleep on her left side on the single bed, her long hair cascading across the flat pillow. My eyes landed on her prominent bump, studying its gentle curve down towards her pubic area. I stood directly over her, casting a shadow over her body and watched her bump for any movement. Other than her breathing, there was none. This worried me. I'd feel much better if I saw a small kick from the baby.

The door opened and Courtney returned, carrying a bowl of warm water, a sponge and a pair of black maternity trousers and underwear.

'Thank you, Courtney. Would you please help me with removing her trousers?'

Courtney nodded and began to undo the buttons and zip on Emily's trousers. She didn't stir. The drugs had well and truly knocked her out, so she was as pliable as a life-sized doll. Between us, we slid her trousers down her legs, then removed her greying pants. We had done this many times together, so seeing a woman naked from the waist down was nothing new, nor was it in any way shocking.

Courtney used the sponge and gently washed Emily's upper thighs while I disposed of the soiled items. Once clean and dry, we dressed Emily in fresh pants and trousers.

'I'm very disappointed that Emily wasn't cleaned and changed immediately after her arrival,' I said as Courtney, and I left the room.

'I'm sorry, ma'am. It won't happen again. I was about to go and . . .'

'I don't want to hear your excuses. I need you to fetch a foetal Doppler and do a scan of the baby while she's still asleep. There seems to be little to no movement. My father wishes to see Emily soon, but before he does, I want to make sure the baby is alive and well.'

'Of course, ma'am.'

'Tell me immediately if anything is wrong. A lot rides on this baby being healthy.'

Courtney nodded and headed away from me.

I stood in the hallway collecting my thoughts after closing and locking the door with the metal key. The red paint on the opposite wall to the door held my focus for a moment while I contemplated the arrival of Emily and her unborn baby.

I turned and looked at the door. Across the width was gold lettering in a spiralling font. My father numbered the room over twenty years ago when it was first built.

He called it room one.

Now, however, as the years and the women have passed through it, it had a new name.

Room 21.

CHAPTER NINE

Kimberley

Muffin and I walk home slowly. I barely have any energy after the events of the day and suffering through two seizures. Some days feel so much harder than others and today is one of those harder-than-most days. I contemplate taking the lift, but Muffin gently pulls me in the direction of the stairs, which are quiet as I trundle up them, pulling myself up each step with the help of the banister. Muffin knows that exercise is good for me. Sometimes I wish she wasn't so on-the-ball. Luckily, none of my flatmates are in when I shove open the front door, which I am exceptionally happy about.

I hate living here. I hate the mess and the noise from the busy London streets outside. I hate having to tiptoe around my flatmates, all of whom I also hate. I wish I had privacy, and I wish Muffin had wide open spaces in which to run and play.

As soon as I set eyes on the messy flat, I make up my mind regarding Jennifer's offer. It's like a lightbulb moment. Screw it. I'm doing it. I've lived in this shithole long enough and paid my dues. Having my own room, to not have to pay rent and have my meals cooked for me is an offer I can't afford to refuse. Living in a city is stifling at times and moving to a remote area of Scotland will give me a chance to breathe free for the first time in my life. Muffin will love the outdoors and be able to play with Frankie too.

To be perfectly honest, I'd made up my mind while I was still talking to her. I didn't want to seem too keen at the time, but seeing this disgusting, tiny flat cements my decision. I'm damn good at my job at Harris Hotel, but this new career will give me chances and opportunities I could never dream about. While the hotel itself sounds intriguing, I'm more interested in the various guests she spoke about, although the idea of seeing Lincoln again is not one that fills me with warm feelings.

Plus, it's a live-in position, which means I wouldn't have to live in this hellhole with other housemates who barely acknowledge I exist. The chance of a lifetime is too good to pass by. I'm not sure what I've done to deserve this opportunity, but I know these types of things don't happen very often to most people, especially people like me who are often looked over for promotion or jobs of any kind when I mention my condition. They say it doesn't happen, that most job opportunities are open to everyone and people with disabilities and severe medical conditions are welcome to apply, but it's mostly bullshit. That's been my experience anyway.

I'm young. I have no ties here. I've never let my condition hold me back before, so this is no different. Although the idea of changing doctors is one that worries me. Jennifer said my epilepsy would be managed properly. And surely any doctor can prescribe epilepsy medication and keep an eye on my health and wellbeing. It's just one of those things I'll have to deal with.

I give Muffin her evening meal, make myself something too, and then we get comfortable on my bed. She lies across my lap while I read my book. However, after a few minutes, curiosity kicks in about the hotel and I use my phone to search for it on Google.

Nothing comes up.

Not one single article, website or mention.

It's like Clifton Hotel doesn't exist. She did say that the guests there liked their privacy, but to hide an entire hotel from the world, from the internet, is both impressive and worrying. What's the main reason she doesn't want it to be found? Is it to do with the guests or the strange things that apparently happen there? What does happen there? I won't find out until I sign the NDA and by then it may be too late to turn back.

While its elusiveness does concern me, considering what Jennifer said about the clients who stay there, it's no wonder it remains a secret. There's a part of me that wonders if this is all a hoax, whether the hotel even exists at all. What if Jennifer is making it all up? Is she luring me out there, but what reason would she have to lie?

Rather than working myself into a panic, I put my worries aside, deciding that going with Jennifer is better than staying here any longer.

I go back to reading my book.

I eventually call it a night when my eyes keep closing and the book falls and smashes me in the face.

* * *

The next morning, I pack a small bag with some personal belongings and clothes. I don't have a lot of items. I'll call and cancel my rental agreement, which is due for renewal in a few weeks anyway. It's perfect timing. My landlord can do whatever he wants with the things I leave behind: the mattress, some old clothes that I should have thrown out years ago and a few nicknacks that I've collected over the years. I have no sentimental attachment to any of them. The thought of living in a lavish hotel with all my expenses paid for is enough to make me giddy with excitement. I could save so much money, something I've never been able to do before because it all gets sucked out straight away to pay bills.

Eventually, I might be able to save enough to buy my own house. Not in London, of course. They cost millions, way out of my price range, but perhaps a nice house in the countryside, somewhere. It's a dream I've never allowed myself to have before, but now I can see it glimmering on the horizon, slightly out of reach, but closer than it's ever been.

I can do this. I know I can.

Being a child of the foster system means I don't own a lot of personal possessions, but I do own one thing which is precious to me, so I grab it and put it in my bag, along with a selection of Muffin's toys and balls.

I exit the flat with a fire in my belly, a fire I know won't go out any time soon, not until I've found out the secrets behind Clifton Hotel's walls. Having slept on it, I'm still nervous about the lack of information regarding the hotel online, but my excitement of a new life outweighs any doubts and fears.

Luckily, the whole flat is still snoring as I slip out into the cool morning air. I walk to Harris Hotel, check in and place my bag inside my storage locker.

I carry out my morning chores. The housekeeper who was off sick yesterday is back today so we are at full capacity, which means I can relax a little. My main job this morning is to ensure all guests are happy and catered for. Then, at ten, I'll head up to the penthouse to see Jennifer.

As I'm walking past the staff reception, I hear a couple of the women whispering. I can't hear much of what they're saying, but I do catch one word.

Lincoln.

I stop and pretend to bend down and buff a scratch off my shoe.

'Yes, that's him. Lincoln. He was in the business suite with Miss Clifton from the penthouse and I swear I heard him say he would kill her if she said anything,' says Lucy, the housekeeper who Jennifer made cry yesterday.

'If she said what?' asks the other housekeeper, Bridget.

'I didn't hear anything else, but he gave me the creeps, you know?'

'Maybe, but he's very attractive, don't you think?'

'They're always the worst ones though. Think they're God's gift to women. I swear, that man is the devil. Thankfully, he didn't stay the night in any of the rooms here. Heard he was going back to Scotland.'

The conversation around Lincoln peters out, so I continue my way around the rooms, ensuring everything is running smoothly, but the words resonate within me.

I heard him say he would kill her if she said anything.

***

At ten, I enter the penthouse to find Jennifer stretching on the floor doing a downward dog, dressed in super-cool leggings and a baggy t-shirt, a get-up that surprises me because I've mostly seen her in designer clothes or a crisp, white bathrobe. Seeing her in sweats makes her appear normal. Frankie jumps up to greet his new best friend.

'Oh, I'm so sorry to disturb you, ma'am. I can come back.'

'No, I said ten and it's ten. You're right on time. It's me who's late.'

I remain where I am while she finishes her stretch. Then she sits cross-legged on her mat facing me in a traditional yoga pose.

'So, what have you decided?' she asks.

'I'd like to accept your kind job offer, ma'am.'

'I'm very pleased to hear that, Kimberley. In that case, we'll be on our way later today. Meet me at the hotel reception at six this evening. It's a long drive, but you can sleep in the limo.'

'Um, today? I haven't handed in my notice or even spoken to Mary about leaving yet.'

'Then I suggest you hurry and make that your top priority today.'

'Yes, ma'am.'

I turn to leave.

'There's the small matter of the non-disclosure agreement to sign too, but if you like I'll give it to you in the car for you to read through on the way. It's . . . fairly long and requires your utmost attention.'

'Thank you, ma'am.'

I call Muffin to tear her away from Frankie. She joins me in the lift as we descend and gives me a look.

'Let's think of this as our next adventure,' I say.

I find Mary and deliver the news. The vein in her forehead almost explodes. I apologise over and over about the short notice to which she replies, 'Short notice? Eight hours is hardly short notice! It's non-existent!' I wholeheartedly agree, of course, but no amount of apologising helps. She finally admits defeat and just tells me to go, but to never expect to work here again.

I say goodbye to my colleagues who are all just as shocked but wish me well and good luck. However, I think they're more upset that Muffin is leaving. It's not like I haven't made friends here, but I don't spend any time with them outside of work. Muffin gets a lot of fuss and treats from all the staff who give her a cuddle to say goodbye, which is more than they give me.

***

My small bag is at my feet while I anxiously lean from one foot to the other, waiting for Jennifer to come down to reception. The porter who helped me the other day smiles at me from the door.

'Waiting for someone?' he asks.

'Jennifer Clifton,' I respond. 'She's offered me a job up in Scotland.'

'Gosh. Well, congrats on the new job. We'll miss you and Muffin around here.'

'Thanks,' I reply awkwardly. I've never really said more than a few words to him during my time here, so his comment seems odd to me.

Jennifer and Frankie arrive five minutes later. She's wearing her oversized sunglasses again even though it's dark outside, which I'm grateful for because her piercing blue eyes make my stomach flip. She immediately hands me a thick folder, which I assume is the non-disclosure agreement. So much for me catching up on my kindle reads in the car.

Jennifer doesn't say a word as she heads outside.

I take one last look at the hotel reception and nod goodbye to the receptionist and the night porter, neither of whose names I know, then follow Jennifer down the front steps where there's a large, white limousine waiting at the kerb. I've seen many limos in my time working in London, but I've never seen inside, let alone sat in one.

The driver is standing waiting for us. She opens the back door.

'Kimberley, this is Valerie, my personal driver. Valerie, this is Kimberley, my . . . new housekeeper.'

Valerie nods at me, but there's no smile. It seems she's not a big talker.

Jennifer and Frankie climb inside the limo while Valerie takes my bag and puts it into the boot. Then, Muffin follows Frankie and hops up onto the seat. I slide my bottom onto the cream leather, trying not to gasp and coo over the gorgeous interior of the car. There's mahogany wood and polished surfaces, along with various buttons and gadgets, none of which I have any idea how to work. Soft music is playing from speakers hidden in the seats.

'Make yourself comfortable, Kimberley. As you read through the document, feel free to ask me any questions. However, I shall be catching up on some sleep during our drive up north. We'll have several stops for food and for the dogs to stretch their legs and whatnot, but we won't be arriving until early tomorrow morning. I prefer to travel at night. Less traffic.'

'Yes, ma'am.'

'If you need anything, just press the button there for Valerie and she can assist you with anything you require.'

Within a few minutes, we're pulling away from the kerb and I say a silent goodbye to my life here in London. My stomach flutters, but Muffin seems perfectly content on the seat next to me. She's sitting and looking out of the window at the passing buildings and cars.

I'm quite glad Jennifer's not a big talker because I find it awkward speaking to her. She extends her car seat so it's lying almost flat, folds her hands across her lap and closes her eyes. At least, I assume she has her eyes closed. I can't tell due to the dark glasses.

Muffin eventually curls up into a ball on the seat next to me, her head on my lap and begins to snore softly. My throat is dry and scratchy. There's a pane of blacked out glass between the back seat and the driver. I lean forward and press a random button to see what it does.

'Hello?'

'Yes, ma'am?'

'Oh, sorry. Um . . . is there any water I can have please?'

'In the mini fridge next to you.'

'Oh . . . thanks.'

A mini fridge in a car. Now I've seen everything.

Once my thirst is quenched, I open the folder and pull out the documents inside. I've always been able to read in moving vehicles, but I rarely get the chance since I mostly walk everywhere in London.

My chest feels a little tight as I slowly turn the pages, my eyes picking up words such as *strict*, *discretion* and *liable*. I can understand why some guests wouldn't want their personal business talked about amongst the staff outside the hotel walls, so that part of the agreement makes perfect sense, but what I don't understand is the part where it says I must never reveal the location of where I work to anyone, nor can I set foot outside the hotel grounds without the strict permission of Jennifer.

Why does it sound like a prison?

The document is twenty-five pages long and comes with several forms to complete, which I expect with any new job, such as bank details for payment, health insurance and a wellbeing form where I list all my medication and details of my condition, which takes a while.

It takes me roughly an hour to finish reading the document and complete the forms. The non-disclosure agreement is slightly odd, but I sign it, nonetheless. It's not like I can ask Jennifer to stop the car because I've changed my mind. We're now outside London on a motorway, heading north.

* * *

Two hours later, I've managed to have a short nap. Jennifer hasn't made a single sound or movement, but the moment we turn into a service station for a pit stop, she stirs and sits up straight. We let the dogs out for a wee and a leg stretch while Valerie fetches us some food for the remainder of the journey.

'How did you find the document?' Jennifer asks me while we walk along the small patch of grass by the car park.

'Most of it seemed fine, but I do have a few questions.'

'By all means, ask away.'

'The part where it says we can't tell anyone that we work for you . . .'

'Clifton Hotel is a unique hotel. Not a lot of people know of its existence, and I like to keep it that way. My father always made it very clear there was to be no advertising of any kind and no word of mouth either. Even our guests don't tell anyone about us.'

'Then how do new guests find out about you to come and stay?'

'They don't find us. We find them.'

'What about having to ask permission to leave?'

'Where else would you go? You'll see when we get there that the hotel is very rural. If you did want to leave, then you'd need to ask for transport.'

'But the staff can leave if they want to?'

Jennifer looks at me and smiles. 'Yes, if they wish, they may leave, as long as I know where they're going.'

'What about doctor appointments? I need regular check-ups.'

'We have an in-house doctor who takes care of everyone. If you require further treatment outside of the hotel, then you will be taken to the nearest hospital. Anything else?'

I stop and wait while Muffin squats on the grass. 'No, not at the moment.'

* * *

The night has well and truly drawn to a close and after one more stop two hours later, I'm ready to try and sleep. Muffin is as good as gold, curled up next to me, so I grab a blanket and pillow from the storage area, recline my seat and secure a sleeping mask over my eyes. It feels weird sleeping in a car, but the rhythmic movement soon sends me off.

I'm woken up by Muffin licking my face. I pull off the mask. It's light now, but only just. In fact, I think we're moments away from the sun rising due to the pinks and oranges cascading across the sky. I'm disorientated as I adjust the seat to an upright position. Jennifer is already awake, her sunglasses fixed in place, her feet crossed at the ankles, ever the polished and neatly turned out professional.

'Good morning, Kimberley.'

'Hi,' I croak as I reach for the bottle of water and take a sip.

'We're just arriving.'

'What time is it?'

'Seven fifteen.'

'Really? Why is the sun only just coming up?'

'It's much darker at this end of the country.'

I peer out of the car window at the cloud-covered sky. Everything seems to have a grey tinge to it, the ground soaking wet from overnight dew. Looking up, there are vast, rocky mountains rising to the sky, a thick cloud of mist surrounding them.

We drive for a further few minutes up a bumpy track. I'm looking forward to getting out of this car. My body needs a good stretch and fresh air, not to mention a decent breakfast. My stomach gurgles on cue.

'Breakfast will be served upon our arrival. I'd like you to join me before I hand you over to my senior housekeeper, Courtney, who will give you a tour of the hotel and show you to your expected duties and your new room.'

'Thank you, ma'am.'

The limo stops at a set of large wrought-iron gates, which open automatically after a short pause. They are black and gold and have Clifton House written in twisted metal across the length of them.

Wow.

This place is something else.

I should have expected the hotel to be spectacular, considering the size of the entrance gates, but nothing prepares me for the grandeur and sheer enormity of the building at the end of the long and winding driveway. The silver stone sparkles in the morning light and there are more windows than I can count. A multitude of huge chimneys reach for the sky, and turrets and doors are scattered around the design. It almost looks like a castle, or a large country estate house that's been transformed into a hotel. The design of the building is segregated into three distinct parts, each with its own entrance. The grounds are vast, but mostly overgrown, left to run wild, apart from the localised garden surrounding the hotel. It truly is amazing. Although Harris Hotel was grand, this seems like it's on a scale of its own, not as glamorous, but far superior in every way. There's even a couple of stone gargoyles set against the turrets. My attention is drawn away from the glorious building as the limo rolls to a stop.

Valerie gets out and opens the door for Jennifer, who exits the car gracefully. Muffin sees her escape route and bolts out of the car, heading straight for a piece of grass to relieve herself.

I get out and rub my lower back, which is aching from the awkward position I slept in during the drive. Valerie opens the boot and retrieves my bag, handing it to me.

'Thank you,' I say.

She smiles at me, then gets back into the limo and drives round the side of the hotel.

'Shall we?' asks Jennifer, jolting me out of my daze. I can't stop staring at the hotel. It's almost hypnotising me with its vast windows, tall towers and overall domineering presence, which is even more foreboding against the backdrop of the misty mountains and rolling hills in the distance.

Muffin and I follow Jennifer up the path towards the large double doors made of dark wood, complete with black hinges that reach almost the whole way across their width.

As we get closer, the doors swing open towards us and an old man stands in the entrance. He's dressed in a smart black suit. I'm guessing he's the butler.

'Jennifer, delighted to have you back with us.'

'Thank you, Bryan. It's good to be back. This is Kimberley, my new housekeeper.' She waves her hand in my direction. I smile and say hello in a small voice. Bryan looks down at me, furrowing his brow. Is it me or does he look angry?

'Delighted, Miss Katy.' His voice may be delighted but tell that to his face.

'Um, it's Kimberley and thanks. Nice to meet you too,' I reply, walking up the steps so I'm level with him. His eyes lower to where Muffin is sniffing at the bottom of the steps.

'Another dog,' he says. 'How delightful.'

'This is Muffin. She's my epilepsy alert dog.'

Bryan's mouth twitches. I wonder if he's fighting the urge to say *delightful*?

Leaving Bryan behind, I follow Jennifer into the reception area and my mouth drops open. My eyes are drawn up to the enormous crystal chandelier hanging from the vaulted ceiling, but it's no ordinary chandelier. It's red. Blood red, which causes sparkling reflections to scatter around the room. The walls are also red, but with white skirting boards. The huge slate tiles are red-and-white chequered.

'Bloody hell,' I mutter.

'Exactly,' replies Jennifer with a wink. 'Striking, is it not?'

'That's one word to describe it.'

'Follow me.'

Jennifer leads me into an adjoining room where a large table is laid out with various breakfast items, including crispy bacon, sausages, toast, as well as pastries, cereals and fruit. A large cafetière sits in the middle; the smell of freshly brewed coffee causes saliva to fill my dry mouth.

I take a seat and help myself. Jennifer does the same, pouring us both a cup of coffee. A housekeeper comes in with two bowls of food for the dogs, who eat side by side without a fuss at our feet. I'm used to decent food at Harris Hotel, but the food here is amazing and I basically inhale a bacon sandwich, a chocolate croissant and a bowl of muesli before stopping to take a breather.

I sip my coffee once it's cooled. 'This place is amazing,' I say. 'How many staff work here?'

'Including you, forty-one,' says Jennifer, keeping her eyes on her phone. She seems very preoccupied since arriving here, constantly typing on her phone and taking short phone calls.

Jennifer stands up a few minutes later. 'This is where I leave you, Kimberley. Courtney will be along in a moment to take over and show you around. I hope you settle in well. Welcome to Clifton Hotel.'

'Thank you again, ma'am.'

She nods and exits the room, Frankie right on her heels.

Chewing the last piece of croissant, I glance around the dining room. It also has a red design, but a deeper shade, burgundy and not as in-your-face as the reception area. In fact, this room is very tastefully decorated, and I especially like the cream floor-length curtains at the large windows which overlook the grounds.

I look up as the door opens. A woman enters. She's dressed in a smart black tunic dress with only a small amount of white around the collar. Her hair is pulled back into a tight bun, and she has black heels on, not too high, but high enough to ensure her posture is perfect when she walks.

'Hi, Kimberley. It's lovely to meet you. I'm Courtney. I'm the Senior Housekeeper here.'

I quickly get to my feet, walk around to her and extend my hand. 'Hi, nice to meet you,' I say. 'This is Muffin.'

As soon as I say her name, she looks up from sniffing around the table and trots towards Courtney, who bends down and gives her a stroke behind the ears, the quickest way to Muffin's heart.

'Oh, my goodness, aren't you just the most adorable thing!' She fusses over her for several seconds then stands back up. 'I assume Jennifer is okay with you having a dog here. If she weren't, you wouldn't be here.'

'Yes,' I say. 'Muffin is my epilepsy alert dog.'

'Oh.' Courtney's face drops. 'I'm sorry. I didn't realise . . .'

'It's fine.'

'Okay, well . . . Follow me, and I'll give you the grand tour and get you settled in.'

'Thank you.'

* * *

Courtney shows me the downstairs areas first: the second dining room, the banquet hall, the ballroom, the kitchen, the library, lounge, sitting room and bar. Each room is decorated differently, but all have the underlying tones of red. I'm not sure which room is my favourite, but if I had to choose, then I'd say the banquet hall. It looks magical, like something out of Harry Potter.

Upstairs is next, which we access via a grand, winding staircase that seems never-ending. As we're walking up it, Courtney tells me about the history of the hotel.

Damien Clifton, Jennifer's father, bought it in 1972. It used to be a hospital for the criminally insane in the 1800s, but was left to rot at the beginning of the 20th century until Damien bought it and renovated it over the next decade. It's a grade II listed building, so a lot of the architecture had to be preserved.

'Oh, and did you know that it's supposedly haunted too,' says Courtney.

'Really?' Of course it is.

'Yes. There are thirty rooms in total, but two of them are supposedly haunted. If you're ever on the rota to clean room eight or twenty, then make sure you take someone else in with you.'

'Okay . . .' I want to ask further questions, but her next statement makes me forget about the haunted bedrooms completely.

'There's just one rule in this hotel, other than the ones stipulated in the non-disclosure agreement. Never go into Room 21.'

CHAPTER TEN

Jennifer

I leave Kimberley in Courtney's capable hands while I head to my office, kicking off my heels as I take a seat on my leather chair. Heels are something I don't think I'll ever get used to. If I'm wearing them for too long, I get hot spots and my lower back starts playing up. I'm in desperate need of a shower, but it'll have to wait until I've finalised a few things for the party and checked up on the special guest in Room 21. In my absence, I've left Courtney mostly in charge as well as Bryan, but Bryan can be temperamental, rather like a pet dog who's been mistreated and doesn't know who he can trust.

I spend ten minutes catching up on emails and then one of the kitchen staff enters with a cup of green tea on a silver tray. I take a sip while I look over the schedule of events for the party. I hate green tea.

Two weeks. I have two weeks to bring everything together. I've watched Damien organise these parties for the past two decades, always working behind the scenes, but without his guidance, it's more difficult than I imagined. The guests have been accustomed to dealing with him over the years, so they are reluctant to liaise with me directly, but everything depends on them coming this year. I need as many of them within these walls as possible. Without them, there is no party.

Usually, there are between twenty and thirty guests who attend the parties. So far, only fifteen have RSVP'd. I'm assuming it's to do with my father not being in charge this year. I send out another email blast, reminding previous guests of the upcoming party, explaining that Damien, of course, will be in attendance.

Lincoln is coming. Nothing would stop him from attending one of these parties. In fact, he'll be here in the next few hours. I'm not quite sure what his plans are for the next two weeks, but he wanted to arrive early to settle in and, in his words, 'take advantage of the opportunity.' Quite what that means, I'm yet to find out, but I don't believe it will be fun.

Finishing up the emails, relieved that a couple more guests have decided to come after all, I swivel on my high-backed leather chair towards the large window which overlooks the grounds. I watch the gardener pruning the hedges around the huge lawn, taking his time to get each trim perfect. Even during the winter months, I like to keep things tidy. Most of the grounds are overgrown with large woods and hedges surrounding the whole estate, helping shield the hotel from view, although the nearest usable road is over two miles away, so the likelihood of anyone driving past the hotel is minimal. They'd have to drive through the wrought-iron gates at the end of the long driveway first, and they hardly ever open. Despite the contract saying the staff can leave if they wish (if they tell me first), most of them don't leave. Why would they need to? Everything they need is here, under this roof. It's the beauty of this place. Once you're inside, you never want or need to leave.

The next few days are jam-packed. I need to go over the menu with the chefs and kitchen staff, who are more than capable of cooking an exquisite banquet for the party, but this is no ordinary party, so I need to make sure they are on top form. There's a level of sophistication needed that's not usually found in the average hotel kitchen. As the party draws closer, the guests will be arriving to settle in. Most of them are expected a few days before the party.

Next, the decorating committee will transform the banquet hall into a dream world. During all of this, I'll need to ensure all the staff know their jobs and what's expected of them. Kimberley will be trained, under the watchful eye of Courtney, who will give me her honest opinion. The housekeeper I'm replacing is long gone. She made her choice. It was the wrong one. If she'd bothered to read her non-disclosure agreement, then she would have seen that blabbing to the police was going to land her in hot water. She won't be making that mistake again, or any other mistake for that matter. She'd only worked here for a few weeks before deciding it wasn't the right fit for her. I thought I'd made the right decision in hiring her, but even I make mistakes. Nothing is going to ruin my party. Nothing. Such a shame to see such young talent going to waste though, but Kimberley will be a perfect replacement. It will take time for her to move up the ranks and earn the trust of the guests. But I have no doubt she has the fighting spirit needed to work here. She will do well.

As I sip my tea, grimacing at the taste, my thoughts drift to my own mother and it causes my vision to blur. It's not often I cast my mind back to my childhood. Sometimes it feels as if I had to grow up fast, too fast.

'Ma'am.'

I blink and swivel round to look at Bryan, who has entered the room silently. 'Yes.'

'There's a problem with the . . . *guest* . . . in Room 21.'

'Oh?'

Bryan nods. 'She is . . . not doing well.'

'In what way?'

'She's . . . refusing to eat or drink anything.'

I sigh. 'I'm sure she will eventually.'

'Perhaps . . . we should consider putting an end to her misery.'

I glance at Bryan, knowing full well that he doesn't mean let her go. 'No,' I say. 'Not yet. I don't care what you have to do, I need her to stay alive for two more weeks, understood?'

'Understood, ma'am.' Bryan bows and exits the room.

Two weeks.

All this will be over in two weeks.

CHAPTER ELEVEN

Kimberley

I bite my tongue to stop myself from asking, 'What's in Room 21?' Instead, I ask, 'Oh, that wasn't stipulated in the non-disclosure agreement.'

'No, it's not. Jennifer doesn't want any written evidence that the room exists.'

I don't point out that since there are more than twenty-one rooms, it would be odd if it *didn't* exist.

'So, why even mention it to the staff? Surely, they must get curious.'

'At first, yes, but most of them know what's inside. I'm afraid that all new staff members must pass their trial period first.'

Okay, this catches me off guard. 'There's a trial period?'

'Of course. Don't all jobs have them?'

'Well, yes, but there was nothing in the contract about one.'

Courtney smiles. 'Don't worry. Only one person has ever failed. As long as you follow directions and orders and have a high standard, you'll be fine. You've got nothing to worry about, Kimberley. Jennifer wouldn't have brought you here if she didn't have faith in you. She's very rarely wrong.'

Why doesn't that fill me with confidence? Should I ask about the one person who failed? Do I want to know what happened to them?

'But she is wrong sometimes, right?'

'Yes, but then, no one's perfect, are they?'

Courtney stops at the upstairs hallway. On the wall in front of us is a huge portrait of Jennifer, holding a dog, who I assume is an ancestor of Frankie. Jennifer is much younger than she is now, perhaps by more than a couple of decades. Her dress sense hasn't changed. She's still wearing the same designer clothes, but something is different about her. I can't, however, put my finger on it. The shape of her nose, perhaps? Maybe she's had a nose job.

'She's really something, isn't she?' says Courtney.

'Yes. Something.' I stare and study the portrait for a few more seconds before finally dragging my eyes away, but Jennifer's bright blue eyes seem to follow me. Muffin sits at my feet. 'May I ask you a question, Courtney?'

'Please do,' she says with a smile.

'Do you like working here?'

Courtney blinks twice, all other expressions frozen on her face. 'Yes.'

'How long have you lived and worked here?'

'Coming up twenty-six years now. I haven't left this hotel in almost twenty years.'

'Really? Why not?'

Courtney smiles again. She looks sincere and kind, but there's a darkness behind her eyes I can't quite figure out. She's not happy here. She's afraid of something, something in this hotel. 'I have no need to leave,' she says.

'Do you have family?'

'No.'

'Do other staff leave to see their families?'

'Jennifer only hires people who have no one on the outside.' She makes it sound like we're trapped in a different world. Everything about this hotel screams secrecy. Jennifer has gone to considerable efforts to ensure it stays invisible.

'I see,' I say.

'I understand you may have questions. Believe me when I say that eventually all of them will be answered, but you must be patient. Patience is rewarded here.'

Makes sense, I suppose. How bad can it be here? Or am I just being very naive?

'You will come to think of this hotel and its inhabitants as family,' she continues.

'Jennifer said something about an upcoming party for the guests.'

'Yes, a grand party is held every year. Usually, Jennifer's father handles the invitations and the planning, but he's taken a recent sabbatical.'

'Where has he gone?'

'He's stayed local,' she replies with a smile. 'But he shall return for the party.'

'What's he like?'

Courtney doesn't respond straight away. She looks up at the portrait of Jennifer and sighs. 'He's very hard on his daughter.' She remains quiet for several seconds, then appears to brush off whatever dark thoughts were circling her mind. 'Shall we?' she asks, pointing to another grand staircase. 'The staff quarters are this way. I'll show you to your room so you can get settled in.'

'When do I officially start work?'

'Not till tomorrow morning, but if you wouldn't mind helping me with something this evening, I'd really appreciate it.'

'Of course.'

'Great. I'll call you when it's time.'

Courtney leads me up another staircase that feels like something out of Hogwarts. A bright red carpet runs up the middle of the stairs, leading the person walking up them higher and higher right up to the rafters, it seems. Everything is exquisitely decorated and designed, even down to the gold-plated door handles.

Various staff members nod their heads in acknowledgement as we pass and Courtney says hello to a few of them, stopping only once to engage in conversation further when a butler has a specific issue he's dealing with. While I wait for her to assist him, I take the time to study a few of the staff members who are milling around outside their rooms or walking up and down the stairs.

One housekeeper, who looks very young, is dusting the nearby photographs on the wall. She notices me watching her and quickly averts her eyes, back to her work, as if she's going to get in trouble if she looks too long in my direction. I wonder how often they recruit new staff members. Should I be worried? The young housekeeper shoots me another quick look and that's when I noticed she's sporting a black eye . . .

'Kimberley . . .'

'Yes, sorry . . .'

I quickly follow Courtney again, trying hard to put the vision of the housekeeper with a black eye out of my mind.

We arrive at a separate area of the hotel that looks much less grand and decadent than the main reception area. It's not run down or anything, but it's much more normal, like a hotel should look. In fact, I prefer it, and instantly feel more at home. I barely have time to think about the relevance of the housekeeper's black eye when Courtney stops outside a door with number twenty on it.

'This is your room.'

'Is this one of the haunted rooms?'

'Oh, no, these are staff rooms. There are guest bedrooms in the main area of the hotel. They're the ones you have to look out for.'

'Got it.' I wait for her to open the door, but she makes no move towards it.

'The door can only be opened by you. No one else can gain access unless they have a code, which changes every hour,' she says with a tad of condescension in her voice.

I frown. 'How is that possible?'

'Your fingerprints are scanned when you touch the door handle. It's a state-of-the-art security system we have in place for every room.'

Looking at the door handle, it looks perfectly ordinary, but as I reach out and touch it, wrapping my fingers around the gold handle, a loud beep erupts and sends me staggering backwards as the door pops open like a sealed safe room.

I cautiously enter and the lights switch on by themselves.

'You can adjust and control the lights, temperature and more with just your voice,' says Courtney, staying put outside the door. 'Give it a go.'

'Um . . . dim lights.'

Nothing happens.

'Oh, looks like they haven't set it up yet. You must sign in and register first.'

'Wait . . . what?'

'Did you not read the contract?'

'Not this bit.' I remember there being something about a security system in place to always ensure privacy, but I don't recall anything about having to sign in and register with an online system.

Courtney smiles. 'It came as a surprise to me too. You'll find this hotel is very tech heavy. Millions of pounds are spent each year to ensure the most state-of-the-art technology is up to date. Guests love it. It provides them complete anonymity and confidence, so they have nothing to worry about when they're here. Once you've logged on and set up your profile then only you can control this room. The keypad to do so is by your bed.'

A double bed with a thick mattress sits in the far corner. This room is more of a studio flat than a bedroom because there's also a small kitchenette and a bathroom off to the left.

It feels like home already. In fact, there's just one thing left to make it perfect.

Almost on cue, Bryan arrives carrying my bag. He clears his throat, announcing his presence.

'Thank you, Bryan,' says Courtney. She takes the bag from him then walks over to me and puts it on my bed. 'Travelling light, I see.'

'I don't have a lot of things,' I explain.

'If you need anything at all, just ask. New clothes, toiletries, footwear.'

'Oh, thanks.'

I unzip my bag and bring out the only item other than the clothes I brought with me.

A teddy bear.

The ratty, old bear is my prized possession. It's the one thing I have from my mother, my real mother. As a foster kid, I was moved around the system from home to home, never settling anywhere, but this bear came with me. Always.

His name is Biscuit.

Biscuit was, apparently, given to me by my mother when I was born. Her one request was that I should have the bear, so I was told. He's sort of like my comfort blanket. I've always wondered what made my mother give me up. She must have cared about me a little, considering she wanted me to have the bear. Inside Biscuit is a small, hard box that used to make a noise whenever I moved him, but the batteries ran out years ago and I've never replaced them. Plus, there was a note from my mother, but it's disintegrated now. I remember exactly what it said though and I always think about her words whenever I'm sad.

I place Biscuit on my bed and smile at his expression. His red ribbon around his neck is so faded now, it's more pink than red. His fur needs a decent wash and a brush, but I can't bear to wash away all the years of tears I've cried into his fur. He's perfect the way he is.

'That's a cute bear,' says Courtney.

'My mum gave Biscuit to me,' I say. I don't elaborate and Courtney doesn't ask.

'That's nice. Right, come with me. I know I said I'd leave you to settle in, but I think it's best I show you what your main jobs will be and explain what's expected of you tomorrow morning when you officially start work. We'll also get you sized up for your uniform.'

I say a silent goodbye to Biscuit and leave the room, Muffin close at my heels, closing the door slowly so that the last thing I see is the bear's cute face looking back at me.

* * *

It turns out I'm taking something of a demotion from my last job as Senior Housekeeper. Courtney is the one in charge here, which is fine. I didn't expect to walk into a senior position, but I also didn't expect to start at the beginning again. My one and only job is to clean rooms. That's it. I'm not to do anything else. I'm not to speak to guests, nor clean or enter any rooms unless I'm told to.

There's one golden rule however. There are many rules, but this rule is the one that, if broken, will get me immediately fired. I'm not allowed, under any circumstances, to be inside Room 21, which has now been mentioned several times.

Courtney explains that Room 21 is on the top floor of the hotel. Even the corridor is off limits to most staff. The only people who are allowed to set foot in the hallway and the room itself are Jennifer, Courtney and a couple of other staff members. I can't say I'm not intrigued, but if I want to keep this job, then I must do as I'm told and be patient.

Courtney shows me the laundry where I'm fitted for my uniform, which will be delivered outside my room first thing tomorrow morning, neatly pressed and perfectly fitted.

'Right, your shift starts at six. Most of the rooms have already been cleaned and sorted, but there's a few left, so I'll start you off slowly and give you one to focus on. Room five.

Here's your list of jobs to tick off in the morning.' She hands me a piece of paper and I briefly scan the list of things to do: wipe all surface areas, hoover underneath the bed, clean bathroom, replace towels. All normal stuff that I'm over-qualified to do. There's nothing there that surprises me.

Then, she hands me another piece of paper with a different list of jobs to complete for the same room. As I take the piece of paper, she watches me. My eyes scan the paper. These jobs are different. They make my insides clench, and a swirl of nausea makes me almost double over.

1. Replace blood bag with fresh one.
2. New plastic gloves in drawer.
3. Clean the tools and weapons in the bottom drawer and replace them.
4. Deliver sex toys and lay them out on the bed.

What. The. Actual. Fuck?

PART TWO

CHAPTER TWELVE

Emily

My body was so heavy, I could barely lift my arms, let alone my head, so I just lay there, waiting for my strength to return. I didn't know how long it would take, but lying still was the only thing I could think of to do that wouldn't involve my heart rate climbing too high. If I stayed calm, then you'd stay calm. I dragged my left hand up and over my bump. A small flutter made me smile. Thank goodness. You were moving again. Not a lot, but enough for now. The relief I felt made tears well up in my eyes, but as I ran my hand down my bump, I felt something that wasn't there before.

I was wearing different trousers.

Looking down, I realised I was no longer damp and couldn't smell urine either. Someone had been in here and changed me, cleaned me. The violation of my privacy made my blood run cold. Why would someone do that? Was it that woman who was in here before? They didn't have to drug me to clean me up. They could have just asked.

Lying down was uncomfortable. I remembered my midwife telling me that after a certain point in pregnancy, it was dangerous to lie flat on my back. Something about the blood supply and oxygen being cut off to the uterus. It could also cause me to become dizzy, so I awkwardly shifted my weight and sat on the edge of the creaky bed, allowing the blood supply to sink back down to my feet. My legs were heavy and swollen, so I reached down and tried to rub my feet, but I could barely reach over my bump. It seemed as if you'd grown in a matter of hours. It always fascinated me how you were growing. My tiny miracle.

I quickly gave up on trying to rub my feet and decided a walk around the room might help bring back the blood flow, but the dizziness returned as soon as I stood. I hadn't eaten the bread I was provided and when I drank the water that woman gave me, I passed out not long after, so the idea of drinking more was not appealing right now, despite my parched mouth and throat. The bread was still on the tray. Surely, they wouldn't drug the food too, but I couldn't risk it.

This was ridiculous. Why were they drugging me? I still had no idea why I was even here. Perhaps I had just been in the wrong place at the wrong time, but after hearing what that woman (Courtney, was it?) said, it sounded like I'd been targeted for a reason. Because of you. They wanted you. Well, I had news for them. I wanted you more and I wasn't giving you up without a fight. While you were still inside me, you were safe. I prayed you stayed put until I could find a way out of this place.

I sighed and decided to spend some time getting to know my surroundings. The silence was almost unbearable. I could hear my own heartbeat. Other than the bed creaking whenever I moved, not a sound could be heard.

'Well, baby, the only good thing about this situation is I can rest now,' I said to you gently, stroking my bump with both hands. Talking to you was something I'd done from the very start, from the day I found out you existed. It was soothing to me, and I needed to stay as calm as possible to not only keep my blood pressure low, but to ensure the stress and anxiety didn't transfer to you.

You were my number one priority. That, and getting out of this room.

I hoped you liked the sound of my voice.

***

An unknown amount of time later, the door opened and the woman I saw earlier peered round the side of it, as if testing to see if I was awake.

'Ah, you're up,' she said as she entered, the door slamming shut behind her. 'I performed a scan of your baby while you were asleep and she's perfectly healthy and doing well.'

My mouth dropped open. 'I'm sorry . . . Did you say . . . *she*?'

The woman's eyes widened. 'Oh, goodness, did you not know?'

I shook my head. Anger swelled within me.

'I am so sorry, Emily. That was very foolish of me to assume you knew.'

I wanted to scream at her. How dare she tell me such an important fact about you without my consent. I felt robbed of the surprise, but I didn't want to cause any issues, so I let it slide.

'It's fine . . . I guess, but . . . she's okay? She hasn't moved much since I've been in here, since the attack.'

'She's absolutely fine. We just need you to rest as much as possible, keep eating and stay hydrated.'

'Hard to do when I've been taken prisoner and you keep drugging my food and water,' I snapped.

'You're not a prisoner, Emily. And I promise I won't drug you again.'

Yeah, right.

'What else would you call this situation? If I'm not a prisoner, then let me out.' I was on the verge of breaking down in tears. My emotions had been all over the place while being pregnant, but even the short amount of time I'd been in this room had heightened them even more.

'This is the best place for you now. For you, and for your baby,' said the woman.

'Why am I here?'

'You'll find out soon enough. In fact, your next visitor should be able to tell you more.' She turned to leave. I sprung to my feet as fast as my pregnant body would allow and grasped her wrist. She shook me off with ease. 'Do not touch me!' she screamed.

Her vicious voice made me jump backwards. 'I'm sorry ... I ...'

'Sorry,' she whispered. 'Never good to sneak up on the staff here. We're all a bit jumpy.' She laughed, but I could tell by her expression that she was serious.

Which begged the question: why were all the staff so jumpy?

I watched her leave, wishing she didn't have to go. I didn't relish the thought of being alone in this room for much longer. However, the person who walked into the room next was the last person I ever wanted to see again.

I stumbled backwards as he closed the door. He stood in the middle of the room with that smug grin across his face, like he was enjoying making me squirm. I was doing more than squirming. My insides turned to jelly, and I wanted to vomit, but there was nothing in my stomach to come up.

'D-Damien,' I said.

'Emily, it's good to see you again.' His eyes landed on my stomach. 'I see you've been busy over the past eight months.'

'She's not yours,' I said quickly, even though it was a lie. I was a virgin when Damien violated me, and I hadn't been with any other man. I may have had a boyfriend, but we hadn't been intimate yet.

Damien raised his eyebrows. 'We'll see about that when she's born.'

'You're not touching her.' My hands folded over my bump, shielding you from your father. 'Why am I here? What do you want from me?'

Damien smiled and I was taken straight back to the night I first met him. He had dazzled me with the same smile, but now, instead of swooning to his natural good looks and charm, I wanted to run away from him and hide.

'My dear, did you seriously think I wouldn't find you? That baby belongs to me.'

'She's not yours.'

'I guess we'll find out for certain in due course.'

'You can't keep me locked up in this room forever.'

'Can't I?'

'You won't take her from me!'

'That's where you're wrong, Emily. If the child you're carrying does indeed belong to me, then you can rest assured she will be safe and secure and well looked after in this hotel.'

'And if she's not?'

'If it turns out to be some other man's seed inside you, then she will be disposed of properly.'

That time I gagged and something like a scream erupted from my throat. 'You're a monster!'

'You can tell yourself whatever you like, Emily.'

'You raped me!' The word *rape* seemed to echo around the small room, making it louder than it was. It sent shivers down my spine as I remembered his hands grabbing me, forcing my face so deeply into the mattress that I almost suffocated.

Damien took a step towards me, but no further. 'I'll be back soon, Emily. If you don't want me to get my hands on that baby, then I suggest you keep your legs crossed for as long as possible, but rest assured, one way or another, that baby will come out of you, and then it shall be mine to do with as I please. In this hotel, you belong to me. Everyone belongs to me.' He turned and walked out of the room. His words cut deep, but one in particular confused the hell out of me.

Hotel?

I was being kept prisoner in a hotel.

* * *

Sometime later, while I was lying on the bed trying to forget about the fact that Damien, the man who raped me, was keeping me trapped inside his hotel, a noise disturbed me. I opened my eyes to find the lights had turned off. Pitch black surrounded me, not even a sliver of light piercing it anywhere. Did that mean it was night-time? The lack of windows in the room made it impossible to tell, so perhaps they were attempting to keep my circadian rhythm intact. I'd been attacked during the night, which meant I must have been here roughly a day. It felt longer. Much longer.

The darkness settled around me, but the noise kept me alert.

Drip. Drip. Drip.

Beep. Beep. Beep.

Right on cue, my bladder signalled it was full. Where was I supposed to go to the toilet? I sat up, disorientated as my blood pressure levelled out. It was so dark, I couldn't see my hand in front of my face, but then I noticed a slight flicker of light that hadn't been there before.

A red light.

In the far corner of the room at ceiling height.

Drip. Drip. Drip.

Beep. Beep. Beep.

I waddled awkwardly across the room towards the red light. It looked tiny, like a light from a piece of equipment. Was it a camera? I couldn't remember seeing one while the lights were on. Were they watching me? Filming me?

I stared up at the red light, then stuck my middle finger up at it.

Fuck you, Damien.

CHAPTER THIRTEEN

Jennifer

Courtney informs me that Kimberley has been shown her room and given the list of jobs for tomorrow morning. I can only imagine what must be going through her mind right now after seeing the list, but I'm satisfied she won't be an issue. Not yet anyway. This first job is merely a test, to see if she has the stomach that's required to progress to the next stage. She needs to work to earn the trust it takes to converse with the guests. At the moment, she's a lowly housekeeper and she'll remain in that job until she can prove to me that she's trustworthy. It may take a day, it may take longer, but the party is in two weeks, and a lot needs to happen in that time. She not only needs to be trustworthy but dedicated to the job. She'll find out more eventually. She has plenty of time to warm up to the idea of what's involved in the running of this hotel.

I must not rush her though. I mustn't drop the bombshell on her too soon or I'll risk losing her forever. It takes time to work your way up to the top, and that's true about any job, not just this one. There's space to do well here.

Courtney, for example, arrived over twenty years ago as a nervous, but dedicated member of the team. Now, she's one of the most trusted staff members. One could almost call her a friend, although I'm wary of forming friendships with the staff. I've been burned more than once by making that mistake.

Only Courtney knows the truth about me. The real truth. Although, I have a feeling that Bryan also knows, but if he does, he hasn't said anything. I don't think he has the guts. He's worked here since Damien first started the hotel. He can't afford to lose this job because he's never known anything else. I'm sure Bryan is wondering where Damien is. No one can get hold of him, and I'd prefer it stays that way. Besides, without him around barking orders left, right and centre, the staff seem a little more relaxed, a little happier. Compared to normal, anyway. Although, the young housekeeper with the black eye doesn't look too comfortable. Perhaps I won't send her into Room 21 again. She clearly got a little too close to our special guest, who may be feeling a little like a trapped wild animal, eager to be free, especially since she knows what awaits her when the day of the party arrives.

The sound of a car horn shatters my thoughts. I let out a long sigh. The first guest has arrived.

Lincoln.

That's not his real name. It's his code name. I don't know his real name. I don't think anyone does, not even Damien. Some of the guests prefer to use code names or fake names, while others are happy to use their real ones. It makes no difference to me. They are promised anonymity throughout their stay.

As I watch Lincoln's black Mercedes trundle up the driveway, I shudder, remembering his smug grin and clammy hands on my body a few days ago. I push myself to standing and make my way out to the front of the hotel, taking my place at the top of the stone steps.

I want to be the first person my guests see upon arrival. It will make them feel important, that the owner of the hotel is there to greet them. Of course, it's usually Damien's job, but since he's not here, then I am in charge whether the guests like it or not. Not that I need to greet Lincoln as he and I go way back, but I like to keep my eyes on him, so keeping him on my side is a must.

Then, once I've greeted the guests and we've swapped pleasantries, I pass them onto the relevant staff member inside, who will look after them for the rest of their stay, always alerting me to any problems that arise. But I do expect my staff to think for themselves and sort out any issues quickly and efficiently.

The Mercedes rolls to a stop in front of me and the driver's door swings open. Lincoln always drives himself. Despite having enough power and money to rule a small country, he doesn't have many staff. He likes to do things for himself, which is respectable, I suppose, but it doesn't make me like him. I don't know how he's come to be so wealthy and, to be perfectly honest, I couldn't care less, but I doubt it's legal. He's an unlikeable man. That's all there is to it. When you're around Lincoln, you must be on your guard because he could very easily lead you into a trap that you can't escape from. I know more than most what that involves, because I've been trapped by him for a very long time. He's a handsome man and he knows it. His black quaffed hair and expertly tailored suits make him stand out from any crowd so that all eyes are on him as he gets out of the car, a brilliantly white smile beaming at me. He may be almost ten years my junior, but that doesn't stop him from taking what he wants from me. I believe the word *psychopath* describes him very well.

Frankie has followed me outside and is sitting at my feet, but when he sees Lincoln he growls, then wanders back indoors. I don't blame him.

'Jennifer, my love, so good to see you again.' He glides up to me and kisses me on the cheek. We only saw each other recently, so his warm greeting is most definitely fake. I know mine is.

'Lincoln, I'm delighted you could make it. I take it the drive wasn't too arduous?'

'Stopped a few times to stretch my legs and stay over in some of my favourite places, but knowing I had such a gorgeous host waiting for me when I arrived kept me going.'

I smile through gritted teeth. 'You mentioned that you may have to pop back down south again before the party?'

'Ah, yes, well, the business is booming as always. It depends how things go over the next few days. It's difficult to drag myself away, but I look forward to this party every year and this one is extra special, wouldn't you say?' He looks past me towards the front doors. 'Where's Damien? Still away?'

'Yes, he sends his deepest apologies, but rest assured, he'll be here for the party.'

'Good to know.'

'It's going to be a night you'll never forget.'

Lincoln grins at me. 'Looking forward to it.'

He gives me a wink and heads past me, up the stone steps and in through the front doors. He knows the drill. Lincoln is one of the regular guests, having attended his first party ten years ago. Damien tracked him down and invited him and he's been coming every year since. Lincoln has got worse over the years. He was a vile human being back then, but now he's pure evil and I'm surprised he hasn't sprouted horns on the top of his head yet or been dragged back down to the depths of hell from whence he came.

I'm about to turn around and head back into my office when the sound of another car coming up the driveway catches my attention. I frown, wracking my brain as to who it could be. I'm not expecting another guest to arrive for five days.

As the car draws closer, I recognise it as belonging to Mr and Mrs Wyatt (not their real names because he's a highly renowned private doctor and she's a politician), the ultimate power couple who spend more on champagne per day then most people spend on rent in a month. They always expect the best when they're here and they always receive it. Mrs Wyatt can be exceptionally picky, but I've learned to read her well over the three years she's been attending with her husband, who started out coming alone, but then brought his wife along. She hasn't looked back since.

The guests at the hotel are treated like royalty (some of them even are) and they always leave satisfied and happy. I've only had one complaint, and I don't intend to repeat it.

But why are Mr and Mrs Wyatt here five days early?

I don't remember seeing an email from either of them informing me of their early arrival. The fact they're here before they were expected is going to have a monumental impact because their suite isn't ready yet.

Shit.

Mrs Wyatt is the first to get out of the luxury car, a white Bentley, top of the range. She beams at me with her pearly whites. It's been a year since I've seen her, and she appears to have aged backwards by at least five years. I don't judge her, far from it, but she appears to have suffered a bad reaction to her lip fillers. Either that or they're supposed to look red and swollen.

'Jennifer, love, so good to see you.' She air kisses each of my cheeks, barely even touching me, as if coming into contact with me will give her an electric shock.

'Mrs Wyatt, delighted to see you, as always, but I wasn't expecting you until next week.'

The woman in front of me flips her hair over her shoulder and sighs heavily — a slightly overdramatic gesture, but then she generally makes a big deal out of every small inconvenience.

'Ah, yes, I'm sorry to say that my husband and I have had a quarrel, and I couldn't spend another moment in his presence, so I decided to come early.'

'I'm sorry to hear that, but I'm afraid your suite isn't ready yet.'

Mrs Wyatt makes some sort of snort and glares at me. 'That is unacceptable.'

'I apologise, but it clearly states in the contract that you must provide me with at least twenty-four hours' notice if you are to arrive early.'

'So, what am I supposed to do? Sit in my car and wait?'

'No, of course not. You can come in and wait and I'll get the suite ready as quickly as possible for you, but it could be at least an hour or two. May I ask, will Mr Wyatt be joining us as usual in five days' time?'

'Who knows,' she snaps back. 'But if he does show his pathetic face then he's not staying in my suite, so you'll have to provide him his own room as far away from mine as possible.'

I inwardly groan because every single room is accounted for already. I'm still awaiting a couple of responses, but after my email blast earlier, I've had a lot more emails ping into my inbox informing me that they'll be attending after all since Damien is assured to be in attendance. Most guests confirm their attendance months in advance, some even book for the next year as soon as the party is over. Rooms are like gold dust here. Once they're gone, they're gone. Mrs Wyatt has now thrown a very large spanner in the works.

'Very well,' I say. 'Do you know if he definitely is coming?'

'You'll have to ask him. Did you get my special request for this year?' she asks, changing the subject, completely catching me off guard.

I blink several times, resetting my focus. 'I did, indeed.'

'And . . . it was . . . acceptable?' She widens her eyes, as if hoping I'll say I struggled to procure her request, but I merely smile and place my hand gently on her bony shoulder.

'Perfectly acceptable,' I respond with a smile. I straighten my spine just enough so I'm a couple of inches taller than her, despite her towering heels. She's quite short without them.

'Good. Now . . . if I must wait for my room to be ready, then I expect to have special treatment to make up for it. Have one of your staff come and find me in the library. I need a glass of champagne to calm my nerves after such a harrowing drive and an upsetting few days.'

'Right away.'

She saunters past me and up the steps into the hotel. Her perfume wafts in my face and makes my eyes water.

I take my phone out of my pocket and dial for Courtney, explaining what needs to happen. I tell her to take Kimberley with her to the suite and prepare it for Mrs Wyatt. I wanted Kimberley to settle in today, but it looks like she's going to be thrown into the deep end. Best way to learn to swim, they always say.

I head into reception to ensure my two new arrivals are happy. Lincoln is already sipping a glass of perfectly chilled champagne and sucking on a plump, ripe strawberry.

My staff are rushing around, fetching their bags from their cars and carting them up to their rooms. The receptionists are smiling and greeting them. I manage to sort out Mrs Wyatt's early arrival and one of the housekeepers is assigned as her personal go-to person for the rest of the day while her room is prepared. Mrs Wyatt instantly orders a massage and a facial.

Despite the brief shock of her arrival, all is well, apart from the small matter of Mr Wyatt not giving me a heads up about it.

Something isn't right.

I know Mr Wyatt very well and he would never not let me know of a change of plans, especially without any notice whatsoever. Not even a phone call. I double-check with reception, and it's confirmed. Mr Wyatt has not made any contact with the hotel to inform us of his wife arriving early or that he'll be needing a separate room.

I stand silently while I watch Mrs Wyatt, throwing her long hair back and sipping a glass of fizz, acting as if the sun shines out of her most-likely bleached butt crack.

I'll get to the root of this.

Nothing will disrupt my party.

Nothing.

CHAPTER FOURTEEN

Kimberley

I keep staring at the list of jobs on the page, reading them over and over until the words blur together and make no sense. I'm not sure what I'm expecting to happen. It's not like they're written in magic marker, and they'll disappear before my eyes. At first, I think it's some kind of sick joke, but Courtney seemed perfectly serious when she handed me the list. She had a straight face and everything. Even when I'm not staring at the list, the words are seared into my brain and no matter how much I try and think about something else, they plague my thoughts and won't allow me to concentrate on anything else.

Blood.

Weapons.

Sex toys.

What kind of people stay here? Or am I just naïve? I certainly never had anything close to this weird to deal with at Harris Hotel, and neither had any other member of staff as far as I was aware. Jennifer did explain that Clifton Hotel was unique and had a specific type of clientele who required a lot of discretion, but . . . I don't know what I was expecting, but it wasn't blood, weapons and sex toys.

There's a knock at the door.

I hide the list behind my back as if I'm afraid to be caught reading something so . . . so . . . Another knock. I answer it and see Courtney standing on the other side.

'Kimberley,' she says, sounding slightly out of breath, 'I'm sorry to disturb you, but I need your help. A guest has turned up early and her suite isn't ready and everyone else is busy, so I need you to assist me in preparing it. She's downstairs waiting as we speak.'

'Oh, yes, of course,' I say. I turn to whistle for Muffin who has made herself comfortable on my bed. She lifts her head, ready for my command.

Courtney inhales sharply. 'Ooh, I'm sorry, but there are no dogs allowed in the suite. Mrs Wyatt is allergic.'

'No problem,' I say, even though the idea of going anywhere without Muffin fills me with trepidation. 'Stay, girl,' I tell her. Muffin whines but lowers her head. She is happy to be left alone for a while, but like me, she prefers us to be together.

I follow Courtney out the door, stuffing the list into my pocket. I'm glad of the distraction to be honest because I'm not sure what I would have done for the rest of the day other than read the list over and over.

'How come Mrs Wyatt turned up early?' I ask, having to break into a jog to keep up with Courtney who is storming ahead like a soldier into battle.

'No idea,' she answers. 'But she's here and waiting for her suite. Plus, it looks like Mr Wyatt may or may not be joining her in five days' time so he may or may not need his own room.'

'Is that a problem?'

Courtney stops at the lift doors and presses the button. 'Yes, it is because we have no spare rooms available. Each one is accounted for already. Mr and Mrs Wyatt always come together, so the fact they want separate rooms is rather unusual.'

'Oh.'

'Yes . . . *Oh*.'

The lift doors ping open, and we step inside. As soon as we arrive at the right floor, Courtney takes off at rocket speed towards the suite at the end of the hall. Brook Suite. It's not as spectacular as the penthouse at Harris Hotel. But it still takes my breath away, but for very different reasons. The decor is unlike anything I've ever seen before.

Dark greens, reds and purples adorn every surface. It's so dark and foreboding that it takes a few moments for my eyes to adjust. Then, the more I look, the more details I see. The skull decorations on the wallpaper. The black crystals on the table. If I didn't know any better, I'd say this was a vampire's lair, which of course is ridiculous, but that's the vibe I'm getting.

'Gosh,' I say. And that's all I can manage before Courtney puts me to work. I take care of the general cleaning: dusting, polishing and wiping, while Courtney sorts out the personal touches, including scented candles, an array of wines in the fridge and setting out a selection of chocolates, snacks and drinks. She also makes the bed, an enormous four-poster with purple hanging curtains surrounding it.

It takes longer than I imagined sorting the suite out. Everything must be exactly to Mrs Wyatt's specifications. I assume that's why Jennifer tested me at Harris Hotel, in preparation for exactly this sort of thing. I don't even get the chance to ask Courtney about the list of jobs she gave me for tomorrow morning. Maybe I'm not even supposed to question them. I'm just expected to get on with them, like any good housekeeper would do.

We work quickly and diligently. I don't pester Courtney with questions, such as how the towels need to be folded because it's all on the list of requirements printed out on the side. I tick off the job once it's done and Courtney does the same. An hour later, we've completed the list.

'I must say, Kimberley, you're excellent at your job,' says Courtney, closing the door behind us. 'You work independently and to a very high standard.'

'Thank you,' I reply.

'Can you find your own way back to your room? I must go and see to Mrs Wyatt and tell her that her room's ready.'

'Yes, no problem. See you tomorrow morning.'

'Don't forget to head down for dinner at six tonight in the staff dining room. Muffin will be provided with food also.'

'I won't. Thanks.'

Courtney hurries away, leaving me standing outside the Brook Suite doors. I could head straight down to dinner now, since it's almost six, collecting Muffin on the way. On the other hand, I could instead head down the corridor and check out the elusive Room 21 that apparently, I'm not allowed to enter.

The sign is right there in front of me, pointing left.

Right: back to my room to see Muffin, have a nice dinner and go to bed.

Left: towards temptation where, if I'm caught, I could lose this job before I've even started.

Decisions. Decisions.

I'm about to take a step forward to go left when I start to feel a bit weird. I recognise the feeling straight away. If Muffin were here, I'm pretty sure she'd be sending me warning signals right now. I decide not to risk it and head right, back the way Courtney brought me.

Shit.

I'm not going to make it back to the room.

I stumble against the wall and gradually lower myself to the floor, mere seconds before a seizure takes over.

It's a small one, but suffering through even a small one without Muffin is something I never want to experience again. Usually, she lies across my legs or stomach and licks my face when I come round, but this time, when I shift into a sitting position once I feel able to move, she's not there to comfort me, and I burst into tears.

I need to get back to my room, back to Muffin.

***

I don't sleep well, if at all. The meal was lovely, and the staff were welcoming, but I didn't stay long. The seizure rattled me more than it has for a long time. My morning alarm sounds just as I'm drifting off from exhaustion. It's not the ideal start to the official day one of my new job, but I'm nothing if not professional and, despite taking a lower-ranking position, I'm still a damn good housekeeper. I'm living in this fancy, technology-laden room for free and no longer have to share a bathroom with three other people, one of whom liked to smoke joints in there, thinking no one else noticed.

I arrive at the staff reception ten minutes early. Courtney is already there with a clipboard and pen, her face contorted into a serious frown.

'Good morning,' I say cheerfully. I may be tired, but I'm determined to make the best of it.

Courtney makes no gesture to say she's heard me. She's staring intently at the paper on the clipboard as if her eyes are glued to it.

'Um . . . is everything okay?' I ask.

'No, it's not,' she snaps.

'Anything I can help with?'

Courtney finally looks at me and huffs. 'No, Kimberley. I just need you to do your job and see to room five, okay?'

'Got it.'

Courtney glares at me, then down at Muffin who wags her tail in response. However, it doesn't seem to melt Courtney's bad mood because she storms off with her clipboard, her low heels clicking across the tiled floor.

Bryan arrives a minute later. He also gives Muffin a stern look.

'You have your list of jobs?'

'Um, yes.'

'Do you have any questions?'

If there was a time to ask questions, this would be it, but how can I ask Bryan, who's an elderly, strange man, about blood, weapons and sex toys and where I'd find such items?

'No questions,' I say.

'Good. Follow me.' Bryan shows me to room five and explains where all the cleaning products are, including my own cleaning trolley laden with top-of-the-range products, which all have weird scents that make no sense together: mildew and chocolate, tangerine and salt, and sweat and blood. Gross.

My curiosity at the last one makes me unscrew the top of the bottle and take a sniff, which I instantly regret as I fight against my gag reflex.

Why would anyone want that smell sprayed around their room?

I hastily put the bottle back, grab my cleaning trolley and input the door code that Bryan gave me to enter room five. As I enter, the lights come on. It's a gorgeous room, highlighted by an enormous four-poster bed with black curtains surrounding it. It seems it's a staple in most rooms.

The room already looks clean to me, but I know how much dirt and grime live under the surface. People look at a room and see clean surfaces, a made-up bed and hoovered floors, but what they don't see is the minute particles of dust on the sides, or the random tissue hidden under the bed or the piece of fluff on the bed sheets.

I do.

I see everything.

So, I get to work.

I have an hour to get this room up to my standard, which I do easily, but when it comes to completing the other list, I'm more hesitant. For a start, where am I supposed to re-fill the blood bag? And where is the weapon drawer? I've cleaned every inch of this room and haven't found one yet. I must be missing something. Damn it. I wish I had asked Bryan now.

I look down at Muffin who's lying patiently by the door. I don't want her transferring dog hair onto the clean and polished surfaces. 'Any help?' I ask her.

Muffin keeps her eyes closed.

Then I remember that these rooms are smart. As in, tech smart. If my own room is voice activated, then perhaps this one is too. It can't have been assigned to the guest who's staying in here yet because I was able to enter freely with a code and I can control the lights with my voice.

'Weapon room,' I say to the room, feeling stupid.

Beep. Beep. Beep.

Muffin flinches at the sound coming out of the walls and I jump as a drawer underneath the huge bed slides open, revealing an array of weapons. Knives, blades, hammers, lances, forks and more lie at the bottom of the drawer, illuminated by their own lighting system. I hold my breath, bending down to kneel on the plush carpet.

I'm supposed to clean these weapons and replace them in the drawer.

I scrabble to my feet and fetch the cleaning trolley, scanning the shelves for anything I can use. I grab a bottle of bleach. Bleach can get rid of anything, right? Then, I can spray the items with the scent listed to cover any lingering smell.

I do what I'm paid to do.

And get to work.

* * *

Time seems to fly by and as I place the last clean weapon back in the drawer, I realise I'm running late. I grab some fresh plastic gloves and replace them, but I have no idea how to finish the rest of the list, so I head back to the staff reception to see if Courtney is back yet or to ask Bryan for help, but there's no one there.

Where the hell do I find a fresh blood bag and sex toys? It's utterly ridiculous. My pulse is pounding so fast I feel out of breath at the idea of not finishing my job properly. I finger my inhaler in the pocket of my uniform. It's not needed just yet, but I'm on the verge of using it. My chest feels tight as I jog along the corridors in search of someone who can help me.

I'm stressed about falling behind. Muffin trots along beside me. She can sense I'm stressed, but her presence is enough to keep me level-headed.

Thankfully, as I round the next corner, I bump into another housekeeper who I haven't met before. Her eyes widen when she sees me, and she mutters something when I cause her to drop the neatly folded towels in her arms.

'I'm so sorry,' I say as I bend down to help her pick them up off the floor.

'Never run anywhere,' she says. 'It makes you look like you're panicking.'

'I am panicking,' I answer back. 'I need a fresh blood bag and sex toys. Where can I find them?' All embarrassment has long since passed.

'Along this corridor, turn left at the end, then take the third right. The code for the door marked *Items* is 6969.' Her face is as deadpan as it gets. 'I'm not kidding,' she adds.

'Right . . . Thanks.'

She smiles down at Muffin. My dog has that effect on most people.

The housekeeper continues her way down the corridor. I stare after her, wait for her to turn the corner and then sprint in the opposite direction, following her directions. I don't care if she told me not to run. I need to hurry and complete my jobs. I can't fail on the first day.

I find the door and input the code.

The door pops open. I brace myself for what I'm about to see. I don't consider myself a prude, nor am I remotely squeamish, but the array of sex toys on the row of shelves in front of me makes even me blush. Dildos, butt plugs, vibrators and more adorn the shelves, all in brand-new packaging.

I don't even know what type of toys this guest needs.

Am I just supposed to guess?

Then I realise that on the shelves are small cards with numbers on. I find number five and grab the items listed on the card, which include a gimp mask and a gag. Then I head further into the room and find a large fridge. I open the door and immediate slam it shut as the sight sears itself into my brain for eternity.

I can't do this.

Bright red bags and bottles of blood are lined up in the fridge. Again, numbers are placed underneath them. The smell that wafts from the cool fridge makes me retch, but I somehow manage to hold it together as I grab the bag of blood and head out the door back towards room five.

I place the sex toys on the bed and replace the bag of blood in the mini fridge.

Then, I sprint back to my room and hurl my guts up into the toilet.

CHAPTER FIFTEEN

Jennifer

Once I wash off the stress of the day and remove the layers of make-up, I crawl under my silk sheets and try to sleep, but even my eye mask and sound machine can't help switch off my racing thoughts. Frankie is cuddled up next to me under the sheets, his warm little body providing comfort. The whole thing with Mr and Mrs Wyatt plagues me more than it should do. It seems particularly odd that Mr Wyatt didn't arrive with his wife. They argue all the time. Hell, one year she even punched him in the face and drew blood, but only an hour later I found them with their legs wrapped around each other in the library. It isn't unusual for them to have a fight, but it is unusual for them to arrive separately and want to stay in different rooms. What's even more strange is that neither of them bothered to inform me in advance!

Now, the next morning, I'm still at a loss of what to do if Mr Wyatt turns up in five days' time and wants a separate room. I haven't managed to put on my make-up this morning, so am hiding away in my office until I get a spare few minutes in which to apply it. I don't like the staff or guests to see me bare faced, only Courtney has that daily pleasure. Frankie is perched on my lap. He never cares whether I've got make-up on or not. I wish people were more like dogs.

Courtney looks positively sick as she approaches my large mahogany desk. My office is in the room next to reception so I can be close to the action, but the staff know not to disturb me unless there's an emergency. There's a huge bank of monitors on ten different screens across the wall behind me, all capturing different areas of the hotel, including the door to Room 21. If I need to see what's going on inside, then I input a code in my computer and log in to a special online viewing area.

The bank of monitors can be swiftly covered up by a sliding panel if I am planning on receiving anyone who isn't privy to seeing them. No one is allowed to sit at my desk. No one. The chair is adjusted to suit my height and weight. The monitors are adjusted so that there's no glare from the windows and are exactly eye-level. Even the keyboard and mouse are positioned precisely so that they don't cause any unnecessary discomfort if I'm sitting here for hours on end, which doesn't tend to happen too often, luckily.

Courtney waits behind the line on the floor until I'm ready to call her forward. I've just finished sending an email to Lord Millington, confirming the time and date of his massage as his personal masseuse is no longer available. Tina, the housekeeper I had to fire, used to tend to his needs, and I can't let Kimberley take over something as important as looking after Lord Millington, so Luna is going to assist him. I just hope she's satisfactory to his needs.

I finally look up. 'Yes.'

'Ma'am, I am afraid there are absolutely no spare rooms available for Mr Wyatt.'

'None at all?'

'None.'

'This is a problem, isn't it?'

Courtney nods. 'Yes. A big problem.'

I sigh, keeping a tight hold on Frankie as I swivel in a full circle in my chair, gazing at the monitors as I pass. 'How are the renovations coming on the attic room?'

'Fine, but it won't be ready in five days. May I suggest something, ma'am?'

'Go on.'

'How about we move our guest in Room 21 somewhere else?'

'Surely, you don't expect Mr Wyatt to stay in Room 21?'

'No, ma'am, but perhaps our new housekeeper could rough it in there for a few days then Mr Wyatt could take her room?'

'That's not possible. Mr Wyatt cannot stay in the staff quarters.'

'It was merely a suggestion, ma'am.'

A change of topic is in order. 'How did Kimberley get on with her first room clean this morning? Any issues?'

'Not that I'm aware of. I believe she was a few minutes late in finishing, but it's all done and appears to be of a high standard.'

'Good. Where is she now?'

'I believe she's in her room vomiting.'

I smile and nod. It's the normal response I expect from new staff. It would normally take several weeks before a new housekeeper would have to deal with such unique requests, but I don't have time to ease Kimberley into it. I need her prepared in two weeks. Slowly, but surely, she'll come around to the fact that it doesn't matter what the guests get up to behind closed doors. It's why they pay us and it's why I pay her to keep her mouth shut.

'Please tell Kimberley to come and see me once she's finished vomiting.'

'Yes, ma'am.'

My inbox pings, alerting me to a response from Lord Millington. I dismiss Courtney who bows and retreats, allowing the door to softly close behind her. It appears Lord Millington is annoyed at having a new masseuse, but there's not a lot he can do about it. Not many women will willingly massage his flabby body with goats' blood instead of oil.

I quickly apply some make-up using the forward-facing camera function on my phone before Kimberley arrives.

***

Fifteen minutes later, I'm closely watching the computer screen. Room 21 is showing on the monitor, its resident lying still on the bumpy mattress. She's been sleeping a lot lately.

A knock sounds.

'Enter.' Footsteps approach, followed by the pitter-patter of paws. Before I look up, I turn off the screen. 'Ah, Kimberley, thank you for coming. How are you feeling?' Frankie jumps off my lap to greet his new best friend. He and Muffin touch noses.

Her face is pale and she's a little shaky. 'I'm fine, ma'am.'

'Would you like something to settle your stomach? I can't have you vomiting all over the place now, can I?'

'I think I'm okay now. Thank you. Did you manage to work out the issue with Mr Wyatt's room?'

'Unfortunately not, no, but it's nothing for you to worry about. The reason I called you in is because I've made you an appointment with Doctor Simmons. She's expecting you in twenty minutes. She'll talk to you about your condition, medication and provide any check-ups or tests you require.'

'Thank you, ma'am. That's very kind.'

'Did Courtney show you where the medical wing is?'

'No, she didn't.'

'Take the lift to the second floor, walk to the end of the hallway, turn left and the medical wing is straight in front of you.'

'Thank you, ma'am.'

I nod and with a wave of my hand, dismiss her. She turns to walk away.

'Oh, and Kimberley . . . it won't take you long to get used to the sight and smell of blood. It's the shit that's hard to stomach.'

Kimberley smiles weakly, turning pale again, then nods and exits the room.

***

After an hour I decide to stretch my legs. Plus, Frankie needs a pee break. I don't get very far before I'm cornered by the last person I want to see.

'Jennifer, might I have a word?'

'Ah, Lincoln, of course you may.'

He's clearly had too much to drink even though it's barely midday because he's unnecessarily touching my arm, waist and shoulders as he guides me to the side of the room. Frankie follows at a distance. Lincoln leans in close to my ear. 'I wonder if I might request something . . . new . . . this time.'

I sigh. 'Lincoln, as I've told you many times, I'm unable to change any agreed-upon requests once you've signed your contract.'

'Yes, I know, but . . .' He licks his lips. 'I didn't think I'd want it this time, but now I'm here, I want to let loose and have some fun, you know what I mean?'

'That is precisely what the party is for. Can you not wait until then?'

'No.'

I sigh again. 'What is it you'd like, and I'll see what can be arranged, but I really must insist you provide me adequate notice next time.'

'Of course, of course.' He leans in close again, so close that his breath tickles my ear as he whispers his sordid request.

I give him my most dazzling smile. 'You are a strange one, Lincoln. I'll see what I can do, but no promises.'

Lincoln downs the last of the dregs of his drink. 'I can always count on you, Jennifer, to fulfil my darkest and deepest desires.' He staggers off towards the dining hall, leaving me with an uneasy feeling in my gut.

Lincoln is a very respectable, wealthy and powerful man on the outside, but on the inside he's a sick, mentally deranged sociopath, and now I have to find someone who's willing to sink to the lowest level and forget they are a human being with rights and feelings.

I cannot allow any of my housekeepers to take the hit. But Lincoln is someone who could cause a lot of trouble if he doesn't get what he wants. I guess it's up to me. He may be sick and twisted, but he's nothing if not discreet.

'Courtney,' I say, touching her on her shoulder. She turns. 'I'm going to be indisposed for an hour or two. Are you okay to hold the fort until my return and take Frankie for a quick walk?'

'Yes, ma'am.'

***

An hour and a half later, I emerge from Lincoln's suite. I've left him sleeping naked on the bed. I have also called in a housekeeper to clean up the mess he's made. Before leaving, I took a shower to wash off the blood, urine and semen that clung to my body. When I arrived, I was wearing a black balaclava over my head to disguise myself. That is what he wanted, what he demanded. He never likes to see the women's faces while he degrades and molests them, but he knew it was me. As I stripped my clothes off in front of him, his eyes lingered on the scar across my abdomen. He didn't question it, despite it probably coming as quite a surprise to him. The last time he'd seen me naked, I didn't have a scar.

It's not often I do these sorts of requests. I like to keep myself professionally distant from my guests, but there are some levels of morbidity I won't subject my staff to. Lincoln and I have an understanding. I allow him to do these disgusting things to me and he won't reveal our biggest secret.

Even though I showered before leaving his room, the first thing I do upon entering my own bedroom is turn on the running water for a bath. I need to soak away more than just the grime on the outside of my body. I'm dirty. Very, very dirty.

As I sink into the soapy bubbles, I can't hold back the tears. I never cry in front of people. Ever. But when I'm alone, I cry until I can't cry anymore. I'm damaged and broken and it's all I've ever known. No one could ever understand what I've been through, what I've had to sacrifice to get to this point in my life. This hotel is all I have and yes, the guests are some of the worst human beings in existence, but it's better for them to live out their sordid fantasies here, within the confines of the hotel, rather than kill, maim and destroy people in the real world. That's what Damien always said. The party is the culmination of what this hotel is all about.

Once I've scrubbed off the top layer of my skin, I wrap myself in my fluffy dressing gown and call down to reception to check everything is okay. Courtney assures me that it is. I settle on my sofa and Frankie jumps on my lap. Stroking his soft fur helps me to unwind. He's such a comfort to me and he doesn't even know it.

But not even his gentle heartbeat against my chest stops the vivid images from flooding my mind of what Lincoln put me through.

Lincoln is a rapist, murderer and psychopath. His sordid fantasies carried out within these walls are the only thing stopping him from inflicting pain and torture on unsuspecting people on the outside.

Little does Lincoln know that this year will be his last.

In fact, this will be the last party this hotel ever hosts, but it will go down in the history books as the best one yet.

CHAPTER SIXTEEN

Emily

How much time had passed was a complete mystery to me. It could have been two hours, two days or two weeks. It couldn't have been two months, or you would have arrived by now.

Something was wrong though and it scared the crap out of me, although technically that wasn't true because I hadn't been able to *go* for however long it was I'd been locked in this room. But I was scared and all I wanted, more than anything else in the world, was to know you were healthy.

My insides ached. No, it wasn't an ache. More of a stabbing, like a blunt, hot knife was stabbing me in the side very, very slowly. I wasn't sure if it was hunger or pregnancy related, but I knew something wasn't right. The pain got worse. Then I started to lose my vision. Then I vomited. Eight times.

By the time the woman I had come to know as Courtney came back into the room, I was writhing around on the floor, moaning like a wounded animal and frothing at the mouth. I just wanted the pain to go away. Surely, I wasn't in labour. I'd read that it started off with light period-type pain and gradually grew. This was a constant stabbing that never let up. Not even for a moment, and it had started so suddenly.

Courtney rushed to my side and got me to sit up, propped against the nearest wall, but it hurt to move, and I cried more. She remained calm and took my temperature, which was high. Too high. My pulse was racing and my breathing erratic.

'I need to get you seen by a doctor,' she said. Then she left the room.

I cried for her to come back. I didn't want to be alone as my insides ripped themselves apart. There was something wrong with you. I was losing you. The stress, the lack of food and water, it was all too much. This couldn't be happening. My vision blurred and I vomited again, not caring that it was over myself. I didn't even have the energy to lean to the side. My head felt like it was about to explode.

Courtney seemed to be gone for an eternity, but when she returned, she was with a young man who I hadn't seen before. The man was wearing a white coat, so I assumed he was a doctor. He immediately checked my temperature and took my blood pressure. Courtney stood to the side, biting her nails and pacing back and forth, waiting for the man to speak.

'I thought you were supposed to be checking on her, Courtney?' said the man.

'I did! She seemed fine the last time I checked. I fetched you as soon as I realised something was wrong. What's the diagnosis? Is she in labour?'

'No, but the baby is in distress. Emily has very high blood pressure. I suggest we operate on her right away. I believe she may have pre-eclampsia. If it gets much worse, we may lose her.'

'Will the child survive?'

'Yes, if we hurry.'

'What about Emily?'

'If we deliver the baby soon, then there's a chance she'll survive.'

'Do it. If it comes to it, save the child first.'

The doctor nodded, but as he did my body started shaking so badly that I toppled over sideways onto the floor and curled up into a ball.

'She's fitting!'

I didn't remember anything after that.

CHAPTER SEVENTEEN

Kimberley

Doctor Simmons is kind, patient and happily answers all my stupid questions, putting my mind at ease about seeing a new doctor after twenty years of staying with my old one. She's treated many patients who have epilepsy before she worked here. She's only been here a short while, just over a year she says, but she enjoys her work, relishing the quiet life outside the busy NHS. She fusses over Muffin who laps up the attention, wiggling her butt so hard that she knocks into a chair. Doctor Simmons takes my blood pressure and performs all the usual checks, asks all the usual questions and requests my doctor's details so she can request my records. She prescribes me a new packet of my medication and fetches it herself from the private dispensary. As I wait for her to return, I notice another door leading out from the main doctor's office, which is locked with a big padlock. My first thought is that that door leads to where the medicine is stored, but Doctor Simmons went through another door to the dispensary, so that can't be it.

Before I have any more time to dwell on it, she returns with a smile and hands me the packet. 'There we are.'

'Oh,' I say, frowning at the name on the side of the packet. 'This is the right name, but the pills don't look the same and it's different packaging.'

She smiles. 'That's not unheard of. Once a branded medication becomes generic, different companies will make their own versions and then each manufacturer will choose its own size, shape and colour for the pill, so one company's pills will look different from another's, even though they're the same medication.'

I nod. 'Okay, thanks.'

'So, how are you feeling in general? When was your last seizure and how long did it last for?'

'Yesterday and only a few seconds really. It was mild. I haven't had a big one for several months now, but I average one or two small ones per day.'

'And do they usually last only a few seconds?'

'About thirty seconds. Sometimes longer, up to a minute or so.'

'Any unusual side effects?'

'Not really.'

'Everything okay with Muffin?'

'Yes, she's my lifesaver. I suffered through a seizure yesterday without her and it was very scary. She lies across my legs usually and not having her there made me feel very alone.'

'That's understandable. Dogs are incredible creatures, aren't they?'

'Especially Muffin,' I reply, leaning down and tickling behind her ears.

'Let me know if anything changes and I'll see you back here in a week.'

'A week?'

'Yes, Jennifer likes all staff to have regular check-ups.'

'Yeah, but . . . every week?'

'It was in your contract.'

'Right.' I almost ask her who does *her* check-ups but decide against it. To be fair, it would be nice to have regular check-ups, just to make sure everything is okay with me medically. It's not that I'm paranoid or anything, but I have noticed lately that my seizures are becoming more frequent. My old doctor was changing my dose, but it doesn't seem to have made much of a difference. Now that I think about it, I haven't officially signed off from his care. I sent him an email the other day, telling him I was moving (remembering not to tell him where) and that I'd be changing doctors. He hasn't replied yet.

'Do you have any questions for me?' Dr Simmons asks.

'Actually, yes . . . this party that's in two weeks' time . . .'

'I'm afraid I'm not at liberty to speak to you about the party.'

'Oh.' I stare at her for a few moments, hoping she'll perhaps offer up an apology or explain a little bit more, but she doesn't say anything else, choosing to ignore me completely and type a few notes on her computer.

'I'll see you in a week then?' she says without taking her eyes off the screen.

I stand up. 'Yes, see you in a week.'

My eyes flick to the padlocked door before I make a swift exit.

* * *

Unfortunately for me, the party is all any of the staff can talk about, but as soon as I try and join in the conversation, they either stop talking altogether or change to another topic. Am I not supposed to know any details about it? Why does everyone else know except for me? It's hard not to take it personally.

I join Courtney on her rounds so that I can learn more about the hotel and where everything is. Some of the staff corridors are like mazes buried deep under the building. There are even secret doors and corridors leading to various rooms, which begs the question: why are they needed? Who needs a secret door in the library that connects to the washrooms in the basement? Weird. Oh, there's also an incinerator in the basement, which is turned on at the same time each day. What on earth are they burning down there? Perhaps it's just normal rubbish, since there aren't any bin men that visit the hotel, so they must have their own means of disposing of their waste. I have so many questions.

The laundry is another area that's always busy. I collect a fresh uniform every single day, which is pressed perfectly.

Courtney leads me through several narrow, dark tunnels beneath the hotel and we appear on the other side without having to navigate the upstairs corridors and rooms. Sort of like a short cut. They will certainly come in useful, I'm sure.

'What were these tunnels originally used for?' I ask as we pass several electric lanterns on the walls, each emitting a glow that causes our shadows to appear twice the size and oddly shaped. Muffin stops to sniff the side of the wall where there's an obvious dark stain.

'No idea,' she says quickly. 'Maybe they were used back in the war.'

'Right.'

We keep going, finally making our way above ground and into the main area of the hotel. We reach a T-junction, and end up in a bright red corridor. Courtney turns right, but I look left. It's then that I recognise where I am.

There it is.

The red corridor leading to Room 21, the one area of the hotel I'm banned from visiting or asking about. Courtney, having realised I haven't kept up with her, returns to my side and gives me a nudge.

'Do yourself a favour and don't think about that room.'

I smile as I respond, 'Easier said than done. It's like asking someone to not think about a pink elephant. Then, it's all they can think about.'

Courtney nods in agreement. 'Yes, but . . . once you find out what's behind the door, then nothing on this earth will make you forget what you've seen. You're better off not knowing for as long as possible. When she thinks you're ready, she'll tell you.

It took me several months of working here before she showed me, and I've spent the rest of my time wishing she never had.'

Courtney walks off in the opposite direction. I take one last look at the corridor. The forbidden door is right at the end, a dim light above it, illuminating the lettering. I finally drag my eyes away, wondering what on earth could be so horrific that's worse than those sex toys and weapons I had to handle earlier.

I'm set to work folding clean towels. There's a certain way they must be folded, and it takes me several attempts before my folding skills are up to standard and I'm left alone to fold over two hundred of the damn things. There are different colours, sizes and shapes and they must be placed on certain trolleys for the housekeepers to distribute to the rooms. It doesn't take me long to work out a system. Muffin soon gets bored and curls up at my feet, snoring softly.

Once I've completed the folding, I'm given the laborious job of shining the silverware ready for the party. Courtney watches over me, but luckily my silver-shining skills from working at Harris Hotel are of more than satisfactory standard.

'Will I be given a role for the party?' I ask.

Courtney stops what she's doing, mid-shine, but doesn't raise her head to look at me. 'It's up to Jennifer. She'll decide if you're ready.'

'Courtney . . . what exactly happens in this hotel?'

'How are you finding your first day?' asks Courtney.

I sigh in frustration. 'Other than the blood, weapons and sex toys, not too bad, although at Harris Hotel I was given much more responsibility.'

'It'll come in time. Who knows, maybe one day you'll have my job.'

'Do you enjoy working here?' I ask. I've asked her before, but she never answered me and I'm still curious.

Courtney looks down at the clipboard in her hands. She doesn't respond. I don't press her for an answer. Her silence tells me everything.

The last thing I need to do is log myself into the online system so that my room reacts to my voice. Bryan walks me through the process, showing me how I can adjust the thermostat and lighting. We sort out the lock so that my room allows only me to enter, and he shows me how an alarm will sound if someone else attempts to open it with the wrong code. Only certain people have access to the codes. I ask him why there's so much security within the hotel.

'Because if there wasn't, you wouldn't be able to sleep at night knowing who was potentially roaming the halls,' he replies, which fills me with as much confidence as if I was attached to a piece of cotton thread about to leap off a bridge to do a bungee jump. Why does everyone have to reply using such cryptic answers? It's starting to really bug me.

* * *

I return to my room, triple checking the security system is working, especially after what Bryan said. It is. Staff eat dinner in various stages. My time frame is between six and seven in the evenings. It's six now and I'm wondering if I should have a shower first before going to eat, but my grumbling tummy tells me the shower can wait, so I reluctantly leave my room and head downstairs to the kitchen, leaving Muffin in the room because she's technically not allowed in the eating areas. I'll fetch her after dinner and take her to eat hers, then go for a short walk around the grounds.

The staff eat in a dining room just beside the kitchen at a long table. We help ourselves to the plates and bowls of food. I slide my bum onto a chair at the end and reach to grab a big bowl of steaming pasta. It smells divine and now my stomach has settled down after the shock of this morning, I'm finding that I'm ravenous.

A few members of staff shoot me looks, but no one engages me in conversation until a timid-looking girl approaches me.

I recognise her as the one with the black eye, which seems to have miraculously disappeared.

'Are you the new girl who has the dog?' she asks me.

I smile up at her. 'Yes, hi, I'm Kimberley and my dog is called Muffin.'

The girl slides her bottom onto the empty seat next to me. 'Where is she?'

'In my room. I'm sure you'll see her around.'

'I love dogs,' she answers. She looks so young. 'Sorry, I'm Michelle.'

'Nice to meet you. How long have you been working here?'

'Less than a year. Guess I'm not the new girl anymore.'

'Do you like working here?'

Michelle shrugs. 'I guess so.'

'You guess?'

'I mean . . . I have to do some pretty weird stuff, but . . . Jennifer's a decent boss. Apparently, before I arrived, she used to be a right bitch, but she's mellowed somewhat since her father went away.'

'Where's he gone?'

'No one knows.'

I raise my eyebrows. 'Someone must know. Isn't he the boss of the whole place?'

Michelle shakes her head. 'Nope. Weird, huh? I've never met him myself.'

I squeeze my lips together. 'Hmm, weird. That seems to be a common theme around here.'

'You'll get used to it eventually.'

I take a bite of food. 'What's the weirdest thing you've had to do?'

Michelle seems to have a think about it. 'I delivered a baby goat to one of the rooms once and I never saw it again.'

'You're joking, right?'

'Nope.'

I look down at my bowl of pasta, having suddenly lost my appetite.

Michelle and I continue our conversation after dinner when she comes with me to feed Muffin and walk her around the grounds. It's nice to talk to someone properly who's around my age. She's actually only nineteen, so I'm a few years older, but she's funny and she's the only person who's shown a genuine interest in getting to know me since I've been here. The other staff still seem standoffish, which she says is normal. They've been working here a long time and have got used to a certain way of behaving. They find it difficult to adjust when a new staff member arrives, according to Michelle, especially out of the blue, like me. Michelle is kind and gives me some tips regarding cleaning some of the rooms, including how to get blood out of silk.

That night, I crawl into bed with Muffin nuzzled next to me. The truth is, the idea of sleeping alone fills me with anxiety, so having a warm body next to me soothes and comforts me, especially after what Courtney and Bryan said earlier.

I dream of walking down a long, red corridor, reaching out my hand and grasping the door handle to Room 21. I open it, but as I step inside, I wake up drenched in sweat.

CHAPTER EIGHTEEN

Kimberley

The next five days pass by in a blur. Considering the hotel isn't full yet, I'm kept busy with errands. It's mainly Courtney who tells me what to do and when. I'm quite glad that I don't have to talk to the guests though because most of them give me the creeps, even the kind, pretty woman I met back at Harris Hotel, the one with the dirty nails. It still baffles me as to why she's impeccably dressed, yet her hands and fingernails look as if they've been used as digging utensils. Lincoln catches my eye several times while I'm carrying towels around and I manage to dodge him by scurrying down the nearest corridor. He makes my blood pressure rise just being close to him and Muffin growls whenever she catches a whiff of his aftershave.

I have one room left to sort out and that's the library. Jennifer and Courtney have been stressing over the fact that Mr Wyatt arrives today, and they still don't have a room for him. Plus, apparently, he's been avoiding all contact, and they aren't sure if he's even coming, but they are preparing just in case he does turn up.

My job is to dust the library shelves and ensure it's in good order and clean out the fireplace, refreshing the log pile and clearing up the ash. Plus, carry on cleaning the glass-ware for the party. It's now in eight days' time and more and more guests are arriving each day. There's even a lord here, who barely makes eye contact with any of the staff, and the couple who I met back at Harris Hotel when Jennifer asked me to remain in the business suite have arrived too. They bark orders and complain about almost everything.

I've been given the night off tonight, so I'm looking forward to an evening of reading in my room. Muffin and I have found a nice little path around the grounds, which is perfect for stretching our legs. Michelle joins us when she can. She's quickly becoming a good friend here, something I've never had before.

Yesterday, I started taking the prescription pills Doctor Simmons gave me. I don't know why, but I'm apprehensive about them looking different. I know it's weird, since they have the same name on the box, but I've been with my doctor since I was five, so seeing a new one is a little alien to me. But, so far, I've had no side effects and, in fact, only had one seizure yesterday, so that's a small improvement.

Bryan enters the library just as I'm finishing in there. 'Ah, Kimberley, might I have a word please?'

'Of course.'

Muffin lifts her head from where she's resting on the rug in front of the fireplace, which isn't lit yet, but I can imagine it creates a fabulous atmosphere when it is, especially in the depths of winter when it's icy outside. Now that it's clean, it's an impressive sight, dominating the room.

Bryan pulls the door closed and faces me, his hands politely crossed over in front of him. 'Kimberley, I am worried for your safety.'

Of all the things I was expecting him to say, it certainly wasn't that. 'Excuse me?'

Bryan's face is deadpan. 'I've worked here a long time and seen a lot of things I shouldn't have. Please believe me when I say I did what I did because I thought it was the right thing to do.'

'I'm sorry, but I have no idea what you're talking about.'

'I think you do.'

I don't say a word.

Bryan flicks his eyes left, then right, finally focusing on me. 'There's still time. You can leave. Right now. Consider this your first and only warning. I will not be held responsible for what happens to you after this.'

I watch Bryan leave the room. My legs remain frozen, unable to move. My palms turn sweaty. Muffin raises her head, comes up to me and barks, then paws at my leg. I gently lower myself to the floor just in time.

***

After Bryan's morbid and, quite frankly, terrifying revelation, I'm finding it difficult to concentrate. I have a television installed on the wall opposite my bed, which has numerous films and shows downloaded onto it. However, despite scrolling for the past thirty minutes, I can't find anything to watch that holds my interest.

My mind is elsewhere.

Bryan's warning.

What the hell was that about? Jennifer told me he was one to watch out for, but to tell me I'm in danger without giving me any proof or specific reason to be worried, seems far-fetched. What is this place? I'm convinced it has something to do with Room 21. Should I ask Michelle about it?

Human curiosity is a powerful and dangerous thing, and it's taking over my mind, so before I even realise what I'm doing, I'm at my door, ready to walk out.

Muffin lifts her head from her new bed, which was waiting for me outside my bedroom door earlier, a delightful surprise and a lovely gift for Muffin. It also came with a dog bowl.

'Sorry, Muffin, but it will be easier to sneak around without you.'

Muffin huffs.

I turn back to the door, put my hand on the handle and twist.

A red bleep sounds.

I try again.

Another red bleep.

Shit. Am I locked inside my room or has something gone wrong with the security system?

I press the button on the control panel next to the door and wait for a response. I've been told this rings down to reception.

But no one answers.

After several rings, the control panel shuts down.

I guess I'm not going exploring after all.

My next shift starts at six tomorrow morning. I'm interested to see if Mr Wyatt turned up earlier and where Jennifer and Courtney found to house him for his stay. I settle back on my bed and switch off the television, choosing to pick up a book instead. I grab my teddy bear and hold him against my chest as I read.

Muffin's gentle snores send me off to sleep.

But I'm woken by screaming.

I launch myself upright, heart beating wildly. But the screaming has stopped. Perhaps it was a dream. I hold my breath, listening for it to start up again, but all I hear is my own thumping heartbeat. Muffin's head is up though, tilting left and then right.

'Did you hear something, girl?'

She whines.

It wasn't a dream.

Someone, somewhere, in this hotel, is screaming.

I call down to reception again. Finally, someone picks up.

'Reception. Everything okay, Kimberley?'

I've no idea who has answered the phone, but it's a male voice.

'Um . . . I've just been woken up by some loud screaming.'

'Ah, nothing to worry about. Probably some over-rambunctious guests.'

'It wasn't excited screaming. It sounded like . . . it was animalistic, like they were in pain.'

'I can assure you, everything's fine.'

'But . . .'

'Have a good night.' And the line goes dead.

I try and call again, but this time the phone doesn't even ring. I'm torn between my job and my conscience. The screaming doesn't sound again, but I lie awake for the rest of the night, listening out for any further sounds. I hear nothing apart from Muffin's snores.

***

The next morning, I rush to get to the staff reception on time. My bedroom door miraculously opens, which tells me I was locked inside overnight. I'm never late, but my head is fuzzy from tiredness and my legs don't seem to want to do what my brain is telling them. I feel . . . weird. I reach the reception just as Courtney arrives, looking fresh and pristine at seven o'clock.

The rest of the housekeepers and I circle around her while she checks our names off the list on her clipboard. Not one of them will catch my eye. Not even Michelle. Did they all hear the screams last night too? Are we just not supposed to talk about it? Were any of them locked in their rooms too? I can't bring it up. It's not my job to probe, to question how they run things here, but it's certainly getting harder and harder to ignore the multitude of questions building up in my head. They're trying to push their way out, escape out of my mouth, but I'm forced to keep it shut for fear of losing my new job.

'Good morning, everyone. We've had several new guests arrive, including Mr Wyatt, who as you may or may not know, is not on speaking terms with Mrs Wyatt and has, therefore, requested to be housed elsewhere. Thankfully, another guest has kindly offered one of their spare rooms in their suite, so Mr Wyatt is now staying in the Harper Suite.'

A few staff members whisper amongst themselves. Some gasp. Others nod along. Who is the guest staying in the Harper Suite? Do I dare ask? Before I can open my mouth, Courtney continues.

'Now, you all have your room assignments. Please be aware that some guests may still be asleep. Any questions come to me directly, not Bryan, is that clear?'

'Yes, Courtney,' comes the chorus from the staff members huddled together.

Wait . . . why *not* Bryan?

What is going on here? I feel like every internal alarm in my body is going off. Something isn't right, yet no one seems to be talking about it or willing to mention it.

The staff scatter in different directions, but I stay and watch Courtney for no other reason than she's drawing my attention like a moth to a flame. She looks tired, drained, like she hasn't slept, even though her outfit and hair are perfect.

'Kimberley . . . Why are you still here?'

I jump, looking around and realising that everyone else has walked away and I'm the only one left standing. 'Sorry, Courtney.'

I scurry off towards the room where our cleaning carts are stored, Muffin close at my heels, and catch everyone else up just as they're picking up their allocated carts.

Some are still chatting about Mr Wyatt staying in the Harper Suite. I see Michelle and smile at her. She rushes over and says hello to Muffin.

'Hey, Michelle, can I ask you something?'

'Sure.'

'Someone told me yesterday that I may be in danger.'

Michelle looks up at me from where she's crouched on the floor next to Muffin. 'Who told you that? Wait . . . it was Bryan, wasn't it?'

My silence is her answer.

Michelle stands up and leans in close to my left ear. 'Don't listen to him. He's just trying to cause trouble. He thinks something bad has happened to Damien and is trying to get to the bottom of it all.'

'Why would something bad have happened to Damien?'

'He hasn't been seen or heard from in like a year. Jennifer says she's in contact with him and he's fine, but Bryan doesn't believe her. Listen, I shouldn't even be talking to you about this. You won't mention it, will you?'

'No, of course not. I'm just finding this place a bit . . .'

'Don't worry, you get used to it.'

'Right. Oh, by the way, who is Mr Wyatt staying with in the Harper Suite?'

'Lincoln. They go way back.'

The plot thickens.

'You've got room thirteen to clean this morning, right?' she asks.

'Yeah.'

'You'll need these.' Michelle reaches into her cleaning trolley and pulls out a surgical mask and a pair of blue surgical gloves.

Great.

* * *

I grab my cleaning trolley and head to my assigned room. There's a sign on the door that says it's safe to enter and that the room requires cleaning. I apply the mask and pull on the gloves, then glance down at Muffin who's sniffing at the small gap underneath the door.

I open the door, and the smell hits me like a slap to the face.

Tangy. Metallic. Sweet.

Oh my God . . .

Muffin whines and refuses to take another step. To be honest, I don't blame her. I hold my breath as I peer into the room.

There's mess everywhere. Everything is trashed. The bed is tipped over and chairs are broken. The elaborate furnishings and decorations have been torn and destroyed, strewn across the entire room.

This is wrong. Very, very wrong.

Whose room is this?

'Something wrong?'

I turn just as Bryan arrives next to me. 'I . . . No,' I say, gulping back the bile rising in my throat.

'Don't just stand there then. Get to work.'

He walks away, leaving me shaking on the spot.

'Stay,' I tell Muffin. I can't have her in this room. There's needles and God only knows what else discarded everywhere. If I'd known what I'd be facing, I would have left her in my room.

I begin by stripping the soiled bedding and dumping it in the laundry basket attached to my cleaning trolley. In fact, most things go in there, including the towels. All the broken items I put in a black bag. Once all the surface items are removed, I can assess the damage underneath.

There's a lot of stains. A lot. Some of them might even be blood.

How am I supposed to remove them from cream carpet?

I quickly check on Muffin who has curled up in a ball outside the door, like my own personal bodyguard. Her nose twitches as she looks at me.

'I know, it stinks,' I say. 'Be good.' And close the door again.

I sigh as I stare around at the stains. Right . . . time to get to work. I roll up my sleeves and grab the bleach.

An hour and a half later, the room looks relatively normal. I've fetched clean bedding from the stores and laid out a fresh rug. I've even opened the windows to let in fresh air because I almost caused myself to pass out from the bleach fumes earlier.

I walk out of the room, pushing my trolley and head back to the staff reception area. Courtney is there.

'I'm done,' I tell her.

She looks up. 'Great work, Kimberley. Any problems?'

'I . . . No.'

'Great. You can now take all the ruined items down to the basement and put them in the incinerator.'

Ah, so that's what they put in the incinerator. Seems a waste to destroy it all. Although, I highly doubt any of it could be salvaged.

I push the heavy trolley down the corridor and towards the lift, steering it down the dark hallways to the basement. A man approaches me and takes the trolley from my grasp. I stand back as he pushes it to the large incinerator, grabs the bags containing the soiled items and dumps them into the furnace.

I guess that's that.

I dust my hands off and head back inside. I feel like I need to lie down. My heart has only just stopped racing, and the smell of bleach is still lingering on my clothes and skin. I catch Michelle just as she's about to head down to the basement with her trolley. She's pale in the face.

'Are you okay?' I ask.

'Yeah . . .'

'You don't look okay.'

Michelle smiles. 'Will you wait here for me?'

'Yes, of course.'

I watch her push the trolley into the lift. Muffin and I stand to the side, allowing other staff to pass by. She returns a few minutes later with the empty trolley and together we push them back towards the staff reception.

'What happens now?' I ask.

'Courtney will give us any other jobs that need doing. How was your room?'

'Gross. Yours?'

'Worse.'

'What's worse than gross?' She gives me a look, her face still pale. 'Oh,' I say. I wish I hadn't asked. 'What the hell goes on in this hotel?'

'You could be fired for asking that question to anyone else.'

'I know, but . . . this is wrong. Something is wrong here and no one's talking about it.'

Michelle stops walking, so I do too. 'I don't know what happens, but your guess is as good as mine.'

'Really? Because my guess is that all the guests are vampires, and they have some sort of drug-fuelled sex orgies in their rooms.'

Michelle bursts out laughing, which eases the tension somewhat. She keeps her voice low as she continues. 'I don't think vampires are involved, but I don't think you're far off from the drug-fuelled sex orgy idea.'

'But that's . . . disgusting.'

She shrugs. 'Rich people are into some weird stuff.'

'Yeah, but . . .' I don't know how to finish the sentence, so I bite my tongue.

'Look, the easiest thing to do is to stay quiet,' says Michelle. 'You get used to it eventually.'

'You keep saying that, but are you used to it?'

'No, but that's what the other housekeepers keep telling me.'

'I'm not sure I can keep quiet,' I say.

Michelle turns to me, leaning in close. 'The last housekeeper who decided to talk to the police wound up disappearing.'

'Wait . . . really? Are you sure? I thought she just got fired.'

'Well, one day she was here and the next she was gone.'

All the blood drains out of my face, and I stumble sideways. Michelle grabs me before I can fall. 'Please,' she says. 'I like you. Don't make the mistake of thinking you can outsmart the system here. Jennifer's a clever woman. Nothing gets past her. Nothing.' Michelle looks up and around, as if to prove a point that we may be being watched.

'What's in Room 21?' I finally ask.

Michelle takes a deep breath. 'I don't know. I haven't found out yet. I'm not sure I ever want to because once you find out, there's no escaping this place.'

'What do you mean?'

'To find out what's behind the door, you must sign a contract to work here forever. If you don't sign, then you never find out the truth of what goes on here behind closed doors.'

'That's . . . barbaric,' I whisper. My chest feels tight. I can't seem to draw in enough oxygen. I don't want to pass out in this room, but the more Michelle talks, the more my head spins and the tighter the vice gets around my chest.

'It just begs the question . . . What's stronger? Your curiosity or your desire for freedom?'

CHAPTER NINETEEN

Emily

It felt as if I was in a never-ending nightmare, constantly trying to wake up, but the more I battled against my subconscious, the deeper down I seemed to fall into the nightmare. There was no way back up. Some moments I could hear voices around me, chattering incessantly, sometimes frantically, but I couldn't understand them. Nothing made any sense. Why were they speaking in a different language? Why were they whispering one minute then shouting and screaming the next?

I kept thinking about you, whether you were okay, safe, alive. Where were you while I was trapped in this forever nightmare? Were you still in my belly? I couldn't move my hands to place them on my bump because I wasn't sure I even had control over them.

Pain would often rouse me from the deepest depths of my nightmare. So much pain. And my brain couldn't distinguish where it was coming from, from what part of my body it originated. Perhaps my whole body was on fire. That's what it felt like. Sometimes I craved the pain because it meant I was still alive. Didn't it? Or was I dead? Was I trapped somewhere in-between, like purgatory?

I had no idea how much time had passed. Was I repeating the same day over and over? It might have been hours, or it could have been longer. Days. Weeks. If it had been months, then where were you? Had I had that thought before? I didn't know. I didn't know anything. I just needed to know *something* before I went crazy. Whenever I looked down at my bump, it wasn't there. In its place, a deflated stomach, the skin stretched and misshaped. This was certainly a nightmare, because I didn't know where you were; you'd been ripped from my body without my permission or knowledge.

The pain was there again. Wave after wave. Labour? No. The pain was constant still, like before. I didn't remember a lot about what happened. I had a seizure, I think, and my temperature was high, too high, like I was burning from the inside out.

Wait . . . What was happening?

A bright light blinded my vison. I tried to bring my hand up in front of my face, but my hands wouldn't move. I wiggled my fingers, but my arms stayed locked at my sides. I wiggled my toes, but again, that's all I could manage. I prised my lips apart to scream, but I couldn't open my mouth.

The light got brighter. Brighter. Too bright.

'Stop!' I cried. Even with my eyes tightly shut, I couldn't block out the white light. It burned.

'She's coming round.'

'She's stable.'

The light grew brighter still, but it was closely followed by a deeply rooted pain in my lower abdomen and pelvis. I couldn't breathe. Couldn't think straight.

Finally, the light dimmed, leaving me with dancing white spots behind my eyelids. I dared not open my eyes in case it caused more pain. I just wanted it to be over. Even with my eyes closed, dizziness flooded my brain. Constantly spinning. Spinning. Why couldn't I just sink back down into the depths again, where there was no pain and dizziness?

'Emily, can you hear me?'

Yes! I wanted to scream.

My mouth didn't work. How could I respond?

'Emily, if you can hear me, squeeze my hand.'

A warm hand slid into my left palm. I did my best, but I couldn't make my muscles respond to my commands. I was there. I could hear her, but I couldn't answer.

My eyes were forcibly opened. The white spots stopped dancing, and I saw a woman peering down at me. Was she an angel? She was beautiful. Her long blonde hair draped over my face, tickling my nose. She quickly noticed and stepped away.

No! I didn't want her to leave me.

'Her pupils just dilated when she saw me. She's in there. Let me know if her condition improves or if she's able to communicate. Keep trying to get her to talk. I need her to talk to me. I need to know where her baby is.'

Wait . . . *What*?

I forced my eyes open and looked down at my belly. My nightmare had become reality. You really were gone, and I had no idea where you were. And neither did this woman.

Where the hell were you? Who had stolen you from me? When I found out, I was going to kill them with my bare hands.

CHAPTER TWENTY

Jennifer (Before)

As I studied my reflection in the mirror, I couldn't help but notice the fine lines crisscrossing around my eyes, like miniature streams. I gently brushed my long blonde hair with my antique hairbrush, but as I did, several strands snapped and embedded themselves in the fine bristles. I picked them out, sighing. It seemed more and more hair fell out of my head every day. Stress, perhaps. At least they weren't turning grey yet. The idea of growing older had never appealed to me. My father constantly mentioned it too. He would do anything to stay young forever. To anyone who didn't know the truth, people would look and think that we were possibly husband and wife, which made my stomach physically sick, but there we have it.

I knew I couldn't live forever, but I'd always wanted a child of my own to carry on my line, my legacy, like my father had with me. Surely, he wanted me to procreate because my brother wasn't going to carry on the line, but every time I brought it up, he dismissed me. That was why I wanted — *needed* — this baby to be found alive and safe. It wasn't biologically mine, but I should know more than most that family didn't need to be blood related.

I was still brushing my hair when there was a knock at the door.

'Enter.'

In the reflection, I saw Courtney enter. 'Ma'am, Emily is stable, and she has managed to speak.'

'What has she said?'

'She keeps saying *baby* over and over.'

'Does she know where it is?'

'She hasn't said. She just keeps saying baby. I think . . . I think she's asking *where* her baby is?'

'But that's preposterous. We don't know. That's why we need her to tell us.'

'I know, ma'am.' Courtney fell into silence and bowed her head.

I sighed heavily and put down my hairbrush. 'Thank you, I'll come and speak to her. In the meantime, I need you to organise a search of the entire hotel. If neither of us know where that child is, then we have a problem. It can't be far. Every room in the hotel must be searched and every guest must be questioned.'

'Ma'am . . . all the guests are still asleep after the party last night.'

'Then wake them up. This is a high priority. Do you understand?'

'Yes, Ma'am.'

Courtney turned and scurried out the door. I looked back at my reflection, studying every pore and fine wrinkle. Dragging a finger down my face, I stopped at my full lips.

How could a newborn baby just disappear? It wasn't possible. Emily couldn't have been alone more than an hour after she'd had her C-section to save her and her baby's life. When we found her, she was bleeding and screaming and the baby was in distress. It was delivered via C-section by the hotel doctor and now it was gone. Emily was still recovering in the medical wing, but the baby . . . It didn't make sense.

Newborn babies didn't just disappear into thin air.

CHAPTER TWENTY-ONE

Kimberley

The rest of the working day I meander through my chores, keeping close to Michelle and doing what I'm told. It's easier to follow orders than try and use my brain right now because it's too preoccupied with trying to figure out what the hell is going on in this hotel. Michelle's words ring in my ears.

Is my curiosity stronger than my work ethic? The only job I've ever wanted to do is be a housekeeper, but I'd like to work my way up the ranks, like I did in my previous job. Was it a mistake to come here? I left a job in a boring hotel as a senior housekeeper to work in a mysterious hotel as a housekeeper who cleans up trashed hotel rooms and lays out sex toys. It certainly feels as if Jennifer hired me under false pretences. She left out several important bits of information that I could have done with knowing beforehand.

That's it. I have to know the truth about this place. I'm in too deep now. I've seen too much. Jennifer wouldn't let me just walk out, would she? I've signed a contract. It's not like I can just blab to the police like the girl I replaced did. Who knows what happened to her. Was she killed or did she really just disappear?

I mull all this over and over while I clean and tend to the jobs I've been assigned to. I notice there aren't a lot of guests milling about the hotel today. Perhaps they prefer to keep to their rooms during the day. There's not a lot to do here for them; not even a spa to relax in.

However, I do come across a guest I recognise around two in the afternoon while I'm passing their room. It's the posh-looking woman with the dirty nails who I saw in the business suite at Harris Hotel. She emerges from her room, bleary-eyed and pale.

'Oh, hello,' she says.

'Good afternoon, ma'am.'

'Goodness, is it the afternoon already?'

'I'm afraid so. Are you feeling okay? Can I get you anything, ma'am?'

The woman puts a hand over her mouth and quietly burps. 'No, thank you. Something I ate last night is just repeating on me. That's all.'

I have a sudden vision of her chowing down on raw meat. I don't know why.

'Has Damien arrived yet?' she asks me, once she's composed herself.

'Damien? I . . . No, he hasn't,' I say.

The woman narrows her eyes at me. 'Something's going on here. Damien is always here. The party is in less than five days. This has never happened before.'

'I'm sure he'll turn up,' I respond.

'You make it sound like he's missing . . . Is he missing?'

'I . . . No, I don't believe so.' Shit, I'm saying too much. I shouldn't even be talking to this woman. 'I'm sorry, ma'am, but I really must get on.'

'Of course,' she replies. Then she watches me walk down the corridor. I'm glad to turn the corner because having her eyes searing into the back of my head makes my body tremble.

* * *

I'm quietly cleaning a side table in reception an hour later. I shouldn't be here, but the housekeeper who was supposed to clean reception had to go back to her room because she passed out during one of her room cleans and she's been dizzy ever since. Room nine, apparently. I don't even want to know what caused her to pass out. I manage to check the room schedule while no one is looking and note that the stern-looking man who I saw at Harris Hotel is staying in there. I volunteered to take her place, mostly so I can catch a glimpse of some of the elusive hotel guests as they make their way downstairs and into the restaurant area to have a late lunch. Each guest is fascinating in their own way. I'm drawn to them, determined to find out more about them, what makes them tick. Who are they? One of them even looks familiar. Very familiar. In fact, I'm almost certain he's a movie star, but when I check his name under his room, it's not him. He could be using a fake name of course. Most of the guests do, Michelle says.

A man walks past me and hisses as the sunlight catches his eyes. He shields them with his hand, then catches me staring at him. My heart stops and I quickly turn, fully aware I've just broken one of the rules. Never stare at the guests. Muffin is next to me. She's become increasingly anxious, whining and not able to settle down and sleep while out and about with me. I do move around a lot, but she's not happy about being here.

I'm suddenly aware that I haven't had a seizure since yesterday afternoon. Almost twenty-four hours. That's unusual.

'You,' a deep, male voice sounds from behind me.

Shit.

I turn and plaster a smile across my face as I set eyes on Lincoln. 'Yes, sir.'

'You're that housekeeper I saw in London. I've seen you a few times over the past few days.'

'Yes, sir.'

'What's your name again?'

'Kimberley, sir.'

'Stop calling me sir.'

'Yes, sir. Sorry, sir . . . Shit.'

Lincoln bursts into laughter. 'I like you. Come with me.' He turns to walk away.

'Um . . .' I glance around, terrified to leave my position. I shouldn't have even looked at him, let alone spoken to him. Now, he wants me to follow him? 'I'm sorry, sir, but I really shouldn't . . .'

He stops and looks over his shoulder at me, his blue eyes blazing. 'It wasn't a request.'

My stomach drops like I'm on a rollercoaster. The last thing I want is it getting back to Jennifer that I didn't do as I was told, but if I follow him, I'm also breaking the rules. I decide it's probably best that I follow him and suffer the consequences from Jennifer rather than make a guest unhappy. The guests are always right after all. That's what I've always been taught, but these guests are not normal, and the idea of following Lincoln anywhere makes me almost gag.

Muffin follows me.

'Leave the mutt,' he says.

Muffin emits a soft growl as she stares at me, crouching low. It almost looks like she's ready to attack him. 'Stay, girl.' She whines.

'Stay.'

I drop my cleaning rag and scurry after him. He's already halfway across reception. As I catch up, I dart my eyes left and right, checking if any of the other staff members are watching me. It looks as if I'm the only one in reception. Jennifer is going to kill me, or worse, fire me.

Lincoln opens a door and holds it for me to walk through. This is the library, a room I had the pleasure of cleaning several days ago. I still can't get over the number of books on the shelves, which circle the entire room, even above the door we've just walked through. I think it's my favourite room in the hotel.

Lincoln shuts the door.

Oh, shit.

'Do you know who I am?' he asks, as his eyes scan my body from head to toe and back up again.

I feel very naked and vulnerable right now. I should not be in here alone with him.

'Yes,' I squeak.

'What has Jennifer told you about me?'

'Not a lot.'

He licks his lips and takes a step closer. My immediate reaction is to step back, so I do but I bump into the wall of books behind me.

'Take your clothes off. Slowly.'

'Um . . .'

His eyes narrow. 'No one says no to me. You might be new, but you'll learn that all the new female housekeepers get a turn with me sooner or later.'

What the fuck? That can't be true. Surely, Jennifer wouldn't allow that. Just because he's rich and important, it doesn't give him the right to abuse his power over women.

'Sir . . . I . . . I think there's been some sort of mistake . . .'

'Take. Your. Clothes. Off. Now.'

My heart is thumping so hard and fast that it feels like it's going to jump out of my chest. Muffin is whining and barking behind the door. My lungs are struggling to inhale. My chest gets tighter. Tears sting my eyes. This cannot be happening.

Lincoln is now so close that he's breathing on my cheek. 'Kimberley,' he says. As I study the lines of his face, I have a strange feeling of familiarity, like a flutter in my chest.

The door next to me bursts open and Jennifer storms into the room, eyes ablaze. I've never been so relieved or terrified to see her, but if I had to choose between her or Lincoln, I'd choose her.

Muffin also rushes in and begins barking aggressively at Lincoln.

'What the fuck do you think you're doing?' Jennifer shouts.

I have no idea which one of us she's talking to, but I answer anyway. 'Ma'am, I'm so sorry. I was just . . .'

'Not you, Kimberley.' She glares at Lincoln who laughs, stepping away from me. My breathing evens out ever so slightly and I take the opportunity to move away from him and towards the open door, ushering Muffin to come to me. The last thing I want is for her to get caught up in this and hurt Lincoln or be hurt herself. Jennifer stares at Lincoln like she's trying to blow up his head.

'Jennifer, my dear. I was merely having a bit of fun with your lovely new housekeeper.'

'I don't remember giving you permission to touch her.'

Lincoln clenches his jaw. 'I'm desperate,' he whispers.

'You'd have thought you had your fill the other night, but now you have to assault my staff. You know the rules here, Lincoln. They are in place for a reason. If you break them, then you're out.'

'Like I said, it was just a bit of fun.'

Jennifer turns to me. 'Kimberley, were you having fun with Lincoln?'

My mouth drops open. 'Um . . .'

'You can tell the truth.'

'No, ma'am. I was not having fun.'

'I thought as much. Please leave this room and go to my office. I'll be along shortly to deal with you.'

'Yes, ma'am.' I dip my head, catching a glimpse of Lincoln, who gives me a wink before I race out the door, through reception, avoiding all the staff who have congregated and along the corridors to Jennifer's office door where I stand and wait, trembling from head to foot. Muffin nudges my legs. At first, I think it may be a warning signal, but then I realise she's just trying to calm me down and reassure me.

***

Jennifer doesn't appear for almost twenty minutes. By the time she turns up, I'm a nervous wreck and in desperate need of a wee. She doesn't make eye contact as she passes me and opens her office door. She holds it open, glancing down at Muffin.

'Come in,' she says. The worst thing is, I can't tell if she's angry with me or not. She seemed angrier with Lincoln in the library, but now we're alone, I have no idea how she's going to react. Am I fired? I know better than to speak first so I stand in front of her desk while she takes her seat and readjusts her chair, never once looking at me.

I keep my head lowered, staring at my feet.

'I am sorry,' she says after the longest of silences.

It's the last words I expect to hear from her, so I lift my head. 'Ma'am?'

She's staring at me, her blue eyes brimming with tears. 'I am sorry, but you're fired.'

My heart drops like a stone. 'Ma'am, I'm so sorry I was in reception. It's just a housekeeper was off sick, and I volunteered without thinking and . . .'

'I'm not finished.'

I clamp my mouth shut and lower my head again, like an obedient servant.

'You're fired as a housekeeper, but you're hired as my personal assistant.'

My head snaps up once again. I'm getting dizzy. 'What?'

'I'm impressed with you, Kimberley. And I like you, but that's not why I need you as my personal assistant. You aren't aware of it, but there's something special about you, and I believe you can help me with the work I do here.'

'Ma'am, I . . . I don't know what to say.'

Jennifer sighs. 'Kimberley, do you know what I see when I look at you?'

'Um . . .'

'I see myself, twenty years ago.'

'Thank you, ma'am.'

'Oh, it's not a compliment, Kimberley. Twenty years ago, I was weak, and I had to put up with a lot of shit. I put up with it for a very long time. Too long, but eventually I had enough and found the inner strength I needed to take a stand. But one thing I did have in spades back then was determination to succeed, and I see the same thing in you. Can I trust you, Kimberley?'

'Of course, ma'am.'

Jennifer stands up and walks slowly in front of her desk, facing me square on. She looks me up and down. 'I need people on my team who I can trust. I'm going to tell you something now that may shock you. You may question my judgement, but if you can trust me, then there's nothing we can't do.'

My heart is beating so hard and fast that I'm worried it's going to beat out of my chest. Am I about to have a seizure? I glance at Muffin who isn't giving me a signal.

'Do you trust me?' Jennifer asks.

'Yes, ma'am.' I do. I really do.

'Thank you,' she says. There's a beat of silence, then she says something that's almost impossible to come back from. 'I'm going to kill every single guest in this hotel on the night of the party . . . and you're going to help me do it.'

CHAPTER TWENTY-TWO

Jennifer

Kimberley stares back at me for several long seconds. She blinks, then blinks again. I can see her inner thoughts, questions, whirling around her head. She's wrestling with her moral compass right now, the decision whether to follow orders or disobey and risk losing her job. That will never happen, but she doesn't know that. I admire her courage and determination to save face in the aftermath of such a revelation.

Frankie is pacing around my feet. He can sense my apprehension and stress-levels since coming back from intercepting Lincoln's unwanted advances upon Kimberley. I think both dogs can sense the tension in the room.

'Did you hear what I said, Kimberley?'

She clears her throat. 'Yes, ma'am, but I'm trying to work out whether or not you're joking.'

'Do I look like the joking type of person?'

'No, ma'am.'

'Then there's your answer.'

'Yes, ma'am.'

'What I'm about to tell you, Kimberley will not only change your life, but the lives of possibly hundreds of people.'

She gulps. 'Okay.'

'Every single guest who stays at my hotel is a serial killer, paedophile, rapist, murderer, sex offender or any other kind of evil human being you can think of. They are the worst of the worst, collected by my father over many decades.'

Kimberley's eyes widen. 'All of them?'

'All of them.'

'Even the nice old lady in room fifteen?'

'Especially the nice old lady in room fifteen. Are you okay? Do you want to sit down? Shall I get you a chair?' I move towards her. She looks as if she's close to toppling over, so I shove a chair towards her, and she takes a seat. I continue to stand before her, just in front of my desk.

'Thank you,' she says. 'I've been feeling a little light-headed recently.'

'Since when?'

'Um . . . since I started taking the medication from Doctor Simmons.'

I nod. 'That's understandable.'

'Why? It's the same medication I've always taken.'

'Let's come back to that, shall we?' Kimberley opens her mouth to speak, but I continue. There're more important things to cover right now. She needs to know the truth and if she doesn't take it well, then she's going to need time to come to terms with it — time we don't really have, which is why I decided to tell her now, five days before the party, rather than leaving it any longer. She's done well over the past few days or so and I know she has many questions. I know she's been asking Michelle questions, and I know she's been wanting to visit Room 21. Her curiosity is growing stronger by the day, and that's good. She hasn't begged to leave yet.

'As I said, every guest in this hotel is evil, some of the worst examples of human beings I've ever come across. Damien, my father, is also one. He's a psychopath. No emotion. No empathy. Nothing.'

'Isn't that a sociopath, ma'am?'

I shake my head. 'No, he's a psychopath. He's always been an expert at blending into society, charming many, many people. He's also highly intelligent and thinks he's God's gift to the world.'

Kimberley frowns. I'm sure she's confused to be hearing me speak about my father in this way. I could say a great many things about that man, but not one word of them would be nice.

'Damien bought this hotel in 1972 and did it up, but thirty years ago he decided to open it up to a special sort of guest, people like him. He turned it into a place where they could all come together to carry out their worst-kept secrets, their darkest desires and fantasies once a year. In a way, he did stop them from killing and torturing victims in the outside world.'

'Are you saying that killers and rapists come here to . . . kill and rape people at their leisure, instead of committing crimes elsewhere in society?'

'Yes, that's right. Everything that happens within these walls is kept quiet. They can come here and do as they please without the risk of being caught.'

'That's barbaric!'

I nod. 'Yes, you're right. It is.'

'Then . . . if you don't agree with what he's doing, then why run the hotel yourself? I don't understand how you could stand by him all these years, whether you're his daughter or not, and let him get away with this. Who do these guests kill? Do you take people off the streets or something?'

'That's exactly what happens. Damien takes people who are of no use to society or who have no family, friends or connections. Sometimes homeless people.'

Kimberley doesn't move. She flicks her eyes back and forth from me to the door, a sign that she may be thinking about making a run for it.

'There's nowhere you can go, Kimberley.'

'I can't be a part of this.'

'You already are, my dear.'

Kimberley's eyes fill with tears. 'You're as bad as Damien is!'

'That's where you're wrong. Let me show you something and then you'll understand.'

I walk towards the door. She stands but doesn't follow me straight away. 'Why are you telling me all of this?' she asks.

'You'll understand everything soon, but I think I need to show you, rather than tell you.'

'Where are you taking me?'

'The one place you've wanted to go ever since you first found out about it.' I don't need to say anymore. Kimberley follows me willingly, Muffin close by and Frankie pattering behind. She walks with me obediently through the maze of corridors. Dozens of pairs of curious eyes follow us as we pass by. Some of the housekeepers and staff have worked here for years and never once been offered this opportunity. I'm sure they're all wondering why Kimberley is so special.

When we reach our destination, I turn to watch her reaction as she takes in the number on the door in front of her.

'Here we are,' I say, spreading my arms wide. 'The elusive Room 21. Behind this door is the answer to all your questions, or at least the reason behind what I'm trying to tell you. I want to introduce you to someone.'

'Someone? You have a person locked up in this room?' Her words are loaded with judgement.

I input a code on the keypad by the door, then push down the door handle. As the door swings open and the lights flicker on, I step into the room, allowing Kimberley and Muffin to enter.

Kimberley gasps when she sees the woman lying on the squeaky metal bed in the corner. She's pale, malnourished, but there's a fire in her eyes that I know Kimberley recognises.

'Kimberley, I'd like you to meet Jennifer Clifton,' I say. 'The *real* Jennifer Clifton.'

The Jennifer on the bed shuffles to the edge but doesn't make any attempt to stand up. Her long, blonde hair is limp and dull, but her eyes are a dazzling shade of blue.

Kimberley stares open-mouthed at me as I carefully remove my contact lenses, revealing my naturally hazel eyes. A flicker of recognition flares in her own as she studies my face.

'W-Who are you?' She takes a step away from me.

'My real name is Emily. I'm your mother.'

PART THREE

CHAPTER TWENTY-THREE

Emily
Twenty-five years before

Let me tell you something. There is no greater pain than losing a child. And I don't only mean losing them as in death. Losing them while they are alive is almost as bad because you have no idea where they are and if they are okay. Were they hurt? Were they being abused? Were they happy?

I know you were a newborn baby when I lost you, but you were so helpless, so small. And I was supposed to have protected you. I failed as your mother before you were even born, and I am sorry. Finding out that you were gone was the worst experience in the world. It felt as if someone had ripped out a piece of my heart, my soul. I wouldn't wish that pain on my worst enemy.

When I finally woke up, I was alone. The pain was still there, lingering in the background, but it wasn't taking over my whole body, making me incapable of moving, not like before. But my body felt wrong. It didn't feel like mine. I pulled against the restraints surrounding my wrists and ankles. I still couldn't move. I couldn't understand why they were tying me down. I wasn't dangerous to them. I wasn't going to hurt myself, or run away, not until I knew where you were. I didn't even have the energy to move, let alone try and escape.

I was in some sort of medical ward. Next to me were beeping machines and I was hooked up to a drip. I could hear doctors talking and smell antiseptic. What was going on? I strained against my weakened abdominal muscles and attempted to sit up, looking down at my body, which was covered in a thin gown.

My stomach was flat. Well, it wasn't flat, it was squishy, but there was no bump. You weren't safely cocooned inside anymore. Where were you? The last thing I remember, I was lying on the floor of that dingy white room and you were still inside my womb.

'Help!' I cried. 'My baby! Where's my baby!'

At my alarmed voice, hurried footsteps approached. 'Emily, please don't attempt to sit up or strain yourself or you'll burst your stitches,' came a soft voice.

I slumped my head back against the pillow, exhausted from my struggle. 'Please,' I whispered. 'Just tell me where my baby is.'

The person who had spoken stood beside me, peering at me over a surgical mask. 'You lost a lot of blood, and the baby was in distress. She was struggling to breathe when she was born.'

'That doesn't explain where she is.'

'We don't know where she is.'

My ears picked up the words, but my brain didn't process them, not straight away. It couldn't be possible. You'd been perfectly safe, cocooned inside me for eight months, but without my body to sustain you, you'd disappeared. Where the hell were you?

'N-No,' I said, but I didn't say it once. I said it over and over until the word made no sense. Maybe if I said it enough, it wouldn't be true.

A warm hand touched my arm, bringing me back to the room. 'Emily, look at me.'

I couldn't control myself for a moment longer. Someone had to pay. 'You did this! If you and Damien hadn't kidnapped me, this wouldn't have happened! Where is she!' I screamed, kicked, but my abdomen exploded with pain, enough to take my breath away and make me see black spots. I closed my eyes, took a few deep breaths before I passed out.

'Emily, I can assure you we're doing everything we can to find her. Do you remember anything? Did someone take her?'

I kept my eyes shut as the tears squeezed through the lids. My heart was breaking in two. 'What? No . . . I don't remember. I woke up just now and she was gone. You were supposed to look after her!'

The woman said nothing.

'What are you going to do with me now? I still don't know why you brought me here.'

'That, my dear Emily, is a little more complicated. You have a lot to learn. I'm afraid you're here forever, but don't worry, you'll fit right in, but we must find your baby.'

CHAPTER TWENTY-FOUR

Kimberley

The air in this room is stale, as if it's from a time long ago. In fact, now I look closer, the room looks like it's from twenty years ago, stuck in the past, the paint on the walls peeling, the bedding faded. The blood is pumping so hard and fast through my veins that I can feel it, hear it. Everything around me is heightened, my senses on high alert. It almost feels like I'm about to have a seizure, but Muffin doesn't give me a warning signal, so I'm safe for now, knowing my reaction is merely because the woman in front of me has just told me something that can't possibly be true.

My eyes flick from the woman on the bed to the woman standing in front of me. The similarities are striking. The Jennifer on the bed is severely malnourished and in need of a decent wash, but her eyes are what seals it for me. They are so perfectly blue that I can barely look away.

Whereas the Jennifer standing in front of me is a more polished replica, minus the blue eyes now she's removed her contacts. I knew they had to be fake! But I could never have realised why she'd have to use them.

My head hurts so much, I can barely think about anything else other than what Jennifer has just revealed. Her real name is Emily and . . .

I look up, my brain suddenly catching up on the rest of that sentence. She said it so calmly, just like she'd told me earlier about killing every guest in this hotel.

'You're my mother? How is that possible?' It can't be true and yet it makes perfect sense. There's no way for me to explain it that doesn't sound crazy, so I do the only thing I can right now and listen.

Jennifer (or I suppose I should call her Emily now) smiles, her hazel eyes sparkling in the light. 'I shall explain everything all in good time. I promise.'

The real Jennifer shuffles her bum to the edge of the bed. She can't move her legs, so drags them using her hands. What on earth has happened to her? 'You're telling me that this is the tiny baby that was born in this very hotel twenty-five years ago.'

I'm startled by Jennifer's voice. It's croaky, rough, like she's smoked fifty cigarettes a day for the past forty years.

'You know me?' I ask her.

Jennifer grins, shifting her legs a bit more, but then she stops, halted by a chain around her ankle. 'I tried to find you when you were stolen from us.'

'Stolen?' I turn to Emily for clarification.

'I was kidnapped when I was eight months pregnant with you and kept in this very room. One day, weeks later, I had a seizure and when I woke up you were gone. I never even got to see you.'

'What happened?'

'That's what I am determined to find out. Once I know who stole you from my womb, I'm going to kill them, but first I'm going to wipe out everyone at the party.'

'But . . . if it wasn't Jennifer who took me, then why keep her locked up like this?' I ask Emily. 'You're as bad as Damien!'

Emily shakes her head. 'Jennifer planned all along to steal you from me. It just so happened that someone beat her to it.'

Jennifer laughs a deep, throaty chuckle. 'You'll never get away with this, Emily.'

'I already have, Jennifer. I've been posing as you for the past year and not one of the staff here has questioned me. Having spent over twenty years working here, I know exactly how you act and speak.'

'You don't think the staff don't know you've been pulling the wool over their eyes? Courtney and Bryan will have noticed.'

'Bryan, maybe, but Courtney definitely knows, yes. She's on my side.'

Jennifer tuts. 'I highly doubt that. My staff are loyal to me and my father.'

Emily shrugs her shoulders. 'Even if they are, it's too late now. The party is in five days. Soon, this whole sick business will be over, and I'll finally be free from this place.'

'Are you saying you've been trapped here since I was born?' I ask.

'Yes. I worked here as a housekeeper, doing whatever I was told because I had no other choice. Someone stole you from me and I've spent the past twenty-five years searching for you, but being trapped within these walls made it rather difficult, but I had someone on the outside who was searching for me.'

'Who?'

'Valerie.'

'Your driver?'

'She does a lot of errands for Jennifer. Over the years, she and I have become friends. She overheard a conversation between Damien and Mr Wyatt one day while she was driving them. Damien has known where you were since you were five.'

'So, who stole me when I was born?'

Emily shakes her head, but it's Jennifer who speaks. 'We still don't know, but someone in this hotel did. My father searched for you for years until he found you at age five.'

'Okay . . . but why was he searching for me? Why has it taken twenty years for me to end up here? If Damien has known where I was, then . . .' I break off, not sure what else to say.

Jennifer smiles. 'Damien is your father too, Kimberley. We're sisters. Or, half-sisters, if you want to be pedantic about it.'

I almost choke as I take a deep breath. The room spins. 'You and Damien were together?' I ask Emily, disgust evident in my voice.

'No, Kimberley. Damien raped me, then he tracked me down, kidnapped me and forced me to be his slave for the next twenty-five years. Trust me, your father is a vile, evil psychopath and I will be killing him when the time is right.'

'But where is he? You said you took over Jennifer's role a year ago? Damien's been gone for a year too, so where's he been all this time?'

Emily turns and walks towards the door. 'Follow me. It's time you met your father. Maybe then you'll understand why I'm doing all of this.'

'My father has been under this roof the whole time?' asks Jennifer.

Emily nods. 'It's not only you who's been trapped here.'

I glance back at Jennifer before following Emily out of the door. She fixes her cold, blue eyes on me. 'I guess I'll be seeing you soon, Kimberley. Mark my words. I suggest you choose your side carefully. You won't get a second chance.'

* * *

Muffin whines at my side while we wait for the lift. She doesn't give me the full warning signal, but perhaps a seizure is close. It's now been more than twenty-four hours since I had one. Something doesn't feel right, and I'm worried that the next time one takes over, it could be a big one.

Emily reaches over and squeezes my arm, but I shrug away. I watch as she puts her contact lenses back in. I'm still struggling to get my head around all of this, and a lot of things still require explaining. There are too many questions to focus on at once and too many holes in Emily's story that need to be filled.

I'm about to come face to face with my father, a rapist, a psychopath.

Emily takes me to the medical wing where I saw Doctor Simmons regarding my medication. She greets us at the door with a smile.

'Good to see you again, Kimberley. How are you getting on with your medication?' She closes the door behind us.

'Fine,' I murmur. I don't have the enthusiasm to tell her about my lack of seizures in the past day. It seems like an unimportant topic right now, considering everything else that's going on.

'Jennifer, delighted as always,' she says, looking at Emily.

'It's okay, Doctor Simmons. Kimberley knows.'

'Ah. That's why you're both here then, I take it.'

'Yes, we've come to see him.'

'Very well. This way.' Doctor Simmons turns and approaches a door at the back of the reception area, the one with the padlock attached, then dips her hand into her jacket pocket and pulls out a key. She uses it to unlock the padlock and then pushes open the door.

Doctor Simmons steps aside, allowing Emily and I to enter the room first. I'm not sure what I'm expecting to see, but it's not a man lying on a hospital bed, hooked up to a drip, dressed in a hospital gown. He looks as if he's sleeping as the machines whir and beep next to him. His skin is sickly pale, his eyes sunken into his skull. I'm sure at one time he must have looked much healthier, but now he resembles a frail old man, his hair and beard greying and long.

'Kimberley, meet Damien Clifton, your father.'

A lump forms in my mouth as I stare at the stranger asleep on the bed. Despite never wanting or needing to know who my parents were over the years, I have, on occasion, wondered what they looked like, where I got my thin nose from and freckles. It's spooky how closely I resemble him. I have my mother's eyes, but everything else I appear to have inherited from him.

'Is he in a coma?'

'No, just asleep. However, we control him carefully with medication, so I can wake him up if you'd like to speak to him.'

I take a step backwards. 'Um, I'm not sure I have anything to say to him. Why are you keeping him here like this?'

'He's a dangerous man and I needed him out of the way while I made my plans. He'll make his appearance soon enough at the party.'

Doctor Simmons clears her throat. 'Emily, I'm expecting Mr Wyatt any minute now for a physical examination . . .'

Emily nods. 'Then we'll be on our way. Thank you, Doctor.'

Doctor Simmons smiles. She catches my eye. 'I'm glad you're beginning to feel better, Kimberley.'

I want to ask her about my seizures, but before I can, I hear footsteps behind me, and I turn just in time to see a man walk through the door. My mouth drops open. No, this isn't possible. He cannot be here. *This* is Mr Wyatt?

'Hello Kimberley. It's good to see you.' He extends his hand, but I don't take it. In fact, I step backwards, closer to Emily.

'No,' I say and then I shake my head over and over again. 'No,' I repeat. 'This can't be true. What are you doing here?' I ask him.

'Why to enjoy the party, of course,' he says with his familiar beaming smile, the one which has put me at ease for the past twenty years.

'Doctor Strong . . . *You're* Mr Wyatt?'

The doctor who has been prescribing my epilepsy medication and who first diagnosed me with epilepsy at age five.

'Yes,' he replies. 'Do you understand yet?'

I shake my head as tears fill my eyes. Muffin whimpers beside me. She always hates it when I cry or get upset.

'M-My seizures,' I say with a stutter.

'Have been controlled by me from the start,' says Doctor Strong. 'They are caused by the medication I have been giving you since you were a child, under the direction of this man . . .' He points to my father on the bed, then adds, 'My brother, Damien.'

CHAPTER TWENTY-FIVE

Emily

As I listen to Mr Wyatt and Kimberley talking, my brain races to connect all the dots. I've only recently found out about Kimberley's epilepsy. I had no idea she suffered from such extreme epilepsy. When I first met her and she explained it, I began to question everything. Yes, people are diagnosed with epilepsy all the time. It's not uncommon, but something about Kimberley's condition didn't add up. The fact she had so many seizures and that her medication did little to reduce them felt wrong. So, I began to dig. I especially dug into who her doctor was, the one who'd been *treating* her since she was five. I remembered that she was nervous to change doctors and that also raised a red flag.

I soon found out who her doctor was, Phillip Strong, and it didn't take long before I figured out that he was none other than Mr Wyatt, who'd been attending the parties as a guest for the past twenty years. I brought Damien round a few days ago so he could tell me the truth. I was surprised at how forthcoming he was with revealing his plan, almost like he was proud of it, and wanted me to know because he knew how much it would hurt me. It did. It really did. I wanted to kill him right there and then, but I stormed out of the room before I could. His time would come soon enough.

Damien admitted to providing drugs, with the help of his brother, to Kimberley from the age of five. It is likely that Kimberley really does have epilepsy, but perhaps a mild form, yet he's been giving her medications to increase the frequency and severity of her seizures, make them more dangerous so she relies on him to survive.

Why did he do it? Because he could. He wanted control over Kimberley's life. Plus, and I can't stress this enough, he's a deranged psychopath who clearly enjoys manipulating others. Perhaps he wanted to punish me; knowing he had control over our child this whole time must have fuelled his ego.

What I didn't see coming was the connection between Damien and Mr Wyatt. Brothers. I knew they were friends, but brothers?

I knew I needed to get Kimberley out of her situation, so that's why I made up the whole job process. I couldn't just tell her all this there and then. She'd never believe me. I'd never met her before. She never would have believed me, even if I'd turned blue in the face from explaining. I needed her here with me, so we could take down this establishment together

Kimberley is trembling as she speaks. 'That's why since I've been here and on the medication that Doctor Simmons gave me, my seizures have reduced.'

'Yes,' I say. 'Doctor Simmons has been slowly reducing the medication you've been taking, giving you the correct dose to control your seizures.'

'So . . .' Kimberley gulps and turns to Mr Wyatt. 'I do have epilepsy.'

'Yes, you do, but a milder form,' replies Mr Wyatt. 'Focal seizures, rather than the tonic-clonic seizures you've been used to.'

Kimberley turns back to Doctor Simmons. 'What about the pills you gave me?'

Doctor Simmons smiles. 'We've had to reduce your previous medication slowly or risk you going through severe withdrawal symptoms, so the process will take some time yet.'

'What is it I've been taking for the past twenty years?' This question Kimberley directs back to Mr Wyatt.

'A mixture of antidepressants, stimulants, tramadol, diphenhydramine and meperidine amongst other things,' replies Mr Wyatt. 'We've been tweaking it over the years, my brother and I, so we don't end up accidentally killing you.' He laughs. 'We wouldn't want that now, would we?'

Kimberley's eyes flood with tears.

I want nothing more than to rip his face to shreds right now, but I control myself. I need to get Kimberley out of here. Enough is enough. I can fill in any other questions she may have, which I'm sure will be many.

I reach forward and grab her arm, pulling her towards the door. 'Let's go,' I say.

Once Kimberley and I are outside the medical wing, she turns to me. 'I'm in,' she says. 'Whatever it is you've got planned, I want in. They can't get away with this.'

I smile. 'Thank you, Kimberley. Now, we have a lot of work to do. I have a feeling that this is going to be one killer party.'

CHAPTER TWENTY-SIX

Emily
Twenty-five years before

You were gone. That was all I could focus on, the only thing that flashed like a warning sign in front of my eyes. Every alarm bell rang, almost deafening in my ears. I'd never felt so helpless in my life. It was like my breath and soul had been stolen from my body. Without you, there was no way I could survive for much longer. I didn't *want* to survive any longer. What was the point?

The only person who could help me now was Courtney, the woman who kept coming in and checking on me. The other woman, Jennifer, the one with fire in her bright blue eyes, was a twisted and psychotic human being. She had no regard for human life. And Damien would have sooner helped me over the edge of a cliff. I had to trust someone, and that someone was Courtney, the housekeeper.

Courtney entered the room, a black robe draped over her arm, complete with a massive hood. I was lying on the hospital bed, not strapped down anymore. I attempted to sit up, but the incision pulled and tightened, forcing me to roll to the side first, then raise my torso.

'Here, put this on,' said Courtney, handing me the robe.
'Why? What's going on?'
'Damien wishes to speak to you.'

Even though Damien was the last person I wanted to see, I obeyed. I needed to understand more about this place, more about what was going on.

Courtney helped me undress and step into the black robe, pulling up the oversized hood so it draped across my face. I couldn't see where I was going, so she led me out of the room by gently pushing my lower back in the direction she wanted me to walk. I wasn't bound by anything. I could make a run for it right now. There was nothing stopping me from ripping off the hood, shoving her to the floor and sprinting for the nearest exit, but how far would I get before I was caught? It still wouldn't bring you back from wherever you were.

As I shuffled along, pain radiated in my abdomen, expanding outwards to my whole body. My stomach felt empty and flabby, not full and tight like I'd been used to. The pain from my C-section almost made me double over. I should be resting, but that was impossible without you.

Courtney guided me along a corridor and through a door. There was silence while she closed the door behind me. I couldn't tell if she'd left me alone or whether she was standing behind me, but I knew someone was in front of me. Their breathing was loud, calm, controlled.

'Take off your hood,' said the deep, male voice.

I did as requested and came face to face with your father.

I scanned the room, searching for anyone else, but we were alone. The room was extravagantly decorated with wooden panels on the walls. Damien was dressed in a pair of navy-blue suit trousers and a crisp, white shirt, with the sleeves neatly rolled up to the elbow. The buttons were open at the collar and his greying hair was slightly damp. He looked just as good as I remembered all those months ago.

'You thought you could take my daughter from me?' His voice was low, barely any tone or depth.

'What do you mean? I told you, she isn't yours.'

'We did a DNA test the second she was removed from your womb. She's mine.'

'Then where is she!'

'Someone in this hotel has taken her,' he said slowly. 'I don't know where our daughter is.'

I started laughing hysterically because if I didn't, I was either going to scream or cry. I couldn't understand how no one knew where you were.

Damien reached out and gently stroked the side of my face, running his fingers down my cheek until he reached my chin, then tilted it up to look him in the eyes. He looked older than I remembered, much older than I was. I recalled the night we first met. We met at a party. Despite the age gap, I found him charismatic, attractive and I warmed to him, allowing him to ply me with drinks and hanging on his every word, as he told me how beautiful I was. Like a fool, I believed him.

As the evening wore on, he began to make suggestions to leave, go somewhere more private. I wasn't sure at first, but after a few more drinks, I followed him into a waiting car.

That was the last thing I remember until I woke up with him inside me, tied to a bed with a gag in my mouth. Once he was finished, I was discarded on the street like a piece of rubbish.

I had no idea why I was used so brutally that night, but now here he was, standing in front of me.

'Did you plan this?' I asked.

He let go of my chin. 'You were special, Emily. I wanted you to be the one to carry on my line.'

'Your *line*?'

Damien's eyes focused on something behind me. The door opened and closed. I turned and looked over my shoulder, watching as Jennifer walked into the room.

'Hi, Dad,' she said.

Dad?

'Wait,' I said. 'She's your daughter?'

'Yes, my love. She will one day take over from me, running this hotel.'

'I still don't understand what you want from me. Why am I here? Why did you kidnap me and my baby?'

'Because one day your baby will take over from Jennifer. I need to keep the line pure, you see.'

'What happens when you finally drop dead?' I asked, not caring about my harsh tone.

Damien laughed. 'Oh, I've made sure to freeze my assets for generations to come. My legacy will live on for ever.'

'You're sick.'

'No, the people who stay at my hotel are sick, but by allowing them their freedom here, it stops them from causing havoc outside these walls. I'm saving a lot of people. It may not seem like it, but I am.'

I had no idea what he was talking about regarding the guests. All I knew is that whatever was going on in this place had to stop. But first, I needed to know where Kimberley was.

'How did the search go?' Damien asked Jennifer.

'I'm sorry, but the child is gone. I've questioned the staff, but no one has seen her.'

'Who was the last person to see the child?'

'I believe it was Courtney.'

'Then I want Courtney brought to me immediately.' Damien turned to me. 'Lock Emily away until she has recovered, then put her to work.'

I scoffed. 'You can't do this to me!'

Damien lurched forward and grabbed my chin, squeezing my cheeks between his tight grip. 'I can do whatever the fuck I want. Don't you ever forget it.'

Then, he spat in my face.

I vowed at that moment, that no matter how long it took, I would get my revenge, and I'd find you.

CHAPTER TWENTY-SEVEN

Emily
The Day of the Party

I've had to put up with a lot over the past year since I've overseen this hotel. It's been stressful and complicated to keep up with the charade of playing Jennifer, getting her personality and mannerisms just right, even down to the way she looks down her nose at everyone. I may have let the mask slip once or twice, but only a few of the staff have noticed. The real Jennifer is extremely high maintenance. I've had to put in bright blue contact lenses every day to cover up my natural hazel eyes. I hate having to stick them in my eyes. I've always had a weird phobia of anything to do with manipulating the eyeball. For the first few weeks, it made me almost gag and I still get infections from time to time when I haven't put them in just right. I've also had to pile on the make-up, wear a push-up, padded bra and do a copious amount of exercise, not to mention keep to a strict diet to get that gaunt, skinny look she seems to like so much.

The real Jennifer has never spent too much time with her staff, so I think that's one of the main reasons why I've been able to fool some of them for so long, but since Damien has been out of the picture, I've had to show my face a lot more.

Now, looking in the mirror is like looking at someone completely different. But it's been a necessary evil. All for my child, who I've finally found after twenty-five years of searching.

I never thought it would take me so long. Sometimes I wonder if it would have been easier to accept that she was gone, move on and leave this life behind, but I made a vow to her when she was still in my belly, a vow to protect her forever, no matter what. A mother's love is a strong and powerful thing. I'd never met my child until a couple of weeks ago, but I knew I'd move heaven and earth to find her, to make sure she was safe, and I'd kill anyone who dared do her harm. No matter what it took.

Now, I've found her, and we can finally raze this hotel and business to the ground where it belongs.

A year ago, I destroyed all of Damien's assets, specimens, samples, whatever he likes to call them (he doesn't know this yet), ensuring that Kimberley and Jennifer are the last of his line. Once Jennifer is gone, then Kimberley will be all that's left. She's different from Jennifer. She hasn't been twisted and brainwashed over decades of living under his spell, not directly anyway. It pains me that she's had such a hard life though in foster care. I wish it hadn't taken me so long to find her, but the fact Damien knew where she was since she was five is enough to make my blood boil. He's taken so much from me, including the first twenty-five years of my daughter's life. How did he even find out where she was? There's still many questions that need answering, but they will come in time.

A knock at the door sounds and I look up from my desk.

Courtney and Kimberley enter. There's another piece of the puzzle I need to understand, and I believe Courtney can place it for me.

'Thank you for all your help over the past few days,' I say. 'Tonight is where all our hard work comes to fruition.'

Kimberley looks at me and nods. 'I've made sure that Lincoln and Mr Wyatt's room has been made up to its usual standard. The whisky they ordered was rather eccentric though, don't you think?'

I nod. 'Yes, it was rather a lot more than I'd budgeted for alcohol but never mind.' Frankie is snoozing at my feet, seemingly not bothered by the extra presence in the room.

Courtney smiles, but her eyes dart back and forth between me and the door.

'Kimberley, I've finally found out who it was who stole you from me and managed to smuggle you out of this hotel under the nose of both Damien and Jennifer.'

'You have?'

'I believe it was Bryan.'

Kimberley gasps, but it's Courtney whose mouth drops open.

Courtney coughs. 'Ma'am, I . . .'

'Yes? Care to offer another explanation?'

'It . . . It was me.'

Kimberley turns to look at Courtney who is trembling like a scared kitten. 'It was you!' Kimberley pales and wobbles, clutching her chest. I quickly grab the nearest chair and move it over to her so she can sit down. She doesn't, not right away, not until I gently take her arm and lead her to it. She sits slowly, staring straight ahead. She sucks in a deep breath. It looks as if she's trying to control her breathing. 'Sorry,' she says. 'I'm still getting used to the medication change . . . although now that's all bullshit, so I guess I'm in withdrawals from the crap I was on for most of my life.'

'It will take time for your body to adjust. Also, you're on the appropriate medication to stop your seizures. Have you had any in the past five days?'

'No, none, but plenty of dizzy and nausea spells. I'm okay. Please . . . continue.'

I nod to Courtney who coughs again and then gulps. 'It was me, ma'am, but Bryan also knew. Twenty-five years ago, I was still a child myself. Barely eighteen. I had no idea about this hotel. Damien never told me anything, but . . . he had something on me that I couldn't risk getting out, so I did whatever he wanted, whatever he told me to do, and that included . . . helping to kidnap you and lock you in Room 21.'

'You kidnapped me?'

'Yes, with the help of Bryan. He was the one who grabbed you. I helped look after you while you were in the room, made sure the baby was okay.' Her eyes flick to Kimberley, then back to me. 'But . . . when I found out what Damien and Jennifer had planned for the baby, I freaked out. Bryan told me to calm down. He said there was a way they could save you by stealing you and smuggling you out of the hotel without anyone noticing. Within an hour of you being born, I hid you in a laundry bin and got you out of the hotel and into a car. Bryan drove you to the authorities. He told them that he'd found you abandoned.'

'Are you telling me that you knew where Kimberley was this whole time?' I snap, squeezing my fists together.

'No! I had no idea where she went after that, but it was better than her staying here.'

'You stole my child from me,' I say, my jaw clenched.

'Ma'am, I . . .'

'Stop calling me ma'am. We've been working at this godforsaken hotel together for twenty-five years. I trusted you, Courtney. I brought you on board with my plan because I thought I could trust you, but it turns out you've been lying to me and keeping this secret from me this whole time.'

'I thought I was helping you, Emily. I wanted to save your baby. I wanted to save you, Kimberley. I can assure you that I've always had your best interests at heart.'

The room falls silent. No one breathes.

I'm still fuming about being lied to by Bryan and Courtney, but there's not a lot I can do about it now. At least I know the truth and, like she said, she did it with the best intentions to keep Kimberley safe from Damien, yet five years later he found her anyway.

I take a cleansing breath. 'Now that's been settled, it's time to get ready for the party. It starts in less than five hours.'

'Is the plan still going ahead?' asked Courtney, wiping away tears that have trickled down her cheeks.

'Yes. We keep to the plan. Kimberley, are you sure you can handle it?'

'Yes.'

'Can I trust you, Courtney?' I ask.

'Yes, Emily. You can. I promise'.

'What about Bryan?'

'Him too. He's been acting like he's on Damien's side, but he's not. He even tried to warn Kimberley, but . . . it's too late for any of that now.'

'What's done is done,' I reply.

CHAPTER TWENTY-EIGHT

Kimberley

My brain is like mud, unable to comprehend a lot of what's been happening over the past five days, let alone the past five minutes or so. How am I supposed to understand what's been going on when I have so many questions still left unanswered? I get the gist, I think, so I take a deep breath, allowing my overactive imagination and racing thoughts to settle.

I leave Emily and Courtney to finish preparations while I head up to my room. Muffin keeps close to me. She's taken to whining every time I leave her alone in my room, so I hate to leave her, but she can't come with me tonight. It's time for me to fly solo. Now I understand the reasons for my seizures, I'm less nervous about having one because yes, I do have epilepsy, but a much milder form than I've been led to believe. If the new medication Doctor Simmons has me on can help lessen the severity of them, then my life will improve dramatically over the coming months. But a horrible thought enters my mind and no matter how hard I try, I can't get it out. What if my body has become so used to the medication over the past twenty years that it can't survive without it, and I'm forced to stay on it and have severe seizures forever?

I need to get things straight in my head. Muffin and I settle on my bed where I begin to slowly piece together what I have learned since I've been here.

Damien Clifton, a sick and twisted psychopath liked to rape and torture young women. He bought this hotel back in 1972 when he was twenty-one years old. All sorts of monsters have stayed within these walls. He sought them out, invited them to stay and every year he held a party where even the sickest monsters could feel safe to carry out their sordid deeds without the risk of being caught by the police.

Almost twenty-six years ago, my mother, Emily, was raped by Damien. Eight months later, pregnant, she was then kidnapped, brought to this hotel and locked in Room 21. I was born, stolen by Courtney, a new housekeeper at the time, and Bryan, who managed to sneak me out under the noses of both Damien and Jennifer, his first daughter. They thought they were doing me a favour by saving me. I don't blame them for anything. They were only doing what they thought was right. If I'd have been raised here, I wouldn't be the person I am today.

After that, Emily was forced to work here. Courtney never told her the truth (for a reason I'm yet to fully understand) and Damien and Jennifer had no idea where I was until at age five, Damien found me and then got his brother, Phillip Strong, a doctor, to prescribe a combination of drugs to give me severe seizures so I'd be dependent on him to survive.

A year ago, Emily found out where I was from Valerie. She then devised a plan and locked Jennifer in Room 21 and pretended to be her, while keeping Damien sedated and hidden from the rest of the staff. As Jennifer, she continued to play the part, inviting the guests to this year's party as normal.

She brought me here using the disguise of hiring me as a housekeeper. But why? Was it because she wanted us to bond as mother and daughter and now wants my help to destroy everyone who has had a hand in running this hotel and ruining her and my life? Or is it for another reason I'm yet to understand?

I get off the bed and head straight to the cabinet where I keep my medicine, including the asthma inhalers. I kept some of the old medication that was prescribed by Doctor Strong and so I compare it to the new medication that Doctor Simmons has me on. She said that I'm on a lower dose because apparently whatever I was on was addictive and dangerous, as well as the appropriate medication to control seizures: lamotrigine, to be taken morning and evening.

It still feels like I'm being drugged against my will. I didn't ask to be given this medication. What about the asthma inhalers? Are they fake too? I certainly have asthma attacks, and the inhalers help me, so maybe that's real. I just don't know anymore. What would happen if I stopped taking everything completely? Would my body cease to function? Would I have a seizure so big that it never stops?

A knock at the door makes me jump. I open it a crack to see Emily standing on the other side.

'I'm sorry,' she says. 'I know you need to get ready for the party, but I also know you have more questions. As do I. May I come in?'

I step aside, holding the door while she walks inside. I close it and turn to face her. 'Do any of the staff here know who you really are besides Courtney and Bryan?'

'A lot of the staff are on my side, especially the ones who have been here for many years. They know me, so no amount of make-up or contact lenses would hide the fact that I'm not really Jennifer. However, as you well know, the staff here have all signed non-disclosure agreements, which means what goes on behind closed doors, stays behind closed doors. They can't say a word.'

'I did wonder about the bright blue eyes.'

Emily smiles. 'Thank God I won't have to wear them for much longer. They hurt my eyes so much. I've had so many eye infections.'

'Which also explains the oversized sunglasses.'

'Yes. Being Jennifer has been exhausting.'

'Haven't any of the guests here noticed you looked different or raised concerns on the whereabouts of Damien?'

'The majority of the guests have no idea. You remember the guests you met at the business suite at Harris Hotel?'

I nod.

'All of those guests have suspicions about me so I had to do some damage control at the time and assure them that Damien would be making an appearance at the party. Everyone else, as far as I know, has no idea.'

'Lincoln knows something?'

'It's possible.'

'Why has he kept quiet about his suspicions?'

Emily avoids my eye contact. 'I have managed to keep him quiet by doing things I'm not proud of, things I never want to repeat out loud.'

I lower my gaze to the floor, blinking back tears. 'Why would you do that? You saved me from him the other day, but you let him abuse you?'

'I didn't *let* him do anything. As a mother, there isn't anything I wouldn't do to protect my child. However, after tonight, Lincoln will get what he deserves, along with Damien, Jennifer and all the other guests here.'

'They'll all be dead by the end of the night. I've been trapped inside this hotel, living my own version of hell, unable to escape or say a word to anyone. I couldn't leave, not without knowing where you were. And whether you were safe.'

'What's going to happen to Courtney and Bryan? She saved me, snuck me out of this place, but then never told you where I was.'

Emily takes a deep breath. 'I haven't decided yet. I can't forgive them for taking you away from me and the fact they never told me . . . it hurts. I thought we were friends, but there's a part of me that's also grateful to them for taking you away. If you'd been trapped here with me, then you would have grown up to be exactly like your father and Jennifer.'

There's a silence in the room. There are things I want to say, but I'm worried I'll offend her.

'What is it?' she asks, reading my mind.

'I just . . . I'm having a hard time getting on board with the whole killing thing. I mean, I am on board, but . . . I understand that what they did to you was awful and they deserve to be punished, but . . . in a way, aren't you just as bad as them for what you're going to do to these people?'

Shaking her head, Emily steps towards me. The last thing I want is to push her away, to give her reason to mistrust me, but if I'm going to join her on this vendetta, I need to understand why.

'For twenty-five years, I've been watching what goes on under this roof. If you knew what these people have done, then you wouldn't compare me to them. They are evil, Kimberley. Pure evil. I've been forced to watch while they raped, murdered and tortured people during these parties, people who were dragged off the streets like I was all those years ago. I'm nothing like them. Nothing.'

I stare into my mother's eyes. My eyes. 'How did you manage to take over the hotel a year ago? I want to know everything. Tell me the truth.'

CHAPTER TWENTY-NINE

Emily

'A year ago, the party was the worst one yet. They seemed to get worse every year. I saw things that no person with a soul should ever see, not if they ever want to sleep again. Cleaning up after the party while the guests slept, I decided that enough was enough. I couldn't put up with it any longer. It was time to be brave, even though I was so afraid of losing everything. I needed to make things happen myself. I wasn't sure I had the courage to step up and take control, but I was wrong about that too.' I stop and take a breath, tears brimming in my eyes.

'You see, bravery isn't about having no fear at all. It's about being afraid but doing the thing that scares you anyway. So, while Damien and Jennifer slept and recovered from the party, I put my plan into action, but I couldn't do it alone. Valerie had found out where you were, but I needed someone else on my side, someone who was close to Damien and Jennifer, someone with inside information. Courtney. She almost cried when I asked her to help me. Turned out, she'd been wanting to do the same thing for decades, but had also been too scared to make it happen. At the time, I had no idea where you were or that you were being controlled by Damien and his brother. I found all that out much later.' At this point, I can feel my breath running away with me, so I walk over to the nearest window and look out at the countryside, something that never fails to calm me.

'If Courtney and I failed, if we were found out, if anything went wrong, then we'd lose our lives. That was inevitable. If I failed, then I'd never see you and you'd never see me. There was more at stake than just being killed. I didn't want to die with you never knowing the truth about your mother. I didn't want you to hate me, to think that I never wanted you, to blame me for your difficult childhood. I wished things had turned out differently, but I was determined to do my best to rectify them, and that meant punishing the ones who started all of this.' I turn and face Kimberley who is rooted to the spot, taking it all in.

'The first thing Courtney and I had to do was ensure all the guests left on time, signed out of the hotel and, if possible, booked their place for next year's party, as in, this year's party. I wanted as many of them to return as possible because this one was going to be the biggest and most elaborate one yet.

'As usual, Damien booked himself in for a full day of treatments at the hotel, including a deep cleansing facial, full body massage and an exfoliating mud bath. It was his normal routine for the day following the party to rejuvenate and relax. However, I added a little something extra into his massage oil, which caused him to fall into a deep sleep. The masseuse was also affected, but she was perfectly okay when she woke up, bar a small headache.' I smile at the thought of how easily he'd drifted off to sleep. In hindsight, he should never have trusted me, even twenty-four years later, but I'd played the part of the trained housekeeper very well over the years, which enabled him to be lulled into a false sense of security. More fool him.

'Courtney and I then transported Damien into the medical wing where we set up a room for him to stay. Doctor Simmons was on my side too. She kept him sedated in a coma until I needed him to wake up and provide me with the information I needed.

'Jennifer, however, was more difficult to capture. The staff noticed Damien's disappearance, but I couldn't reveal the truth to most of them. Some of the staff had been working for him for so long that they couldn't even think for themselves. They were more like trained sheep, following the leader, not having any clue about what they were doing or where they were going. It wasn't their fault. It's this place. It was Damien. He brainwashed them.

'Courtney suggested to Jennifer that she go away for a few days to recuperate after the party. She was a workaholic and often kept working long into the night, researching future guests, and ensuring that the goings on at the hotel were kept quiet. It took a lot of, shall we say, bribery to keep the hotel out of the news and off the police radar. Jennifer was a very powerful and talented woman. She and Damien knew a lot of high-up, important people: newscasters, journalists, politicians, even royalty. I knew that if I was going to pretend to be her, I had to not only look like her but be just as ruthless.'

Kimberley opens her mouth, possibly to say something, but I'm on a roll now, so I quickly continue. There will be time for questions later.

'She asked me about her father's disappearance, but she didn't seem too phased by it. I had a feeling that she thought it would be easier to run the hotel without him. He'd taught her everything over the years, but she kept behind closed doors a lot of the time, waiting for her moment to shine. It was one of the reasons why most of the staff didn't suspect anything when I pretended to be her. They weren't used to seeing her face. I wondered whether, if she'd been brought up by a normal father, she'd have turned out normal herself, whether he made her into a vicious killer himself, or whether she was born one, like he was.

'Jennifer was too dangerous and too unstable to keep around. She finally agreed to go on a road trip to get some space from the hotel and it was during this trip her car was involved in a near-fatal accident where she lost the use of both her legs. Obviously, it was all arranged and kept out of the news, thanks to her not wishing anyone to know she was injured and out of commission.

'She woke up from her coma in the hospital, paralysed. Her once beautiful face was now disfigured, which helped to explain why the shape of her face changed when I took over her identity. While Jennifer was recovering in hospital, I was undergoing a transformation of my own. My dark hair was bleached blonde. I put myself on a super strict diet, which caused me to lose almost two stone in two months, not something I'd recommend. But, slowly and surely, I made myself look as close to Jennifer as I could, including the blue contact lenses.

'When she was finally allowed to return home to the hotel, the staff anxiously waited to greet her. They'd been briefed by Courtney that Jennifer looked different and would be in a wheelchair while she had physiotherapy to regain her strength. Therefore, when I turned up in the wheelchair, they had no idea that I wasn't Jennifer.

'The real Jennifer was sedated and transported straight to Room 21 where she stayed locked up. She did partially regain the use of her legs, but she still cannot walk properly. She will never be up to full strength again. I spent the next few months building the strength in my own legs and putting on a show for the staff, ordering them about and conducting the various duties once performed by Jennifer. It was no easy task, but I was determined to see it through.' I finish my story and look at Kimberley.

'Thank you for telling me that,' she says softly. 'I had no idea you went through so much to get to where you are today.'

'As have you.'

'I guess we've both been fucked over by these twisted people.'

'So, you agree they should be punished?'

'Yes, but what happens afterwards?'

'That's the beauty of it. Anything we want.'

CHAPTER THIRTY

Kimberley

Emily's story left me both horrified and astonished at the level of dedication she's put into her plan over the past year. After her long captivity here, her determination to bring this place down has been nothing short of miraculous. And I'm a part of it. I always have been. I can't let her down now, not after everything she's endured, everything she's done for me.

I've always said I want to do something worthwhile, something people will remember me for. My mother has single-handedly collected the worst people in the country and gathered them under the same roof and has plans to wipe them all out in one go. And I'm supposed to help her. Do I want to be remembered for being a vigilante? Is that what this is, or is this just cold-blooded murder, no better than what the guests do behind closed doors? Then again, no one will ever know about this, no one outside of these walls will know the truth about what is about to happen here.

I am silent for a moment. The truth is, I have no idea what to do. Whichever decision I end up making is going to have drastic repercussions for me and everyone involved.

I can't just walk away from this. I know too much about the hotel. My mother found me for a reason.

'I'll do it.'

Emily closes her eyes and smiles. 'Thank you, Kimberley. Thank you.'

'What do you need me to do?'

CHAPTER THIRTY-ONE

Emily

The next few hours pass by smoothly, running like clockwork. The kitchen staff finish their preparations for the food and set up in the main banquet hall where the lavish party is to be held. The decorating committee finally finish transforming the room into a fantasy wonderland, complete with a fountain of fake blood and chocolate and strings of twinkly lights. The guests normally have real blood, but they won't know the difference unless they taste it, which they may still do, but it'll be too late by then to do anything about it. I once saw a guest dancing in the blood fountain and drinking the blood like it was water. I seriously question the mental state of some of these serial killers. Often, serial killers are quite smart, easily able to manipulate and outsmart their victims and those around them, while others are just in it for the killing. It's animalistic in nature.

A huge gold-plated statue of a naked woman adorns the centre of the banquet hall. It's surrounded by black and purple candles, which will be lit when the party is underway. The circular tables are laid with black tablecloths and a magnificent black and purple centrepiece in the middle. No expense has been spared. Every guest has their own personalised goodie bag, which contains the highest quality products from flavoured lube to hand-crafted weapons and gorgeous perfume. Each guest is also given a mask to wear, each one hand-painted and designed with the individual in mind. While most of the guests know each other, it's important to keep identities a secret as much as possible. That's why names are changed, masks are worn, and no contact details are swapped while here.

The staff who are going to be in attendance all have their assignments and will also be wearing masks, but their masks are identical, as are their black and purple uniforms. Their masks are purple with black butterflies dotted around the outside with sparkles.

My outfit tonight is nothing short of spectacular, fitted and designed to perfection to emphasise my figure. I'm still a size or two bigger than the real Jennifer, especially now that she's spent the past year on bed-rest, but the staff have been too disciplined to mention it. My evening gown is black with purple diamonds encrusted into the material. Every time I move, they catch the light and sparkle like stars. It fits my figure perfectly, and emphasises my breasts, pushing them up towards my chin. My mask sits across my blue eyes, a simple purple one with delicate swirls of lace and leather. I have begrudgingly put the blue contacts back in, relieved that this will be the last time I have to wear them.

I stand in front of the full-length mirror, studying my body and face. If anything goes wrong tonight, then it's all over for me, but I don't even care about surviving tonight, as long as Kimberley does and as long as all the monsters under this roof don't.

Everything about tonight is perfect. Yet, I'm so nauseous I can barely sip the champagne from the crystal flute. I am due downstairs in ten minutes and must shine like the sparkling star I am, but my feet are rooted to the spot in front of the full-length mirror, and I can't seem to tear my eyes away from my reflection.

I am the star of the show. The party can't go ahead without me. I remember the night of my first party like it was yesterday, but back then I wasn't the star of the show. I was a mere servant, one of the staff who blended into the background, ignored by all the guests unless they wanted something.

I'll never forget that first party when I saw human beings rip each other apart, enjoy slicing pieces of skin off and eating it, raping innocent victims who'd been taken off the streets. It opened my eyes to the brutality and evilness of mankind. These people were the worst kind of humans, but they were hiding their true selves behind normal exteriors; businesspeople, politicians, royalty, celebrities, all of them hid dark secrets, putting on a show for the outside world so they couldn't see the rotten souls beneath.

Little did I know that that night would change my entire life and I'd never be the innocent young girl I was before. My baby was gone and I was being forced to work for an evil man.

Now, all these years later, I've finally taken control. I will end this disgusting hotel once and for all, but I'm not full of excitement like I probably should be. Fear grips my inside like a torture device that squeezes me tighter and tighter until I either pass out from lack of oxygen or I learn to live with the gut-wrenching feeling.

Tonight, all eyes will be on me.

Tonight, nothing can go wrong.

Tonight, every single guest in attendance will die.

It truly is going to be one killer party.

With one last look at myself, I turn and exit my room, heading downstairs where I'm due to greet each guest as they enter the banquet hall, the room where they'll take their last breath.

CHAPTER THIRTY-TWO

Kimberley

The next few hours are spent getting the final preparations ready for the party. The banquet hall is decorated with black and purple, the round tables laden with the finest glass and cutlery. Emily spends a long time ensuring everything is perfect. The staff mill around her, obeying her every command like trained dogs, most of them still unaware of her true identity. Only a select few know. Once the party is over and the guests are dead, what happens to the staff? Has Emily even thought that far ahead or is she hell-bent on killing everyone, including the people who work here? She said that we could do whatever we wanted when this was all over, but what if the police find out? This hotel isn't known to the outside world. It's not on any maps, any website, but that doesn't mean someone won't blab about it.

'Kimberley, I need you to do something else for me,' says Emily once we're alone in the banquet hall. The preparations are over. There's nothing left to do but count down the hours until it starts. 'It's dangerous, but he doesn't trust me anymore. I can't do it. I need you to go and see Lincoln. I need him to ask you to be his plus one for the party.'

'Why?'

'He has something I need, and I think you're the only one who can get it.'

'What is it?'

'Information.'

'What sort of information?'

Emily turns to me. 'Lincoln is a very powerful man. He knows a lot of people, a lot of powerful people, a lot of very bad people. He always keeps a small black notebook on him. On there are the names and locations of all the known serial killers in the country. Damien has been working very closely with him for several years, collecting the data. Since Damien's disappearance a year ago, Lincoln has taken it upon himself to contact these killers and tell them about this hotel. But I have no idea who they are. I do suspect that Lincoln knows I'm not the real Jennifer. He may know I'm planning something tonight, so I need you to keep an eye on him. I need the black notebook.'

A mind-numbing wave of fear washes over me as my mind goes back to that afternoon when he trapped me in the library and demanded I take my clothes off. I'd just stood there, frozen. My throat constricts.

'I . . . I can't.'

'He'll see you as a prize he hasn't yet collected. He'll ask you to the party just to vex me. It should be easy to swipe the notebook.'

'No, I mean . . . I can't . . . b-breathe.' I lean forward, clutching the back of a nearby chair. Emily takes my arm and helps me sit down while I attempt to catch my breath. It feels as if I'm trying to breathe through a straw. It's enough to survive, but every breath in is laboured. I'm fighting against my own body.

Just breathe, dammit!

'Where is your inhaler, Kimberley?'

I reach into the pocket of my dress, but before I can take a puff, Emily snatches it out of my hand. I don't have the breath to demand it back. She steps aside and looks at the blue inhaler. Then, to my utter confusion, presses the depressor button, letting out a small puff. Then she takes a puff herself.

What the . . .

'Kimberley, where do you get your inhalers from?'

I frown at her and reach forward to grab it from her. 'G-Give!'

'Kimberley, listen to me very carefully. This inhaler is not prescription. Where do you get them from?'

'W-What . . . are . . . you . . . n-need.'

Why won't she give me my inhaler? Is she trying to kill me?

Then she says something that almost makes me faint. The room spins and seems to be fading further and further into the distance.

'This inhaler is filled with air.'

A lump gets stuck in my throat. I collapse forward onto the floor on all fours. Vicious coughs wrack my body. Spit flies from my mouth and onto the floor.

A warm hand touches the back of my neck. 'Breathe, Kimberley. Focus on my voice. You're okay. You're safe. Breathe in for five and out for five. Come on. You can do it.'

I wish I had the oxygen in my lungs to tell her to fuck off and give me my damn inhaler, but I'm expending all my energy on not passing out, on trying to get my lungs to work.

Breathe in.

Breathe out.

My inhaler is filled with air.

What does that mean? How is that possible? Surely Damien and Doctor Strong haven't faked that too?

I'm not sure how many minutes pass, but each agonising second seems to tick by slowly. It's torture. She's going to let me die here on the floor of the banquet hall.

Her warm hand stays on my neck.

It's soothing. It's like her energy is flowing into me. Eventually, my body stops fighting against me and breathing gets a little easier, smoother. The straw I'm trying to breathe through gets wider and wider. Black spots stop dancing in front of my eyes and my vision comes into focus. The blacks and purples in the room spring into full, vibrant colour again.

I'm okay.

I'm not going to die.

Eventually, the energy I need to sit up straight returns and I look into Emily's eyes. 'Who provides you with these inhalers?' she asks. 'Is it also Doctor Strong?'

My mouth opens and then closes. 'Y-Yes.'

Emily sighs and closes her eyes, as if she can't quite believe what she's hearing.

'Are you saying he's also been giving me fake inhalers?'

'It's possible.'

'I don't believe this. Do I have asthma or not?'

'I'll have Doctor Simmons run some more tests once this is all over. I'm so sorry, Kimberley. I wish I could fix all this for you, take all the years that were stolen from you back, but I can't. All we can do is punish those responsible.'

I nod. 'I'm ready.'

'Good. Now, I think it's time you got ready for the party. Remember what I said about Lincoln. It's up to you to get that notebook. I doubt he'll bring it to the party, so you need to get into his room beforehand. He usually likes to have a drink in his room before the party starts. Once we have the notebook, then we can carry out the rest of the evening's activities. Just do yourself a favour and only drink the champagne you're given, nothing else.'

'I don't even want to ask why,' I say solemnly.

***

After Emily leaves the room, I head back upstairs to get dressed and look through each of my inhalers. Each one has been prescribed by Doctor Strong, aka Mr Wyatt. It says to take two puffs three times per day, or whenever I experience an asthma attack or feel short of breath. I'm due to take the next puffs now, but now my mind is wondering what would happen if I didn't take it? Maybe the medicine within the inhaler is part of the cause of my seizures, along with the drugs they've been giving me.

I depress the inhaler, watch as it emits a puff of *whatever it is* and sniff the air. It has no odour at all. There's a term for what he's done to me, isn't there? And it's been going on since I was five years old. What about all the different foster homes I went to? Some of them were outside the area covered by the doctor's surgery where Doctor Strong worked, so how come I had to keep going back to him? My foster families said he was the best doctor for my medical condition, but that wasn't true, was it? Were the foster families in on it? If they weren't, then how did Damien and Doctor Strong coerce them into ensuring they kept taking me back to his surgery?

My stomach roils. It's abuse. Long-term abuse where someone who I trusted has created a medical condition that I don't have, just so they can control my life, keep an eye on me. To make it worse, he's my uncle. Doctor Strong is my uncle, and my father has been working with him this whole time.

The more I think about it the more freaked out I become, so I stare at the array of inhalers and medication laid out on my bed. My whole life has been a lie. I've grown up thinking I'm severely unwell, almost dying on several occasions due to a severe epileptic attack, having to avoid so many triggers. But it's all been a lie.

I look up at the ceiling and scream, letting out a loud, animalistic sound as I lunge forward, grab the inhalers and pills and hurl them at the wall where they break apart upon impact. I keep throwing them until there are none left, then I pick up the nearest object, a hairdryer, and throw that too. Then I kick the side of my bed, scream some more, before collapsing on the floor in a heap. My heart is beating erratically. Muffin shimmies over to me, her tail between her legs.

'I'm sorry to scare you girl,' I say, kissing her on the top of her head.

As I wait for the black spots to stop dancing in front of my eyes, I sit up against my bed and stare at the dress, which is on a hanger on my wardrobe door. It's a beautiful dress. Stunning. Mostly dark purple with a thick, black waistline. The skirt of the dress is silk whereas the top half looks like lace. There's a matching mask lying on the side table.

Anger is still pulsating through my body at the reality of what Doctor Strong has put me through over the years. But then, he was just following orders. It was Damien, my father, who was pulling the strings all this time. I know Emily wants to kill him tonight, but I need to talk to him before she does. But first, I need to get this notebook from Lincoln.

The plan is in motion.

CHAPTER THIRTY-THREE

Emily

The first guests begin to arrive in the banquet hall an hour later, dressed in their finest suits, dresses and various other outfits matching their tastes. I greet each of them at the entrance and they are handed a glass of champagne by a waiter who's standing next to me.

'Good evening, Mrs Wyatt,' I say as the graceful woman approaches me dressed in a skintight black sequin dress that skims the floor and shows off a great deal of cleavage. She gives me two air kisses on each cheek and takes a flute.

'Jennifer, you've surprised me. This party looks to be even more spectacular than usual.'

'Thank you, I appreciate that.'

'Did you hear from my husband at all? Is he here?'

'Yes, ma'am, he is.'

'Where's he staying?'

'In one of the other rooms with another guest.'

Mrs Wyatt raises her eyebrows. 'Is he indeed? Who is he staying with?'

'I'm afraid I'm not at liberty to reveal that information,' I reply coolly. I'm enjoying watching this woman squirm. I don't need to feed her with compliments or bend over backwards to keep her happy any longer. It's about time she got a taste of her own medicine.

She stares at me as if I've said a vulgar word. 'Careful, Jennifer,' she says. 'You wouldn't want your father to hear about this, would you? Will Damien be here soon?'

'Yes, I can assure you, he's on his way.'

'Good.' At that moment, a very handsome and well-groomed man appears behind her and places a hand on the small of her back. He's tall, over six foot, and has gorgeous thick, black hair. His beard is expertly trimmed and styled, and he smells as good as chocolate. His black mask obscures his upper facial features, highlighting his chiselled, strong jaw. It seems she's met one of the other guests already to replace her husband.

'Have a lovely evening,' I say.

As more guests arrive, the banquet hall comes alive and is buzzing with chatter, music and the scent of wealth and power. It's intoxicating.

Courtney appears at my side, as perfectly turned out as ever. 'Are we ready, ma'am?'

'Yes. I believe so. Let the party begin. We're just waiting for one more guest.'

'Lincoln. I hope Kimberley can handle him.'

'I have no doubt she will.'

CHAPTER THIRTY-FOUR

Kimberley

Stepping into the exquisite dress makes me feel like I'm stepping into a different world full of money and splendour. I feel like a different person, and that's exactly what I'm counting on right now. I need to be a different person to make this work. I can't be shy and unassuming like I normally am.

Chances are that Lincoln won't even recognise me. The last time he saw me I was dressed in a housekeeper's uniform and cleaning the reception area with a damp cloth. Now, I look like I'm about to step onto the catwalk at London fashion week. I haven't added too much make-up because my face mask hides a lot of my features.

The classical music from the banquet hall is being played throughout the hotel. I find the tone of the music unsettling, considering the intended audience and as I walk down the large halls towards Lincoln's room, my stomach clenches and my palms sweat.

I reach his door and knock straight away before my body catches up to what my brain is telling me to do, and that's to run away. I hold my breath while I wait for him to open the door, which seems to take an eternity. Seconds feel like minutes as I shift my weight from foot to foot, fighting the urge to turn and sprint down the corridor in my high heels.

'Ah, Miss Johnston, what a delightful surprise.'

The man who opens the door isn't Lincoln.

It's Doctor Phillip Strong.

I do my best to hide my surprise, but it must be obvious to him. It had completely slipped my mind that he was staying in Lincoln's room. Damn it.

'I'm sorry, were you expecting someone else?'

'I . . . Sorry, I just forgot you'd be here.'

Phillip (it feels weird to call him by that name) opens the door wider to reveal Lincoln standing behind him. My mind whirls and twirls as it attempts to fit two and two together. Now that I think about it, how do they both know each other? Are they lovers, friends or something else?

'There's no need to look so shocked, Miss Johnston. Lincoln and I go way back, isn't that right?' Phillip turns and looks at Lincoln who curls his top lip in a creepy grin.

'You could say that,' he says.

'Would you like to join us for a pre-party drink?' asks Phillip, stepping aside and holding the door open.

It's like being invited into a hungry lion's den, but it is what I came here to do, isn't it? But I hadn't counted on Phillip being here. He presents a big problem.

'I'd love to,' I say with a smile before stepping over the threshold of the den. Phillip closes the door behind me with a soft click.

Phillip is dressed in a deep purple velvet tuxedo. On anyone else it would look like a lame Halloween costume, but on him it looks positively enthralling. I can barely drag my eyes away from him. It fits him expertly in all the right places. His greying hair only accentuates the overall look.

'I must say you look incredibly beautiful tonight,' says Phillip, moving towards the side of the room where there's a built-in bar set up.

Eww, is my uncle coming onto me?

The difference between the staff bedrooms and the guestrooms is quite staggering. This one is the grandest bedroom I've been in so far. It isn't just one room, but several adjoining rooms. We're in the lounge/dining/living area and there's even a balcony which looks out over the lavish estate, but the dark evening means I can't see a lot from where I'm standing.

'What can I get you to drink?' asks Phillip.

'What are you having?'

'Macallan 'The Reach' single malt, aged eighty-one years.'

'Sure, sounds good.' I smile. I know exactly what it is because I was the one who delivered it to the room. It costs more than an average house to buy.

Phillip smirks as he turns to the bar and picks up an intricately designed bottle that was resting on a plinth of three hands holding it up.

Lincoln steps up beside me and stands a little too close than what is deemed appropriate. My body wants to flinch away, but I stand rooted to the spot as Phillip turns and hands each of us a glass of golden single malt. I made sure to watch him as he poured it, so I'm almost certain he didn't slip anything into the drink.

Just to be safe, I wait to take a sip. 'Thank you,' I say.

Lincoln takes a drink.

Phillip smiles and does the same.

Then I raise the glass to my lips and take a small sip. Heat and fire explode in my mouth, and I fight back the urge to cough as I swallow.

'That sip is probably worth over a thousand pounds,' says Phillip.

'W-What?' I stutter.

'This is a two-hundred-and-fifty-thousand-pound bottle,' he says, as he replaces the glass back on the bar.

'Oh,' I say, looking into the glass in my hand. 'It's . . . um . . . nice.' It's really not.

Phillip laughs. It feels as if he's making fun of me. 'So, my dear, you've risen from a lowly housekeeper to the belle of the ball in a short space of time. I take it dear Jennifer has taken a shine to you.' The fact he's called her Jennifer throws me for a second.

'You could say that,' I reply. I take another sip for no other reason than to settle my nerves and stop my bottom jaw from trembling. The second sip goes down a little smoother this time. It still burns, but it doesn't make me want to retch. I think that's enough though. I don't want my mind to be too fuzzy for the party.

'Not that it's not lovely to see you, Doctor Strong, or should I call you Mr Wyatt? Or Phillip? You have so many names, I'm not sure which to use.'

'Yes, I'd appreciate it if you could use my pseudonym within these walls.'

'Very well. I was hoping to spend some time with Lincoln this evening,' I continue, not daring to look at Lincoln.

Mr Wyatt raises his eyebrows. 'I'm afraid that won't be possible because Lincoln is mine for the evening.'

'Yours?'

'Yes, we've made an agreement, haven't we, Lincoln?' Phillip glares at Lincoln who reaches towards me and slips an arm around my waist, sliding his palm over my bottom as he does so.

'Change of plans, old boy. If Kim here wants to play with Lincoln tonight, then who am I to say no?'

I shudder and fight the urge to flinch away.

Doctor Strong, or should I say Mr Wyatt, inhales deeply. If I didn't know any better, I'd say that Lincoln just hurt his feelings. I can't say I feel sorry for him. I do intend to speak to him at some point this evening to find out exactly why he's been medicating me all these years. I also keep forgetting that he's my uncle, which makes this whole thing feel even more weird and wrong.

'Very well,' Mr Wyatt says. He steps towards the door. 'However, if it's not too much trouble, I would like a dance with young Kimberley tonight. It would be my honour to dance with my niece.'

I nod my head, then he leaves the room. I almost call out to stop him because the thought of being alone with Lincoln turns my stomach, but as I turn to look at him, he looks a little pale, like he's just seen a ghost.

'Um . . . Lincoln, everything okay?'

'Did Phillip just say you're his niece?'

'Yes. It's a long story.'

Lincoln frowns, his eyes look anywhere but at me. What the hell is going on?

'Something wrong, Lincoln?'

Lincoln hesitates for a fraction of a second. He narrows his eyes at me and gently slides his hand off my backside. 'No. Let's forget what's just happened and have some fun, yeah?'

'Um . . . what did just happen? I'm confused?'

Lincoln's eyes grow dark as he scans my body from head to toe. 'It doesn't matter. Come here.'

'I'm good where I am, thanks.'

'Then what are you doing here alone with me in my room? You're the one who wanted to have some alone time with Lincoln, so I suggest you make the most of it.'

'Do yourself a favour and stop talking in the third person. It's creepy.'

Lincoln turns his whole body to face me and steps closer. I immediately regret my choice of words and tone of voice. For a moment, I thought maybe he'd like the confident approach I was taking, but now I see that he likes his women to be obedient and hang on his every word rather than the other way around.

But I'm not ready to roll over and take orders. Not from a man. Not like this. For a job, yes, as a housekeeper, but not in my personal life.

'Careful what you say to me, Kim,' he says with a hint of a growl.

'I'm not afraid of you, Lincoln. Not anymore. And my name is Kimberley.'

He looks me up and down, smiling like a Cheshire cat. 'I disagree with that statement. You're trembling and your heart is beating over a hundred beats per minute.' He leans close and sniffs me. 'Plus, I can smell your fear. It smells . . . delicious.' He licks his lips and slides his hand against my bottom again.

I put the half-drunk whisky tumbler down on the side. 'Lincoln, I'm not quite ready to . . .'

'To what?'

I'm not quite sure how far I have to push him. I know I need to get close to him, both physically and mentally, but being in his presence is enough to turn my stomach. The way he stares at me like I'm a piece of meat is disgusting.

The muscle in his jaw is tight and the vein on his forehead looks ready to burst. I'm almost worried he's going to give himself a brain haemorrhage.

'If you don't want to have fun with me, then why are you here, Kim? What do you get out of being here tonight?'

'I told you. I just want to spend some quality time with you . . .' I have a horrible feeling that he's not buying my performance. I need to do better.

Physically swallowing the saliva that rises in the back of my throat, I take a step closer to him. 'I guess I'm curious about you,' I say.

Lincoln beams his kilowatt smile. 'It seems my reputation precedes me. Another drink?' He nods towards the bar, already walking over towards it. I lean against the nearby table, a little woozy from the whisky already. I need to focus. The notebook. Where's the damn notebook? Emily said that he usually has it on his person, but would he really take it down to the party with him?

'I'd better not,' I say. 'Need to save something for the party.'

Lincoln pours another whisky into his own glass. 'What exactly do you think happens at these parties, Kim?'

I inwardly cringe at his constant use of a shortened version of my name. I've always hated being called Kim. 'I'm sure whatever I have in my mind is nothing compared to what really happens.'

Lincoln raises his eyebrows and lowers the glass from his lips just as he was about to take a sip. 'Hmm, now that is interesting, Kim.'

'How is it interesting?'

'I pride myself on being in the know when it comes to this place, but it appears that you know more than I do.'

'Lincoln, you're clearly a smart guy. And considering how close Jennifer and you are . . .' I stop, unwilling to say any more. I don't want to give him any extra ammunition against me.

Lincoln holds my stare for a moment then downs the rest of his drink. 'Shall we head down to the party?' He brushes off the odd conversation we've just had as if it's nothing. What was that all about? He seemed genuinely thrown to find out Phillip was my uncle. He offers me his arm. It seems our little chat is over. As he extends his elbow, his jacket opens, revealing a black notebook tucked into his inside pocket.

Bingo.

I take his arm with a smile. 'Yes. Let's.'

At least I know where it is. Now, all I have to do is remove it without him noticing.

CHAPTER THIRTY-FIVE

Emily

I almost topple off my heels when Mr Wyatt walks towards me with a scowl across his face. An unhappy guest is never a good thing. It's the last thing I need tonight. Quickly, I compose myself. It never bodes well to see Mr Wyatt looking as if he wants to murder someone. How did I not notice the similarities between him and Damien before? I could have sworn, many years ago, I saw them . . . I must have been mistaken, although I wouldn't put anything past Damien. He's not only into women and he likes things slightly, shall we say, *different*. But they're brothers, so if I did see them doing something they quite possibly shouldn't be doing, there's also incest to add to his list of indiscretions.

'Mr Wyatt, how lovely you could join us this evening,' I say with a flourishing smile as he stops in front of me. He leans in and kisses me on the cheek, but somehow keeps the scowl on his face.

'Jennifer, delighted as always.' I see he's also keeping up appearances this evening.

'I've been meaning to ask you if you'd received any of my messages? We'd been trying to contact you for some time after Mrs Wyatt turned up alone.'

'No, I'm afraid not. I've changed numbers, you see, and email addresses. I had a bit of trouble with the law. You understand.' I can understand the trouble with the law, but I don't think that's the reason why he didn't respond to my urgent messages. Even if he had changed his number, he could have emailed or contacted me somehow to say he wouldn't be arriving with his wife. It completely threw me the other day, not to mention the fact he's been medicating my daughter for the past twenty years. There's a special place in hell waiting for him, rest assured.

'Not to worry,' I say. 'Your wife should be around here somewhere. Have you touched base with her?' I like to play too, and make people squirm.

Mr Wyatt averts his eyes. 'Ah, I take it, she hasn't told you?'

'Told me what?' I ask innocently.

'We've separated. About four months ago.'

'Oh, I'm so sorry. I had no idea. No, she didn't tell me anything.'

'That's typical of her,' he mutters.

I'm unsure whether to say anything else at this point because I can't tell whether their separation will affect the party tonight or not. The last thing I want is squabbling spouses to disrupt the evening's activities. That's the only thing that bothers me. I couldn't care less if their marriage has broken down.

'Well,' I say, 'I'm sure there will be plenty of young ladies available for your pleasure tonight.' Mr Wyatt locks his eyes on me. I feel my cheeks heat up. 'Oh,' I say. 'My apologies. I take it you're after something . . . closer to home.'

'You could say that. I was hoping to spend the evening with my nephew, but it seems his loyalties lie elsewhere tonight.'

'Your nephew,' I repeat, not quite sure I've heard him correctly.

Wait . . .

He doesn't mean . . .

'Did you not realise Lincoln was my nephew?' he asks.

'I . . . I had no idea.' I really didn't. Shit. This family connection goes a lot deeper than I thought. They're all a bunch of incestuous killers. One big killer family. My stomach churns.

'How about we cut to the chase . . . *Emily*.' The way he pronounces my name sends a shockwave of adrenaline through my body.

He knows. Of course he fucking knows. He's Damien's brother. How could he not know?

Mr Wyatt moves his body closer to mine — too close. The smell of expensive whisky is almost overwhelming, but it's his presence, the sheer power in his body that frightens me the most. He could kill me with one swift movement.

'Whatever you've got planned for this evening is not going to work. I suggest you bring out my brother and my niece, and let's get all this out in the open. You're nothing, Emily. You've always been nothing.'

'How did you know about me?'

'Did you seriously think I wouldn't recognise you? I've been coming to this hotel since the start. Jennifer is my niece.'

'Why didn't you say anything?'

'You played your little game, and I played mine.'

At that moment, Kimberley and Lincoln appear at the top of the steps and start their descent. Mr Wyatt, or should I call him Phillip now, grasps my arm so tight that his fingernails dig into my skin.

CHAPTER THIRTY-SIX

Kimberley

As I clutch Lincoln's arm, walking to the banquet hall, I scan the area, looking for Phillip, for Emily, for Courtney, anyone I recognise. I feel naked and exposed in this dress, too much cleavage and leg on show for my liking. I am so far out of my comfort zone, about to walk into a room full of serial killers and the most deplorable human beings in existence.

As we enter the banquet hall, Michelle appears with a tray of champagne flutes. She locks eyes with me for a second and then lowers them, directing her gaze at the flute on the left. I take it.

'Thank you,' I say.

Michelle offers Lincoln another flute, which he takes and necks the contents in one go, immediately picking up another. I'm quietly glad about having something in my other hand that's not entwined with Lincoln's arm. I've always found it awkward at parties standing around without a drink. What are you supposed to do with your hands?

There's Emily, standing with Phillip. I can't wait to make him pay for what he's done to me. I might never fully recover from the damage he's wreaked on my body. Already, I can feel the strange withdrawal symptoms from the medication I've been taking. I know I don't need it, but I do . . . I either must try and give it up completely or continue to stay on some form of it, which will continue to give me severe seizures, albeit not as often as before.

Something's wrong.

The closer I get to Emily, the faster my heart beats. She's staring at me with a forced smile. I may not have known her for very long, but she's my mother. We have an unspoken connection.

'Kimberley, Lincoln, so delighted to see you,' she says, her smile not reaching her eyes.

Lincoln grips my waist tighter. 'Jennifer . . . *Phillip*.'

'I was just telling our wonderful host how beautiful the room looks,' says Phillip, glancing around the banquet hall. I must admit, it is glorious, the poshest and most elaborate event I've ever attended. However, the fact that all the guests are killers is a new experience.

'It does look spectacular,' replies Lincoln. 'When are we expecting the man himself to arrive?'

'Any time now,' says Emily with a squeaky voice. Phillip has his hand around her arm, squeezing tight. Shit. Okay, something's definitely wrong. I need to get Emily away from these two men before everything kicks off.

'Lincoln, would you mind if I stole Kimberley for just a moment?' asks Emily, attempting to move away from Phillip who lets her go, but not before digging his nails hard into her flesh.

Lincoln lets go of my waist without a word and stands next to Phillip.

'Ladies,' says Phillip, raising his champagne flute and then taking a sip. He and Lincoln walk towards another group of guests, all of whom greet them like old friends.

Emily pulls me in the opposite direction and out of the banquet hall, shoving me into a corner, away from the gaggle of guests who are appearing in the hallway.

'Ouch! What the hell . . .'

'Kimberley, I was wrong. I was wrong about everything. They've all been playing me from the start. They've known all along that I'm not Jennifer. They've probably known that Damien and Jennifer are hidden somewhere in the hotel. Also, Lincoln is Damien's son.'

I almost choke. 'What?'

Emily shakes her head, as if she can't quite believe it herself. 'I know. Don't ask. I never saw this coming.'

'Wait . . . so Lincoln is my half-brother? He's Jennifer's half-brother too?'

'Yes.'

My stomach gurgles and I quickly cover my mouth with my free hand. 'I feel sick.'

'We have to be careful. They could be planning anything.'

'What are you talking about? Who's *they*?'

'Everyone!'

'Everyone? Everyone knows?'

'Yes!'

I bite my bottom lip. 'What does this mean?' I whisper.

'It means we're royally fucked. That's what it means. They know something is going to happen tonight. We no longer have the element of surprise.'

I click my neck from side to side. 'Well then, I suggest we give the guests what they came here for, don't you agree? When are Damien and Jennifer due to arrive.'

'In about an hour.'

'Then let's enjoy the party until then.'

'Kimberley, I don't think you understand. It won't work. My plan won't work. They know too much.'

'They don't know everything. I still have a little something up my sleeve that even you don't know about.'

***

An hour later, all the guests have arrived and are congregated in the banquet hall, sipping champagne, nibbling on appetisers, and some are even dancing and swaying to the music. There's laughter and loud chatter; the whole room is buzzing with excitement.

After speaking with Emily, I returned to Lincoln's side and have remained there ever since. Damien and Jennifer are due to arrive at nine o'clock exactly. I have twenty minutes to work my magic and retrieve the notebook from inside his jacket pocket.

But someone has been keeping a close eye on me the whole evening.

Phillip.

Every time I look over at him, he's staring at me, at Lincoln. It seems that jealousy is rearing its ugly head, and I think it may work in my favour. Is it jealousy though? Perhaps he just doesn't like the fact that Lincoln is spending time with me. I can practically feel his negative energy from across the room. He's talking with a young man but doesn't appear to be paying him any close attention. His wife, on the other hand, is doing her best to prove that she's over him and is sandwiched between two male suitors, both of whom are plying her with drinks.

Emily told me earlier that it's best if we play along as much as possible and continue with our plan. I agreed with her but added a few ideas of my own about how the evening should go.

I have twenty minutes.

Then, it's showtime.

I take a deep breath and make my move, leaning into Lincoln's body as if only he can stop me from falling over. I'm not drunk. I've only had a few sips of my champagne, but Lincoln doesn't know that. He's been handing me drink after drink and I've been casually swapping them with empty glasses whenever Michelle walks past with a tray. We time it to perfection each time and she gives me a smile.

'Lincoln, can we go somewhere private real quick?' I ask, whispering into his left ear as he converses with another guest. The fact he's my half-brother is enough to make me want to puke on his posh jacket, but since he seems to like a bit of incest, I need to keep up the charade. Perhaps that was why he reacted so strangely when he found out Phillip was my uncle.

Lincoln's body stiffens as he cuts his conversation with the other guest short. He turns and looks at me. 'I don't want to miss the party.'

'We won't. We'll be back in time for Damien to arrive.'

'What I have planned for you will take much longer than twenty minutes,' he says with an evil hiss. 'In fact . . .' He runs a hand down my cheek and over my bare shoulder, '. . . perhaps I should give you a quick taster of what's to come.' Without waiting for my answer, he grabs my arm and drags me out of the room. I almost trip over my dress as I stumble against his back.

He strides towards the library, pushes open the doors, then shoves me inside.

Fuck.

This was a bad idea.

He slowly begins to unbutton his jacket. 'Are you bleeding?' he asks.

'Wait . . . What?' I ask. My heart rate spikes. I can barely catch my breath.

'Are you menstruating?'

Eww. 'No,' I say as confidently as possible.

'Shame.'

I fight back a gag as he steps closer. This man is the epitome of sick. His jacket is open and as he takes it off, I see the notebook cocooned in the inside pocket. I need to get that damn notebook.

I can't let him get started on what he wants to do to me. I have to stay in control.

'Lincoln, give me your jacket,' I say, holding out my hand. It's shaking, and he notices.

'Come and get it,' he replies.

He holds it out in front of him. I take a wobbly step forward, my right hand grasping the soft fabric. But then he's on me and I don't even have time to react. His body slams into mine, pushing me against the wall. My hand is still grasped around his jacket, so while his hands roam my body and his mouth devours mine, I finger the fabric until I feel the supple leather notebook between my fingers. I shove it behind me onto the library shelves, hiding it among the other books.

He's hurting me. I can't breathe.

How am I going to get out of this?

Then it hits me like a sledgehammer.

A seizure.

I slump to the floor, twitching and jerking as saliva drips from my open mouth.

***

My eyes flick open to see Phillip staring down at me. At first, my brain is slow to respond, but then like a puzzle, piece by piece, it connects.

'Welcome back,' he says. He helps me into a seated position, my back resting against the bookshelves.

Lincoln's notebook.

It's too risky to retrieve it now. I'll come back for it later.

My eyes scan the room for Lincoln, but he's gone.

'You gave Lincoln a bit of a fright,' says Phillip.

'How awful for him,' I reply.

Phillip laughs as he helps me to my feet. 'It was clever of you to fake a seizure.'

I brush my dress down. 'Yes, well . . . there wasn't much else I could do to get him off me.'

Phillip extends his arm. 'You were lucky he didn't decide to take advantage of you while you were indisposed. Shall we? It's almost time.'

I take his arm, and we walk out of the library towards the banquet hall just as Emily stands at the top of the entrance stairs. She glances at me, and I respond with a slight head nod.

It's showtime.

The lights go out, plunging the hall into darkness.

CHAPTER THIRTY-SEVEN

Emily

The darkness is thick and deep. The music and chatter continue, but at a lower decibel, and then a scream slices through the dark like a knife. It's so loud that it disrupts the flow of the music and the band stops playing, catapulting the room into a silence so eerie that my skin crawls. Within two seconds another scream, one that makes my blood turn to ice, rips through the air.

The voices of the guests simmer to hushed whispers, then cut out completely. They aren't afraid. Not even a little. Because they think the entertainment is about to begin. The air is practically vibrating with excitement. They are wrong.

The lights stay off. I wait patiently, praying that Kimberley is right to continue with the plan. She has something else planned that I don't know about and it's sending all my nerve endings tingling. I don't like the uneasy feeling that's swirling around in my gut, making my toes go numb. And it has nothing to do with the fact that when the lights went out, Lincoln was staring at me from across the room. All I can think about are his eyes searing a hole in my brain.

I saw him come running into the banquet hall ten minutes ago, looking positively sick. He ran up to Phillip and dragged him out the door. I assumed that Kimberley had orchestrated her ploy to grab the notebook. Her nod just now confirmed it.

The screams subside. Then, as if by magic, the candles flicker to life, the ones in the huge candelabras placed on all the tables. Electric, a nice touch.

The first thing I see through the fake candlelight is a crowd of people congregating near the entrance doors. The second thing I see is a woman being held at knifepoint by a man. At least, that's what it looks like. It's difficult to see from so far away. My insides clench as I step closer, but I must be careful not to disrupt the plan.

I can't see Kimberley anywhere. My eyes scan back and forth across the room, but it's impossible to pick anyone out thanks to the colour-coordination and everyone wearing masks.

Then, someone grabs my left arm so tight that it starts to cut off the circulation to my hand.

I turn to confront them. It's Lincoln.

'Watch and learn,' he says, his lips merely centimetres from my ear.

No . . .

'What is this?' I ask.

I can barely see the man and woman at the front now because the crowd has thickened, blocking my view of the entrance doors.

I pull against Lincoln's restraint, my body craving escape, needing to see who it is who's in trouble, to help them. Lincoln drags me back towards him so roughly that I stumble in my heels straight into his hard chest.

Then, I stamp on his foot with my left heel. He hisses in pain, releasing my arm. I spring forward and start pushing against the crowds towards the front of the room. There's muttering and grumbles as I shove my way through the guests.

As I break through the front of the crowd, I see who it is now, and my heart sinks in my chest.

Courtney is the one being held at knifepoint.

By Damien. And he's no longer in a coma. He's standing, very much awake. And he looks . . . happy? Why is he happy?

Courtney's face is tear-streaked and bloodstained. Damien's face is beaming as he presses the tip of the knife into the side of her neck. A bead of blood is blooming just beneath the tip. One swift movement and it's all over for Courtney. I have no idea how I'm supposed to deal with this.

Where is Kimberley?

Phillip is standing just off to the side. He glances sideways at me. His hands are open, showing his palms to Damien. He's not a threat to him. Damien glares at me, ignoring Phillip completely.

'Brother, what's this about?'

'Oh, shut up, Phillip and get back in your box,' Damien says. His words are meant to sting, filled with venom, but his voice is pleasant, soothing in tone.

A collective intake of breath can be heard across the room. Like me, the guests here know Damien well enough to understand when he's serious. They're probably all wondering where he's been for the past year.

'This is the bitch who stole my Kimberley away from us,' says Damien, staring straight at me.

I step closer, my hands out. 'Yes, I know.'

'I told you I'd make the person who stole her away pay one day.'

'Yes, but . . .'

Before I can get out another word, Damien slices Courtney's throat open. Blood spurts across the bustling crowd, but instead of being disgusted and appalled like normal people would be, an almighty cheer erupts. A couple of people even rush forward, desperate to be drenched in the blood, which is still spurting from Courtney's throat.

It's so perverse, so inhuman, yet I can't tear my eyes away. Damien lets Courtney go and she drops to the floor like a sack of potatoes, her legs crumpling underneath her so she lands at an unnatural angle. Her body jerks a few more times, then lies still, bleeding out, the blood seeping across the tiled floor like an expanding puddle.

There's no point in trying to help her. She's gone. Damien hasn't taken his eyes off me, even as he wipes the blade of the knife against the sleeve of his suit jacket.

'There, isn't that better,' he says.

'You didn't have to kill her, Damien.'

'Yes, I did.' He finally looks away from me and addresses the room full of guests. 'Ladies and Gentlemen, welcome to the party of the year. I'm sure that those of you who have been coming since the start will agree with me when I say that time has flown by, and each party is more successful than the last.' A murmur of agreement spreads across the room. 'You may have noticed my absence over the past year. My lovely daughter, Jennifer, has been dealing with the running of the hotel during this time . . . except, this isn't Jennifer.' He stares at me without blinking, without an inch of humanity in his gaze.

Every single pair of eyes in the room swivels in my direction.

'Wait . . . she's not Jennifer?' comes a small voice.

I search the room for the owner of the voice. It's Mrs Newton, the elderly woman who walks with a cane.

'No, my dear Mrs Newton,' continues Damien. 'She is not.'

'Where is the real Jennifer?' comes another voice from another direction.

'That's a good question,' replies Damien. 'Bryan, if you will.'

A hush descends on the room as a nearby door opens. Bryan enters, pushing Jennifer in a wheelchair. She's so pale, so thin, that it doesn't look as if her own body can support her. I knew she was weak, but she appears to have deteriorated drastically since I last saw her.

Damien walks down the steps towards her. 'My dear child, it's good to see you. It's so wonderful to finally have all my children in the same room together. Lincoln, Kimberley, please join us.'

Lincoln strides into view, straight to Damien's side. He leans down and kisses Jennifer on the top of her hand, placing a hand on her bony shoulder. She looks up at him and smiles. She may look weak and helpless, but I know how truly evil she is.

Kimberley is nowhere to be seen. Good. I hope she stays away. It's my fault she's been dragged into this mess.

'Kimberley,' says Damien in a sing song voice. 'Come out, come out, wherever you are.'

'Kimberley, I suggest you stay away,' I call out.

'Who's Kimberley?' shouts a voice.

'Silence!' demands Damien. His eyes blaze with fire. 'Find her.'

The guests part like the red sea and begin to split up, following his every word. I watch while they pull the banquet hall apart. Tables are flipped over, decorations are ripped down, vases of flowers are smashed.

'Stop.' Kimberley's voice echoes across the room.

'Ah, the youngest daughter has arrived. Finally.' Damien waves his hand, signalling for the crowd to part once more. Kimberley steps into the light.

'Hi, Dad.'

'My dear. Welcome to the family.' He spreads his arms wide.

Damien, Jennifer and Lincoln smile at her.

'It's time to choose, Kimberley. Either you're with us, or you're with *her*.' At this point, he extends his finger towards me.

Kimberley must choose.

CHAPTER THIRTY-EIGHT

Kimberley

I'm standing in a banquet hall, wearing the most exquisite gown, holding a glass of champagne and looking at my new family in front of me.

They want me to choose.

Tick tock, Kimberley.

Tick tock.

Choose now.

And . . . go . . .

I just hope Emily goes along with me on this one.

'I'd like to raise a toast,' I say, stepping closer to Damien, Lincoln and Jennifer. Michelle appears beside me with a glass of champagne. I take it. Then, like clockwork, ten waiters spread across the room, handing flutes out to all the guests, who take them, holding them aloft.

Everyone takes a fresh glass. Those who already have a glass in their hands down the contents and grab a new one. Emily takes one, locking eyes with me as she does.

'Please, I'd like everyone to join me in congratulating my father on the many wonderful years of running this hotel.

This place truly is a unique and captivating place. Each guest deserves their place here tonight. Thank you for being here. I'm honoured to be joining the family tradition. Cheers.'

I hold up my glass, then take a sip.

'Cheers,' comes the chorus of voices around the room as each guest takes a sip of champagne. My gaze stays locked on Damien. His eyes are dark, glaring back at me. Jennifer takes a sip, then Lincoln raises his glass to his lips, but Damien reaches out a hand and stops him before his lips touch the glass.

Emily also drinks.

No one speaks. No one moves.

The seconds seem to tick by at a glacial pace. Then someone in the room coughs, followed by another. Coughs erupt like fireworks.

One by one the guests drop their glasses, clutch their throats and drop to the floor in perfect synchronisation. It's beautiful to watch.

PART FOUR

CHAPTER THIRTY-NINE

Damien
Twenty-five years before

He'd finally found her. The woman he'd been searching for. She was eight months pregnant too. That was a surprise. Not planned at all, but nonetheless, he'd make it work, as he'd made it work with his previous two children. Each of his children were special, especially his eldest.

Jennifer.

She was a young woman now and already on her way to learning the ropes and joining him as his business partner. Her mother, Caroline, had been a wonderful woman. He'd met her when he was eighteen and, despite struggling with displays of emotion, he had fallen for her. It felt normal to have a woman by his side. It made him appear to others as normal and that's exactly what he needed people to think because, the truth was, he knew he was different to most people. And not in what would be described as a good way.

It had been a wild romance, culminating in an unexpected pregnancy. The birth had been traumatic, and Caroline had tragically lost her life after a massive haemorrhage only a few minutes after delivering Jennifer into the world. He knew then that Jennifer was special. Only just born, merely seconds old, and already she'd taken a life.

Damien didn't blame her. He doted on her. His little murderous daughter, who had ripped her mother apart as she'd entered the world. It was a sign. Yes, he knew he'd miss Caroline, mourn her, but Jennifer was all he had now; a part of Caroline would always live on in her.

He had nurtured Jennifer's murderous instinct from a young age.

Then, ten years later, came Lincoln. The woman he had raped refused to have an abortion, then turned up at his door one day carrying the child, his son. Damien didn't want him and turned her away, giving her several hundred thousand pounds in compensation to keep her quiet. She took it and ran back to Peterborough where she lived, and he didn't see or hear about Lincoln again until one day, many years later, he saw a news bulletin about a vicious rapist patrolling the streets of Peterborough. He knew without any proof whatsoever that the rapist was his son. It was poetic somehow. He had a connection to his children even he couldn't understand.

They had no leads of course. The police never did. By now, his hotel had been running for two decades. He wanted, needed, his son to join him there. Jennifer would always be number one in his eyes, but this rapist was special. He did things to his victims, things that went beyond anything Damien could ever imagine. In fact, during one of his dalliances at the hotel, he tried what his son had done to multiple women, and found he didn't have the stomach for it.

Lincoln was worse than him.

Most of the women Lincoln left behind ended their own lives rather than live with the mutilations he'd inflicted on them. It was no way to live.

He tracked Lincoln down and invited him to the party at his hotel.

Then came his third child. Kimberley.

He met her mother, Emily, eight months ago at a party. She'd been all over him, despite him being much older than her. It had been too easy to ply her with drinks and drag her into a waiting car where he'd then had his sordid way with her. She'd been conscious during most of it, muttering something about him stopping and trying her best to push him off, but why would he do that? It was fun, and she was screaming. He liked it when they screamed. It did things to him that delighted and aroused him.

That was who he was.

He couldn't get it up if they didn't fight back a little bit. How else was he going to fulfil his desires?

After he dumped her on the side of the road, he went back to the hotel after telling Bryan, his faithful butler, to keep an eye on her. Bryan said she was in a bad way but had survived her ordeal. However, Damien hadn't had his fill of Emily. She was a sweet young thing and he wanted to make sure no other man touched her.

But she disappeared.

He was furious with Bryan, of course, who promised he'd keep searching for her for as long as it took to find her. It took eight months.

Now, it was time to claim his prize.

A sweet, new offspring who he could teach and mould to his desire. If it was, in fact, his. He'd have to be certain before he raised it. A DNA test when the child was born would see to that. The mere thought of another man touching his Emily made his blood boil. He just hoped she hadn't betrayed him. It was bad enough she'd run away from him after their dalliance.

He had Jennifer. He had Lincoln. Now, he'd hopefully have whoever this child turned out to be. His own flesh and blood. Another chance to keep the family business alive. That was what it was all about after all. One day he'd be gone, dead, but his children would ensure his legacy would live on for ever.

Clifton Hotel was his legacy.

One day Jennifer would take over.

Lincoln was already proving himself to be a viable candidate also, especially since his appetite for the extreme had expanded lately. Lincoln was different to Jennifer. Whereas she was level-headed, serious and confident, he was outlandish, reckless and slightly unhinged. Damien suspected he had an even worse blood lust than he himself did. Once, he found Lincoln with a half-naked, half-dead girl in his bed while he . . . Well, it took a hell of a lot of cleaning and covering up once he was finished.

How would the new child turn out?

It was a question that intrigued and excited Damien. He sent Bryan to fetch Emily. Then, once she was safely in Room 21, he would plan his next move. She was the twenty-first woman to stay in the room. It was a ritual he'd kept up for the party, always bringing a girl off the streets as the highlight of the evening. Often, the women were never seen again. The party guests would take part in a silent auction and whoever won claimed their prize. But Emily was different. She was carrying his child.

The baby wouldn't be harmed of course, but what to do with Emily once she'd provided him with his new and future heir? She was the only mother of his children who was left alive. Lincoln's mother had been killed years ago, most likely by him. And Caroline had died during childbirth. Emily was special. He didn't want to just let her go. No, she needed to stay somewhere he could keep an eye on her. He was selfish and territorial, especially with his women. Perhaps he'd keep her here as one of the housekeeping staff.

But then, everything went wrong.

The child was born. A girl, and she was indeed, his offspring. Then, she was stolen from under his nose.

Jennifer didn't have a clue where she was or what had happened. Lincoln wasn't around. He was living it up somewhere in London. Someone in his hotel had betrayed him.

His precious child was gone. He was determined to find her, no matter what it took, and when he did, he had the perfect plan to control her until she was ready. His brother would help.

CHAPTER FORTY

Emily

The guests drop like flies, one after the other. Some vomit. Some froth at the mouth like an overworked racehorse. Some lash out in anger, grabbing others by the throat as their life drains from their bodies. Jennifer twitches and slumps in her wheelchair, but there are three people left standing.

Damien, Lincoln and Phillip.

The bastards knew what we had planned and didn't drink, but they let Jennifer die anyway.

'My dear Emily,' says Damien slowly, emphasising each word. 'You have just committed mass murder. I do believe you're worse than any of the people here.'

'If you knew what I was planning, then why allow it? You could have stopped it,' I reply.

'That wouldn't be nearly as much fun.' He looks down at Jennifer, who has grown still, a sliver of drool and blood oozing from her mouth. 'Such a shame, but since her accident, she is no longer useful to me. I cannot have a cripple take over my hotel.'

Lincoln scoffs and straightens his jacket. He locks eyes with mine. I know it was him who rammed the van into

Jennifer's car. I was the one who asked him to do it, after all. He was more than open to helping, especially since the accident would benefit him too. That's the thing about bargaining with a psychopath; if it benefits them, there's nothing they won't do because all they think or care about is themselves.

'I suppose that means you've made your decision, my dear child,' says Damien, directing his steely gaze to Kimberley who has now arrived at my side.

It feels as if we're on a battlefield. Us against them. Men against women. Mother and daughter against father and son (and brother).

'I have,' says Kimberley. She reaches for my hand without looking for it and grasps it tight. I blink back tears. I've never felt her skin against my own. Never.

Damien sneers.

Phillip shakes his head in disappointment, but his eyes are watering. His jaw clenches and he coughs, then spits blood onto the floor. 'What?' he asks, mostly to himself.

'Uncle?' asks Lincoln seconds before he also begins frothing at the mouth.

'I guess that two-hundred-and-fifty-thousand-pound bottle of whisky isn't so tasty after all,' says Kimberley.

CHAPTER FORTY-ONE

Kimberley

Emily turns her head slowly to look at me, probably confused about what's going on. I couldn't risk either Lincoln or Phillip not drinking the champagne, especially if they knew we had something planned, but men are predictable, especially men like them, who adore the finer things in life, like ridiculously overpriced, rare whisky.

'It seems you forgot one thing,' I say to both Lincoln and Phillip as they collapse and writhe on the ground. They are still conscious, so they can hear my genius plan before their lives end. I always find it ridiculous in murder mystery films or books when the whole plan is revealed at the end as if the reader or the watcher isn't smart enough to figure it out for themselves, but in this instance, I feel like everyone left alive in the room deserves to know exactly how I beat them, considering what they've put me through for the past twenty-odd years.

Phillip is having a seizure, his teeth clamping down through his tongue. Blood pours from his mouth. I should know what a seizure looks like, I've spent my life having them at his expense.

I let go of Emily's hand and step closer to Phillip, leaning over him as he twitches. 'I'm a housekeeper at this hotel and it was my job to ensure your rooms were exactly as you expected them to be. I even delivered the bottle of whisky you requested in your welcome pack and set it up on the bar in pride of place. Oh, and I slipped several dozen of the pills you've been forcing me to take for the past twenty years. Plus, a little something extra. They've taken longer to work than I imagined, but how poetic that you should die by having a never-ending seizure. Lincoln, on the other hand, looks as if he's choking on his own vomit. And why didn't I react badly after taking a few sips? Because I've had the past twenty years to build up a resistance to the pills whereas you haven't.'

Phillip's eyes widen and then glaze over. His body is jerking so hard that his limbs are flailing about wildly. I manage to block his left arm as it almost slaps me across the face. I leave him to die on the floor and return to Emily, who is smiling like a proud mother at their child's first concert.

Lincoln is also fitting, but it doesn't take long before he gives up and dies. He hasn't been able to breathe for the past two minutes.

Damien hasn't moved a muscle. He's stock still, like a statue. The fact that he's just watched his eldest daughter, son and brother be murdered, along with every guest in his hotel, and he hasn't shown a single ounce of emotion or made any attempt to help anyone, is the most disconcerting experience I've ever witnessed. I am in the presence of true evil.

'Bravo,' he says. 'Both of you have exceeded my expectations. Emily, my dear, I thought you were this weak, delicate flower, incapable of standing on your own two feet, but you're the most beautiful and extraordinary specimen I've ever met. And Kimberley, my child, the culmination of my entire existence, you are who I've been searching for my entire life. I thought Jennifer and Lincoln were special, but you . . . you are more conniving and stronger than both of them put together.'

I hold his gaze, not blinking. 'As flattered as I am to be compared to two psychopathic serial killers, I must disagree with you, Damien. You may have been controlling my whole life without my knowledge by medicating me, but you didn't count on one thing.'

Damien folds his arms, waiting.

'That it would actually make me stronger, not weaker.'

Damien curls his top lip into a snarl. 'You're forgetting that you are in my hotel and in my hotel, my staff listen to me.'

'Actually,' says Emily, stepping forward. 'They listen to me. I am Jennifer after all, and I've been treating them better in the past year then you or the real Jennifer have for the past two-and-a-half decades. Who do you think they'll listen to now?'

On cue, the double doors open and in walk several dozen members of staff. They spread out, blocking the doors. There's no way Damien is getting out of this room alive. Some fold their arms, others look a little scared and hide behind their colleagues, but they're here to show him that he can't control people with fear anymore.

He's lost.

'It's time to make a choice, Damien,' says Emily. 'Either you take the gun I know you have tucked into the waistband of your suit and shoot yourself in the head, ending things on your terms, or you refuse and die the hard way.'

Damien blinks several times. He's on the back foot. He doesn't have the element of surprise anymore and he knows he's cornered, like a wounded animal with no way out. Time will tell if he's the type to stand and fight to the end, or he'll end things quickly because he's a coward.

Damien slowly reaches his arm round to his back and pulls out a gun.

I hold my breath, not daring to move in case it sets him off. He raises the gun to his temple and grins. 'I am always in control, even of my own death,' he says and pulls the trigger.

Click.

The staff gasp and begin mumbling their surprise.

Click.

I smile. 'It seems you've underestimated me again. As a housekeeper here, it's also my job to supply the rooms with weapons, but it seems you're so used to your staff following orders that you didn't even bother to check if the gun was loaded.'

Damien throws the gun on the floor. 'You fucking bitch,' he says with a growl.

I shrug my shoulders. 'Like father, like daughter.'

And I pull a gun out from the folds of my dress and shoot my father. I miss his head, but I catch his shoulder. At least I hit him. It is the first time I've fired a gun. He stumbles back and grunts, so I shoot again. And again. I keep shooting as I walk forward, my eyes trained on him until he slumps to the floor, dead. Very dead.

CHAPTER FORTY-TWO

Kimberley
The Days after the Party

The clean-up operation will go down in history as the biggest and most time-consuming one yet. Luckily, since the hotel has its own incinerator in the basement, all the bodies go there. One by one, the staff load them onto trolleys and wheel them down into the dark. Emily and I oversee everything. We don't say a lot to each other. There's plenty to say, but now isn't the time. Once this hotel is cleaned and every shred of evidence burned, removed or wiped away, then we need to decide what we're going to do with the building.

The staff who are left will need to be questioned, most likely put into therapy for what some of them have been through. All the while, we have to keep this from being broadcast to the world's media. If word of this murder hotel got out, then it would be catastrophic for all of us involved. But the fact that several dozen of the world's worst serial killers, rapists and paedophiles are all now dead must be something worth celebrating, even if the world will never know what happened here.

We've saved hundreds of people from being killed or raped or tortured. Maybe the crime rate will drop in this country now that all these killers are gone, never to be seen or heard from again. They don't deserve to be remembered by anyone. Every shred of evidence from their rooms is also burnt, along with any personal belongings. The incinerator is roaring for days afterwards.

It takes several days to return the hotel to its former glory. All the vile decorations come down, a fresh coat of paint is administered and all the bedding, weapons, sex toys and paraphernalia are also burned or destroyed. Day by day, the hotel is transformed, all evidence of the past covered over or removed. The memories will always live within the walls, possibly trapped for ever, but I hope that destroying the monsters who created this place will go some way to restoring the hotel's equilibrium.

And I checked out the so-called haunted rooms of the hotel. Turns out, it was some bad wiring and hearsay. Emily admitted they were forced to keep up the story of the haunted rooms and play around with the lights and temperature. I must admit, I found myself a little disappointed.

Doctor Simmons was found after the party unconscious and bound in her office. It appears that when Damien was roused from his coma, he managed to inject her with a heavy dose of sedative that had been intended for him. He was supposed to have attended the party heavily sedated in a wheelchair, but he quickly turned the tables on her. Having been in a coma for so long, his body and mind hadn't been quite as switched on as usual, so he injected himself with a dose of adrenaline, giving him the edge over poor Courtney, who in the end met her own fate in the dining hall.

Over the following days, after recovering herself, Doctor Simmons adjusts my medication some more. I don't have any more seizures, but the headaches and nausea are quite bad. She says I may have to stay on a very low dose for a bit longer to lessen the side effects from the withdrawal process. I'll never be cured of my epilepsy, but now I'm on the correct medication, it can be controlled.

Muffin still follows me everywhere. She has a job to do after all, but how do I explain to a dog that she doesn't need to always be on alert anymore? She's always looked out for me, and I want her to enjoy her life now and not have to worry about me as much. We play fetch in the grounds and snuggle by the fire at night.

Emily finds us one evening when the hotel hallways are quiet, and everyone has gone to bed. Some of the staff have left already to live their lives outside of these walls, but others have nowhere else to go, so they are staying here until Emily and I decide how to proceed.

'May I join you?' asks Emily.

Muffin raises her head from my lap. She's snuggled beside me on the plush sofa. 'Yes, of course.'

Emily takes a seat on the other side of Muffin and strokes her back. Her tail wags a few times, then she returns to sleeping.

'Growing up, I always wanted a dog,' says Emily with a sad sigh. 'But my parents never allowed it.'

'She's one in a million,' I reply.

'How are you?' I don't reply straight away because my silence speaks volumes. 'I know,' she says. 'I know what you must be thinking. I'm sorry about everything, but the monsters are dead now, and that's all that matters.'

'What happens now?'

'That's why I've come to talk to you. I have an idea as to what I'd like to do with this hotel. Since the building isn't listed publicly, and the majority of the guests who know about it are dead, then it creates the perfect opportunity to start afresh.'

'What do you mean?'

'A year ago, while Damien was under the influence of a sedative, I managed to get him to sign the deeds over to me.'

'You did?'

'He had no idea about it, of course. Neither did Jennifer. All this time, the hotel has officially and legally belonged to me. Which leads me on to my suggestion of what to do with it, if you're on board, of course?'

'What do you have in mind?'

Emily pauses for a moment, then speaks slowly. 'What do you think about turning this hotel, which was once a place of pain and murder, into a refuge, a retreat, for victims of rape and abuse, or for the families of those who have been murdered?'

I smile. 'It's the most perfect use of the hotel I could have imagined.'

'Perfect, but I do have one condition. We run it together . . . as a family business.'

My lips curve up into a huge smile. 'Let's do it.'

***

That evening, I'm upstairs in my bed. Biscuit, the teddy bear, is on the shelf opposite me.

The note inside was destroyed, but I can never reveal the truth because the truth is something that would destroy everything I've worked so hard to build.

The only person who knows my secret is Bryan. How he knows, I have no idea, but it's a secret he's willing to keep for me.

I close my eyes and think the words on the note in my head. I do have a brilliant memory, after all.

'My dear Katy, I'm so sorry I had to give you up, but I had no other choice. Three months after you were born, I was diagnosed with terminal cancer. I'm not going to make it to see you grow up or even reach your first birthday, so it's better that I hand you over to be adopted. I don't have anyone else who can take you. I have no family.

'You may not keep the name I gave you, but you'll always be my Katy. Your father was killed in a car accident before you were even born. I'm sorry I couldn't give you a better life, but I hope you have a wonderful life, and I know that whatever happens, whoever you turn out to be, you'll make a difference in the world one day. I love you. Your mother, Rachel Evans.'

EPILOGUE

Kimberley
Two Years after the Party

Sometimes, when I wake up, it feels as if I'm still dreaming. I've come a long way from the nervous, epileptic housekeeper I once was. Now, I'm the co-owner of Hylton Manor, a secluded retreat for those needing to heal after suffering abuse, whether it be from a relationship or a random attack. It took almost eight months before we opened our doors to the public, but now we're almost always fully booked. And the best part is that it doesn't cost the people who come here a single penny.

My belief is that you shouldn't have to pay to recover and heal from abuse, so the doors of Hylton Manor are open to all who need our help. Most of the staff stayed on to help run the place. They are paid a fair wage and are allowed to leave whenever they like, although the isolation of the manor is still a hindrance to most, but that's the beauty of the location. Guests come here to get away. Not hide away but get a change of scenery and admire the beauty and tranquillity of the Scottish Highlands. It's not therapy. There's no yoga or meditation, but there are people who listen and who can help when you're feeling your worst.

My epilepsy has all but gone, although I still do struggle through migraines. Unfortunately, Doctor Simmons was unable to wean me off the medication that Damien got me addicted too, so it's at the lowest possible dose now, which gives me little to no side effects. I did have a very mild seizure about two months ago and, despite not having to alert me for almost two years, Muffin immediately remembered what she was trained for and gave me a warning signal.

I expect I'll be on the medication for the rest of my life. In a way, Damien and Phillip still have control over me from beyond the grave, but I'm glad that I can now live relatively seizure free.

Emily and I have grown closer as mother and daughter, and now have a strong, healthy relationship, which I never expected to have. We're more like best friends than mother and daughter, which, I suppose makes sense since I'm not her real daughter. She often tells me how guilty she feels that she missed out on my childhood years, but is proud of who I am today, despite her not being involved for the first twenty-five years of my life.

Obviously, I cannot reveal that she's not my mother, that Damien got it all completely wrong and Bryan tracked down the wrong person on purpose. Perhaps he wanted to keep the real Kimberley safe. I cannot be sure of that, but all things considered, I think I've turned out pretty well. I often consider tracking down the real Kimberley, but I think it's better this way. I've always thought I'd been dealt a bad hand by the universe, growing up in foster care, having severe medical conditions, but now I realise they were all there to test me, to turn me into Kimberley, daughter of a vicious psychopath.

I took that upbringing and Emily and I decided to add our own little twist on Damien's hotel.

About a year ago, Emily and I began work on a special side project.

One of the issues I had was that, even though the guests of this hotel have escaped their abusers and come here to heal, there's no closure. Their attackers and abusers are still out there in the world, having got away with it and are carrying on with their miserable lives. Sometimes they're inflicting the abuse on someone else, having moved on from abusing the ones who have sought refuge here.

This didn't sit well with me.

Which is why Room 21 is now being used again, designed specifically for the purpose of providing closure for our guests. Not everyone is required to take part. It is completely up to them, but so far, we haven't had anyone turn down our offer.

Emily and I are sitting behind the bank of monitors in the main office, watching our newest guest pick up one of the items on the table while her abuser is tied to a chair in the middle of the room. It took a long time to find him, but we finally located him, dragged him here and wiped his existence off the face of the earth.

Our guest takes the claw hammer and whacks her abuser across the head with it.

Blood spurts out and splatters the white walls.

I turn to Emily. 'Looks like we're going to need to redecorate again.'

THE END

ACKNOWLEDGEMENTS

To all my loyal readers who stick with me, you're amazing and it means I can keep writing books and making up twisty stories!

Thank you to Aimee Louise for helping me with the epilepsy sections. As someone who has epilepsy, her advice and information was invaluable to making Kimberley's condition true to life and believable. Thank you for taking the time to talk about such a difficult subject.

To the amazing team at Joffe Books, who have supported me and edited this book. It was a twisty one for sure! And thanks for picking up on a massive plot hole I had in originally! Your advice and guidance is amazing and I hope to work with you all on future projects.

Thank you!